The Witness

i

The Witness

The Witness

A Novel

by

Susan Burke

The Witness

Table of Contents

"I am confident that there truly is such a thing as living again, that the living spring from the dead, and that the souls of the dead are in existence."

Socrates

Part I
Chasing a Dream
April - June, 2019

Chapter 1

Samantha's eyes flew open, her senses on alert. It was 2 a.m. and the whole world seemed to be holding its breath. Straining to hear anything amiss, she only noticed the soft patter of a light spring rain. After a few minutes she allowed herself to relax, pulled the duvet up to her chin and tried to return to her preferred mode of sleep... dreamless oblivion.

Within minutes shattering screams filled the air. "Help, help me! Stop! You're hurting me!"

Samantha jumped to her feet and hurried into the bedroom across the hall. She knew what to expect but it was always horrifying to see her three-year-old daughter fighting off some invisible demon. She sat carefully on the side of Bonnie's bed and spoke softly to her. "It's okay, honey. I'm here, nothing is going to happen to you." She'd learned the hard way not to touch her daughter in the midst of a bad dream or she would battle even harder.

Bonnie's blonde corkscrew curls were dripping wet and her nightie was damp as well. "Go away! Get off me! You're hurting me! I hate you!" She was kicking her feet and squirming around violently in the bed. Her breathing was ragged as she gasped for air.

Finally, as Bonnie's eyes started to flicker, Samantha stroked her hair and said softly, "Calm down, my darling, calm down. We are the only ones here and you're safe. You've just had a bad dream." Samantha passed her the inhaler, always at the ready.

After a few grateful breaths, Bonnie looked up at Samantha and said "He keeps hurting me down there, Mama. Tell him to stop."

This new detail got Samantha's attention. "Down where, honey?" Bonnie pointed between her legs.

Suddenly fearful that someone, somehow, might have sexually abused Bonnie, Samantha said, "Come on, let's put on a fresh nightie." As she pulled off Bonnie's damp nightgown, she took an extra minute or so to check things out. There was no sign of any sort of abuse. "Everything's fine honey. I think you just had another bad dream." Having nightmares of lions, tigers and bears was one thing. Dreaming of sexual abuse when you were just three years old was an entirely different affair.

Samantha put her arms around Bonnie and rubbed her back while looking around the pretty pink room for anything that could suggest monsters hiding in dark corners or boogie men under the bed. But there was nothing; just a row of dolls on the window seat, staring out at her with their blind, vacant eyes… witnesses to nothing.

Now, as usual, Samantha crawled into the canopied bed with her whimpering daughter who was softly saying "I want my Daddy. I want my Daddy."

"I know, my darling, I know." But she didn't know. How on earth could Bonnie be crying out for Hank when she'd never even met him?

Samantha held Bonnie close until her breathing returned to normal and she started nodding off. What am I going to do she asked herself for the hundredth time, as she leaned back against the headboard. Dammit Hank, where are you when I need you? Despite knowing better, not a day went by when she didn't miss him and wish he were back - not just because she'd been so much in love with him, but because now their child needed help and she was at a loss as to what to do.

3

Once back in her own bed, her last thought, as she dozed off to sleep, was the grim acknowledgment that she and Bonnie were two lost souls... both in need of salvation.

Chapter 2

*L*uckily, Samantha was able to secure an appointment within a week for Bonnie to see her pediatrician. It was a Friday, and Samantha took the day off from work.

Dr. Jefferson was in his sixties, very kind and caring, and his young patients loved him. They also loved the chocolate MARS bar they received on the way out, which might explain why they were always on their best behavior.

When they were invited into the doctor's office, Samantha asked if Bonnie could stay in the reception room for a few minutes. so that she could speak privately with the doctor. "Don't worry, hon. It's just about some financial stuff. I'll be back to get you very soon." She thanked the receptionist for keeping an eye on Bonnie, and gave her one of the many jigsaw puzzles stacked up for Dr. Jefferson's patients.

Once inside, with the door closed, they shook hands and Samantha took a seat. "It's only been about six months since I last saw Bonnie," Dr. Jefferson said, as he reviewed her file. "Is something wrong?"

"Well yes and no, Doctor. Physically she seems just fine. But... " She paused trying to come up with the right words to describe why there did indeed seem to be something wrong.

"Yes... but what?" Dr. Jefferson said.

"Nightmares, Doctor. She has lots of nightmares."

Nodding his head, Dr. Jefferson assured her that nightmares were a common phenomena in children. She needn't worry, they would go away gradually.

Samantha took a deep breath and pressed on. "That's not why I'm worried. It's what she's dreaming about that frightens me. Bonnie has been having nightmares for a long time, but she's been unable to describe them in any sort of understandable way. But about a week ago, after another of her midnight battles, she said, and I'm quoting, 'he keeps hurting me down there, Mama. Tell him to stop.' When I asked her where 'down there' was, she pointed towards her vagina. Of course I checked for any sign of abuse, but I didn't see anything. How could she have dreams of sexual abuse, Doctor? She's too young to even know what she's talking about!"

Dr. Jamison frowned. "It is very unusual. How long did you say this has been going on?"

"Well, she's always been an uneasy sleeper... crying out, wiggling around. But without any words to tell me what was upsetting her, I just put it down to baby stuff... teething, gas, wanting to be picked up. That sort of thing. Over the past year, she's been saying 'Go away. Get off me. I hate you. You're hurting me.' The new bit came last week after she woke up and said 'Tell him to go away, Mama. He's hurting me down there.' "

"The poor child. It sounds like she's really suffering, psychologically at least." Glancing at his chart, he said "You're still living alone, correct? No men around the house?"

"Yes, I still live alone. I haven't seen Hank since before Bonnie's birth, and there are no men around the house."

"Okay. Let me chat with her for a few minutes and give her a short physical exam. Is that all right with you?"

"Of course. Shall I get her?"

"Why don't you wait outside, and I'll ask Tracy to bring her into my exam room. I think she's known me long enough to be comfortable without you, and she may feel more open to talk. Okay?"

6

Samantha felt the first hint of an oncoming storm. "Yes, of course. I'll wait in the reception room." Rising to go there, she started to worry about where this might lead. But thirty minutes later they returned, both smiling, one digging into her MARS bar.

The doctor took Samantha aside for a minute and said "I couldn't find a single thing wrong. She seems happy, well adjusted and just tired of having bad dreams. I assured her they would go away soon, and hopefully they will. Don't worry. I going to do a little research on this subject, and I'll get back to you within a day or two. Thanks for bringing her in." They shook hands and Dr. Jefferson waved a cheery goodbye to Bonnie.

As they walked out, Samantha felt relieved and disappointed at the same time. Sometimes no diagnosis is worse than knowing what's wrong. Bonnie skipped along by Samantha's side, holding on to her hand and singing "Old MacDonald had a Farm." As they got into the car, and Samantha was adjusting Bonnie's seatbelt, she wondered how her daughter could seem so normal by day and so disturbed at night. The belt clicked into place. Clearly there would be no answers today.

==

At 10 a.m., the very next day, Billie Jo Collins sat in her car reviewing the case file on her lap. There was very little in it, but she took a quick glance so she wouldn't forget the names of her soon-to-be clients. 'Samantha Mitchell, 35 years old, a working mom, divorced. Bonnie Mitchell, 3 1/2 years old, her only child, physically well, but currently having recurring nightmares of being hurt 'down there.' Pediatrician: Dr. Albert

Jefferson. Called Westchester Child Protective Services to report possible incidents of sexual abuse.'

Billie Jo took a deep breath. These meetings were never easy, but it was always her goal to be supportive and empathetic. The last thing she wanted was an angry, defensive mom. Putting her papers away, she walked up the steps to the door of a white Colonial house. It looked like the idyllic home, in the idyllic town of Pelham Manor. Not North Pelham, not Pelham Heights, but Pelham Manor, where many affluent upper/middle class residents lived. It was referred to as a 'bedtime community,' since so many of the locals commuted daily into New York City. Of course, in cases like this, outward appearances meant nothing. She pressed the bell, and patted her greying curls into some semblance of order.

"Hello. Can I help you?" said a very attractive young woman, who was no doubt Samantha.

"Yes. Are you Mrs. Mitchell, Samantha Mitchell?"

"Yes."

"My name is Billie Jo Collins." She reached in her pocket for a card, which she passed to Samantha. "I'm from Child Protective Services. Would it be alright for me to come in and talk to you for a few minutes?"

"What? Child Protective Services? Why on earth would you be coming here?" Samantha stared at the card as if it said The Planet of Mars.

Billie Jo could tell that Samantha was nervous. They always were. Mothers hardly ever think their child might need help from CPS.

"I know this must be a surprise, and I'm sorry for not calling first. We received a call from Dr. Albert Jefferson. He said he was at a loss to explain your daughter's nightmares about possible sexual abuse. It's the law in cases like this for CPS to be notified so that we can do an investigation."

Samantha did not look happy but reluctantly stepped back and said "Of course. Come in. Can I get you a cup of tea or coffee or anything?"

"Oh no, I'm fine. Let's just sit down and have a chat." Samantha led her into the living room which was modestly decorated, with lots of personal touches. Billie Jo admired how comfortable the room looked; a place to live in rather than just visit with company. There was one table by the sofa full of silver framed photos of a child, from infant-hood on up. She paused to look at the pictures of a smiling, golden haired little girl who just radiated happiness. "Is this your daughter, Bonnie?"

"Yes, um, yes. If you'll just excuse me for a minute, I'll ask her to go to her bedroom with a coloring book while we talk."

"Actually, with your permission, I'd like to talk with Bonnie first… alone. Perhaps she could show me her bedroom and we can talk up there."

"You mean I can't be in the room?" Samantha's voice had gone up a notch.

"Oh, don't get concerned. This is just our policy in cases like this. I'm sure Dr. Jefferson talked with Bonnie alone too. I have years of experience talking to little girls, Mrs. Mitchell. My own and hundreds of others. Everything will be all right. After all, my sole purpose in being here is to help you and your daughter."

Samantha seemed to accept this explanation, even though she still looked worried. But what mother wouldn't be?

She disappeared for a moment, and then returned with Bonnie at her side. "Bonnie, I'd like you to meet Mrs… ?"

"Collins."

"Yes, I'm sorry. Mrs. Collins. And this is my daughter Bonnie."

"Hello Mrs. Collins."

9

"It's nice to meet you, Bonnie. I have a daughter who looked a lot like you when she was young. How old are you?"

"I'm free." She held up three fingers. "But almost four!"

Billie Jo smiled. "I love your dress. Did you pick that out?"

"Yes. Every day Mama lets me pick something to wear."

"I'll bet you have lots of pretty dresses. I'd love to see them. Could you show them to me?"

Bonnie glanced at her mother, who nodded her head.

"Sure! They're up in my bedroom. This way... " and off she went. A girl on a mission.

Billie Jo mouthed "thank you" to Samantha and followed.

Bonnie's bedroom was a study in pink. A trellis of pink flowers on the wallpaper, and a four-poster bed with a coordinating rose pattern on the duvet, dust ruffles and canopy. Bonnie had opened the door to her closet and was starting to rapidly take out dresses.

"Oh don't take them all out, honey," said Billie Jo, who had walked up behind her. "I can see them from here. I bet your favorite color is pink!"

"Yes! How did you know? I love pink, and so do my dollies." She pointed to the window seat, where Billie Jo counted at least a dozen dolls dressed in shades of pink and rose, lavender and lilac."

"Oh my, you have the Barbie and Ken dolls. I had them too when I was your age. I didn't know they were still being sold."

"These are my Mama's dolls." Bonnie picked up Barbie and gave her a hug. "I play with them a lot."

"I see you only have one boy doll, Ken. And I know you don't have a brother. Is Ken the only boy who's ever in your bedroom?"

"Yup. This is a girls-only room." She flashed a bright smile and giggled.

Billie Jo chuckled. "Can I sit on your bed, Bonnie? It looks so comfy."

"Sure! I jump on it sometimes, but my head hits the canpee."

Billie Jo sat down and Bonnie climbed up via a small footstool, upholstered in the same pattern as the bed linens. "It's too high for me, so Mama got me this step."

Billie Jo smiled too. It was hard not to smile around this infectiously happy child. "Bonnie, I understand that you have been having pretty bad nightmares. Can you tell me about them? Maybe I can help in some way."

Bonnie's smile faded away. She looked down at her lap for a moment, then said, "My dreams are scary. A man is on top of me and he hurts me... down there." She pointed between her legs.

"Oh, my dear. That does sound scary. I'm so sorry. Do you know who this man is?" Billie Jo's voice was full of caring concern.

"I think his name is Mike. He was a friend of Carrie's."

Billie Jo reached in her bag for a pad and pen. "And who is Carrie? Someone in your daycare school?"

Bonnie's response stopped Billie Jo in her tracks. "I am Carrie. And Carrie is me." For the first time in her life, Billie Jo couldn't think of a thing to say. Out of my league was her first thought. She had no intention of playing psychologist.

"I see. Is there anything else you can tell me about Mike or Carrie?"

"No. Not right now. Let's go downstairs." And with that, she jumped off the bed."

"Bonnie, before you go, I just wanted to thank you for talking to me. You are a very brave little girl, and I am going to do my best to help you."

"Okay. Let's go down now." And off she went.

Back in the living room, Bonnie climbed up on the sofa and gave her mother a hug. Samantha said "Hi, my darling. Everything ok?"

"Oh, yes. I showed Mrs. Collins my dresses and my dolls. She likes my bedroom. Can I have a chocolate chip cookie now?"

"Of course. Let's go in the kitchen. Mrs. Collins, I'll be right back." The two of them went off, Bonnie skipping every other step.

When Samantha returned, she looked over her shoulder to make sure Bonnie wasn't following her. "Well, what did she say?"

Billie Jo understood Samantha's concern, but explained that she would prefer to finish her investigation before sharing Bonnie's comments.

"She's a darling girl, Mrs. Mitchell."

"Yes, thank you. I think she is too." Samantha selected a chair that allowed her to sit up straight, crossed her feet, not her legs, and clasped her hands in her lap. She looked like a perspective employee being interviewed for a job, or better still… a truant teenager in the principal's office.

"What do you want to know?"

"First of all, I want to assure you that my sole purpose in being here is to help you and to make sure that your daughter is safe. As I said, by law, Dr. Jefferson had to call us because Bonnie apparently said 'he keeps hurting me down there,' when she was describing her nightmare. This type of thing can be a sign of sexual abuse. I'm not saying that it is, but it can be. So, by law, we need to follow up with you and see if we can figure out what's going on."

Samantha leaned forward and put her head in her hands. "Oh God!" Then sitting up straight, she said "Bonnie has not been sexually abused! I can't explain that comment or her nightmares, but since she is never left alone, it's impossible that she was abused."

Billie Jo understood Samantha's anxiety. No mother ever wants to believe that their child, whom they love so dearly, could be the subject of sexual abuse on their watch.

"Samantha… is it all right if I call you that?"

"Yes, of course."

"My suggestion is that we just start at the beginning. Although I have Dr. Jefferson's report, why don't you tell me what has been happening."

Samantha told Billie Jo everything she had told Dr. Jefferson, including that he said Bonnie showed no signs of being hurt in any way.

"I see," Billie Jo said. "So, this is a mystery. Well let's see if the two of us can solve it. First, could you tell me a little about your life… yours and Bonnie's?"

"Where should I begin?" Samantha asked, crossing one leg over the other.

"I know that you're separated and are raising Bonnie on your own. Tell me where you work, and the flow of an average day in the lives of Samantha and Bonnie Mitchell."

"All right. Yes, Hank and I are separated. He left when I was about six months pregnant, and to this day I have no idea why. In fact, neither Bonnie nor I have seen him since." Samantha stood up abruptly and asked if Billie Jo would like some water.

"Sure. If you're having one I will too." She could tell that Samantha did not particularly like talking about her ex.

Samantha disappeared into the kitchen and returned in a few minutes with two glasses of iced water. After settling down again, she resumed her story.

"I'm a Senior Financial Advisor at Charles Schwab, in the City, and have worked there for about ten years. I took off three months after Bonnie was born, and then hired a nanny to take care of her so that I could return to work. Mercedes Hernandez is her name, and she has worked here for about three years. I'd be lost without her. Mercedes is in her early sixties, has several grown children of her own, and lives in Mt. Vernon, about twenty minutes from here. Bonnie adores her."

Billie Jo looked up from her note-taking. "She sounds wonderful. And it's not easy finding a good nanny."

"You asked about our daily routine. Well, Bonnie and I get up about 6:00 a.m. I help her get dressed, although she always knows exactly what she wants to wear, and we have breakfast together. Mercedes arrives at 7:30 and I usually catch the 8:15 train into the City.

"Mercedes takes Bonnie to daycare, which starts at 9 a.m. and is taught by Patricia Henderson. There are eleven other children in the group who all live in Pelham Manor. According to Mrs. Henderson, Bonnie is out-going, into art, and loves playing with the other kids. Mercedes picks her up at noon, brings her home for lunch, and then maybe they go the park, or play in the yard, or have indoor games… what-have-you. But Bonnie is never on her own."

Billie Jo stopped note-taking again and asked, "Does Bonnie have any friends she plays with in the afternoon?"

"Yes. She often plays with Allison, the girl next door, who is the same age. Her mother is also divorced."

"I see." Billie Jo said. "And is her ex-husband ever around?"

"I've never met him, but I can't say that he has never been there." Samantha took a sip of water.

"All right. What happens after you finish work?"

"I usually catch the 6:14 train. If I'm going to be late, I call Mercedes and she stays until I return. Bonnie has had her bath and is in bed when I get home, a little after seven. If she's still awake we talk for a while or I read her a story. I wish I could be home earlier to have dinner with her and playtime afterward, but unfortunately I do have to juggle work and mothering. We usually spend the whole weekend together though, and I often plan special activities for us. Going to the Central Park Zoo is her new favorite."

"That's a lovely zoo. My children used to enjoy going there as well. They loved talking to the seals."

"How many children do you have?" Samantha asked.

Billie Jo smiled. "Well, I've had five of my own, but I often feel like a mother to some of the children I meet in my work. Helping children is really what my life is all about.

"If you don't mind, let me ask you a few standard questions about Bonnie. Has she displayed any atypical behavior? Aside from her nightmares, I mean. For instance: does she show any signs of aggression, or does she become fearful of anything or anyone, is she uncomfortable being around adults... of either sex?"

"Her daytime behavior hasn't changed at all." Samantha said. "She's a very happy child, with a winning personality. Oh, she might complain from time to time, but not over anything important. You know... I want pizza tonight, not liver. That kind of thing. She seems to enjoy being around adults and can even carry on a conversation, of sorts. I've never seen her be fearful of anyone, except whoever is showing up in her dreams. She doesn't even act out before going to bed, which you might expect. It's like her life is divided into two parts that rarely intermingle. Does that help you?"

"Yes, it does, and it's nice to get a better picture of her. Now, on to you. Do you ever go out on dates? You're young and attractive, three years have gone by since your separation, I should think you'd attract lots of men."

"Well, thank you, but no. At the moment, my life is just too busy for men."

"So there are no male visitors here?"

"No. In fact, aside from a handyman every now and then, I can't think of the last time a man was here. I do go out with friends from time to time, or to the odd party, but no men come home with me. Ever."

Samantha seemed to be challenging Billie Jo. As if to say 'so now what?'

"You said that Mercedes stays late when you are delayed coming home. On the weekends do you ever need to hire a babysitter? You know, when you want to see your friends, or go shopping or something?"

"Fortunately, I don't have to hire one," Samantha said. "My next-door neighbor is always happy to have Samantha over to play with Allison, and if she's not free, my mother also lives in town, just about a mile away. She loves to have Bonnie come over to visit, and even spend the night sometimes. She lives alone, since my father died about a year ago."

Billie Jo put her pen down. "Oh, dear. I'm sorry to hear that. Losing a parent is so difficult. You have my condolences." She reached over and patted Samantha's hand. They were both quiet for a moment, then Billie Jo sat back and continued.

"All right… from what you have told me, it seems that the only adults who spend time alone with Bonnie are you, Mercedes, Mrs. Henderson, the next-door neighbor and your mother. Did I miss anyone?"

"Nope, that's about it."

"Okay then. My job should be fairly easy. If you don't mind, please write down the names and phone numbers of those people. I will need to meet with each of them and see if I can find any clues to Bonnie's behavior."

"What? You're going to tell them that Bonnie might have been sexually abused? That would be terrible! I'm sure than none of them will be able to offer you any more information than I have, and they might start to wonder what kind of mother I am. Oh, no, this is a bad idea!" Samantha rose and started pacing the room.

Billie Jo was not surprised at her reaction. "Oh, my dear, I know how hard this must be on you. But this is a necessary step in our investigation, all our investigations. Think about it this way; these are your friends and family. They love you and Bonnie, and they are on your side. They will be anxious to help in any way they can. And sometimes people don't even know what they know."

Samantha finally sat down in a soft club chair and let out a sigh. "Okay. You're right, I'm sure they will be understanding. Everyone except my mother that is. She will definitely think that whatever is going on is my fault. Just give me a moment and I'll make a list for you."

"Great. Hopefully I'll be able to see each of them within a few days, and then I'll get back to you."

As Samantha went over to the secretary and started writing her list, Billie Jo thought over Bonnie's strange comments about Carrie and Mike. It almost sounded as though she had a split personality, although she'd never heard of such a thing in a child so young. She wanted to talk to Samantha about it, but thought it better to wait until she'd gathered information from everyone close to Bonnie. Someone might just say something off-hand that would help her figure this out.

As she was saying goodbye at the door, Bonnie came down and took her mother's hand. They were the picture of a perfect mother and daughter.

==

As promised, within two days Billie Jo had completed her interviews. Unfortunately, or fortunately depending on how you looked at it, there were no clues to Bonnie's dream-life and no one had ever heard of anyone named Mike or Carrie. Although Billie Jo said their names had come up in her conversation with Bonnie, she did not say anything more. Particularly not that provocative last sentence. They each voiced shock and dismay that this sort of an investigation was even necessary since, in their minds, Bonnie was so loved and well-cared for.

In describing her, Mrs. Henderson used adjectives like smart, curious, creative, outgoing, well-behaved and congenial. Sort of sounded like the words put into a report card, but Mrs. Henderson was very genuine. She had not observed any of the worrisome behaviors that Billie Jo probed for, nor had any of the others.

Mercedes, the nanny, was distraught that there was even a suspicion of sexual harassment. She loved Bonnie like a daughter, and was always careful to keep an eye on her whenever they went out. She concurred, to the best of her knowledge, that Samantha did not go out on dates and, in fact, was usually home just as Bonnie was getting into bed. When asked about Bonnie's playtime behavior, Mercedes spoke glowingly about how much she liked to dress up. She even dressed up her dolls. Then they would all sit around and pretend to have tea. Including Mercedes.

Elaine Cameron, who lived next-door, was very concerned when Billie Jo explained the reason for her visit. Not only for Bonnie, but for her own daughter as well. She was adamant though, that neither child had ever been left alone with a man, or was left unsupervised. When asked about whether her ex-husband ever visited, she laughed.

"Absolutely not! He is not only living with someone else now, but the two of them are in London. So you can rule him out."

Eleanor Murray, Samantha's mother, was last on her list. Despite her daughter's concerns that she would be very critical, she was the opposite. She was distraught that Bonnie was having such terrifying nightmares, which she'd never been told of, and she had no idea what might be causing them. As fate would have it, on the few times that Bonnie spent the night there had been no problems. Like everyone else, she thought Bonnie could do no wrong, and that she was a happy, well-adjusted child.

On Wednesday, Billie Jo called Samantha at work and asked if she could come over that evening, after Bonnie had gone to bed.

She arrived at the house close to 8 p.m., and Samantha opened the door immediately. This time she ushered Billie Jo into the living room quickly and forgot the niceties of offering her something to drink.

"I know you're anxious to hear what I learned, so I'll just dive into it," said Billie Jo, pulling the file out of her shoulder bag. "First of all, let me assure you that you and Bonnie are well loved, and everyone was upset to learn what you are going through. No one has noticed any symptoms of fear or anxiety in Bonnie and they had only good things to say about her. In fact, I'd say that you should be proud. You are clearly a good mother."

"Well that's nice to hear. How about my mother? Did she have any clever insights to offer?"

Billie Jo smiled. What is it about mothers and daughters anyway? I'll bet that Samantha has tried hard to build a closer relationship with Bonnie than she had with her own mom. "Actually, she was not snippy at all. Of course she was upset, but just wanted to help in any way she could. I expect you will be hearing from her soon, and I don't think she blames you in any way."

Samantha breathed a sigh of relief, but then became frustrated. "So where does that leave us? What do I do next to figure out what's going on?"

Billie Jo asked if they might have a cup of tea, saying that there was something else she wanted to discuss.

Samantha said "Of course. Come on out to the kitchen." A cloud of concern had returned to her face.

As they sipped their tea, Billie Jo told her about her conversation with Bonnie. "At first we talked about easy things; her clothes, her dolls, her pretty bed. After I felt that she was comfortable with me, I explained that you had told me about her nightmares and I asked if she knew who the man in her dreams was. Much to my surprise, she did. She said she thought his name was Mike and that he was a friend of Carrie's."

Samantha put her teacup down. "What? But we don't know anyone named Mike, or Carrie either for that matter."

"Well brace yourself, 'cause there's more. When I asked if Carrie was one of her playmates, she said no. She said, and I'm quoting now, 'I am Carrie and Carrie is me.' " Both women just stared at each other. "Does this make any sense to you?"

"Absolutely not. How could she say such a thing?" Suddenly Samantha paused and closed her eyes. "Wait a minute. I just remembered something. About a month ago I took Bonnie to the Central Park Zoo. After we left, we were standing on the corner of 65th and 5th waiting for the bus, and I noticed Bonnie tilting her head way back, looking up at something. I asked her what she was looking at and this is what she said. I may not have the exact words, but it was something like this. 'Mama,' she said, 'you can see the zoo when you is up there.' Then, in a sad little voice, she added,

'Carrie loved to look out that window.' Just at that moment the bus pulled up, and I was distracted from her comment. Later I assumed she was making up a story, which is something she likes to do, so I didn't ask her about 'Carrie.' What do you think this is all about?"

"I don't know, Samantha. But though I can find no signs of Bonnie being sexually assaulted, I do suspect something out of the ordinary is going on." She leaned forward and took Samantha's hand in both of hers. "She has conjured up something in her mind, my dear. Something way beyond her years, and I have no idea how that's even possible. My recommendation is that you find an excellent child psychologist. Something is wrong, but neither of us has the skill to figure it out."

Chapter 3

*F*or the remainder of the week, Samantha fretted over what to do. When several days went by without a nightmare, she even started to hope that it had all been a phase.

Saturday morning Samantha slept gratefully until eight, when she was awakened by Bonnie quietly crawling into her bed. As usual, she moved as stealthily as a cat and softly put her nose right up to Samantha's to make sure she was really asleep. This always made Samantha laugh, prompting Bonnie to squeal with delight.

"Oh, goody! You're awake! It's time to get up, Mama! Can we have pancakes this morning?" She started jumping up and down on the bed. As she started to land nearer and nearer to the edge, Samantha reached out for a leg.

"Yes, yes, okay! Pancakes it is. But please honey, no more jumping on the bed. One of these days you're going to land on the floor with a great big thump! Come on, let's go brush our teeth before breakfast."

The bathroom that she and Bonnie shared, at least for the time being, was the only room she had completely redone. It was large, with a spa tub, a glass-walled shower, and two sinks, his and hers... now hers and hers.

Bonnie rushed in and hopped up on the short stack of stairs in front of her sink to start brushing her teeth. "Now remember," Samantha said, "you have to brush just as long as I do. Then we'll get to the fun part!" A few minutes later they were both filling their mouths with water, swishing and spitting several times. Samantha had to admit that this was an odd bonding ritual, but hey, whatever works.

Downstairs, while Bonnie played with her Barbie and Ken dolls, Samantha padded around the country kitchen in her pajamas, mixing the batter and mulling over Billie Jo's recommendation. With the dawn of a new day, sun shining in the window and bacon sizzling on the stove, she wondered whether it had been too extreme. But when she glanced over at Bonnie, she saw that Ken was lying on top of Barbie and in a low enticing voice Bonnie was whispering "Come on Carrie, you know you like it, you little bitch!" Samantha froze. She stared at Bonnie as though her daughter had suddenly been hijacked by a perverted ventriloquist. Why was Bonnie talking like that? Who on earth *was* this Carrie person? And wherever did she hear the word bitch?

Putting down the batter bowl and switching off the burner under the bacon, Samantha did her best to sound casual. "Bonnie, love, who is Carrie?"

"Carrie is me. And Ken," Bonnie held the doll aloft, "is Mike, and he's mean!" She then smashed the Ken doll on the floor.

Samantha sat down on the floor next to her, fiddled with the broken Ken doll and said, "Do you know someone named Mike, honey?"

"No, but I 'member him."

"You remember him from... when?"

"From when I was Carrie!" Bonnie seemed a little frustrated that Samantha didn't understand her.

Samantha was unnerved. "But you were never Carrie. You have always been Bonnie, my little girl!" She desperately wanted this to be one of Bonnie's stories. "What happens in this story, hon? Does Mike pull Carrie's pigtails?"

Bonnie's reply made her blood turn cold.

"Mike killed me, Mama! He lied on top of me and hurt me... down there. I screamed and then he put a pillow on my face, and I couldn't breathe! I kicked and tried to scream some more, but I couldn't!" With that startling outburst, she put her forehead down on her raised knees and started to cry.

Samantha was totally taken aback and folded Bonnie in her arms. "It's okay, pumpkin. Mike isn't here, and you're safe with me. Everything's going to be all right." To herself though she thought, oh God, Billie Jo was right. Something terrible is going on.

Yet still, after Bonnie had calmed down and breakfast had been served, Samantha tried again to find a logical explanation. "Honey Bun… do Carrie or Mike live near here?"

"No," Bonnie replied, now speaking in a calm matter-of-fact manner. "Carrie lived in the big city, the one with the lady standing in the water and holding a candle." She hopped off her stool to demonstrate that lady, with one hand held up to hold her torch. Climbing back up, she added, "but Carrie died. I don't know where Mike lived." And then, as if nothing had happened, she poured buckets of syrup on her pancakes and dug in.

Could Bonnie really be talking about the Statue of Liberty? She didn't think Bonnie had even seen a picture of it, and they'd only been to the City once… to visit the Zoo. And that thought brought Samantha back around to Bonnie's statement about Carrie living in the penthouse apartment across the street from the Zoo.

I give up, she thought. It's time to find someone who can figure all this out.

==

It took several weeks of research for Samantha to find Dr. Karadamand, a well respected child psychologist, who appeared in New York Magazine's annual list of 'Top Doctors.'

Born in India, he had lived in America for twenty years and studied at Princeton for both his undergraduate and graduate degrees. His specialty was childhood trauma. Although anxious to see him right away, when Samantha tried to make an appointment, she was forced to wait a month. Isn't that always the case, she thought. During that time, the nightmares continued and Samantha became increasingly anxious.

About a week before their appointment, the doctor called Samantha. He explained that he liked to speak to the parents before a first meeting, so that he could understand what was happening and appropriately question the child. "And, please, just call me Dr. K," he said. "That's usually easier for everyone."

After explaining that there was no father on the scene for him to interview, Samantha started spilling out what was going on.

"My three year old daughter has several nightmares a week, and now they seem to be increasing. She has said that someone is hurting her 'down there.' So, of course I took her to see her pediatrician, Dr. Jefferson. He couldn't find anything wrong, but reported the visit to Child Protective Services. Someone came over immediately to interview me and Bonnie as well as everyone else who spends time alone with her. But in the end she could find no signs of sexual abuse. However, she thought I should find a child psychologist because of something Bonnie said. Apparently, when she was being questioned about her dream, Bonnie identified the man who was hurting her as Mike, a friend of Carrie's. When asked who Carrie was, she said 'I am Carrie, and Carrie is me.'

"And then several days later she told me that she, or Carrie, I don't remember which, had been sexually assaulted and then smothered with a pillow by that man named Mike! I'm at a total loss, Doctor. She's too young to even know what she's talking about! Yet it all seems so real to her." Her words all poured out on top of each other as she tried to explain the craziness of the situation.

"I can certainly understand how troubling this must be," Dr. K said. "How long did you say these nightmares have been going on?"

"She's never slept well from the day she was born. I thought things would improve as she got past those infant years, but they only seem to be getting worse." She was trying to sound calm and in control, but was on the verge of tears.

"Let's not get into any more on the phone," Dr. K said. "I've treated many children with terrible nightmares and creative imaginations. It doesn't necessarily mean they have any psychological problems. Rest assured, Mrs. Mitchell, I will do my best to get to the bottom of whatever is going on. Just try to remain calm. Okay?"

"Yes, Doctor. I'll try," Samantha said, knowing how unlikely that was.

"Good. My office is at 310 East 72nd on the first floor. See you next Friday?"

"Yes, okay Doctor. See you then."

==

As she was getting dressed on Friday morning, Samantha glanced at herself in the mirror and was surprised to see that she looked just the same. Instead of seeing a tired, worn-out, anxiety-ridden woman on the verge of a nervous breakdown, her reflection showed an attractive thirty-five year old, who had a peaches and cream complexion, thick, wavy, auburn hair full of reddish glints, blue eyes and a smattering of freckles across the bridge of her nose. Taking heart from the phantom in the looking glass, Samantha took Bonnie into the City.

On the train, when Bonnie asked where they were going, Samantha explained that they were going to see a nice man named Dr. K. "But I'm not sick, Mama."

"I know, honey. But this doctor may be able to figure out why you have so many nightmares and make them go away. You'd like that, wouldn't you?" Bonnie nodded, but looked doubtful.

After filling out the necessary paperwork in the reception room of Dr. K's office, they only had to wait a few minutes before Dr. K, himself, came out to greet them. He was short and dark skinned, about fifty, wore black rimmed glasses, a white doctor's coat over his blue shirt, and had a warm, welcoming smile. He shook Samantha's hand, introduced himself to Bonnie and invited them both into his office. Upon being asked to take a seat, Bonnie boosted herself up onto the chair next to Dr. K's desk, her blond curls jumping. Dr. K opened his laptop, readying himself to take notes.

"Well, Bonnie, it's so nice to meet you. Did you have a nice trip on the train?"

"Yes," she replied softly; clearly a little nervous.

"Tell me Bonnie, how old are you?"

"Free. My birfday is May 23 and then I is four." She proudly held up four fingers while eyeing the lollipops on Dr. K's desk.

Glancing at Samantha for approval, Dr. K said "Here... have one," and he extended the bowl of candy to her. "Bonnie, your mother has told me that you have a friend named Carrie. Can you tell me about her?"

While unwrapping the lollipop, Bonnie calmly explained, "Carrie is not my friend. Carrie is me and I is Carrie."

"I see. Are you always... Bonnie *and* Carrie?"

"I am me on the outside and Carrie on the inside."

Dr. K nodded his head. "Does Carrie speak?"

Bonnie looked thoughtful while sucking on her lollipop. "Not during the daytime so much. But she does at night, when I'm sleeping."

"I see," Dr. K said, "and what does she say then?"

"She's afraid. She's screams and says 'get off me, go away, stop!' "

"Who is she talking to, Bonnie?"

"Mike. I don't like Mike. He was mean to Carrie."

Dr. K was busy typing. "In what way was he mean to Carrie?"

"He tried to touch her... down there." She put her hand between her legs for a minute, then pulled it back quickly.

"Was Carrie upset by that?"

"Oh yes! It was very scary."

"Then what happened?"

"Carrie screamed and Mike made her dead wif a pillow."

Samantha was horrified, but Dr. K continued on calmly. "Oh my, that's terrible! Bonnie, do you know who Mike is?"

"No. But I hate him," Bonnie replied, as she angrily kicked one foot into the side of his desk.

Samantha and Dr K looked at each other in surprise at this sudden change in temperament.

"Bonnie," Dr. K asked, "Do you know Carrie's last name?"

"Yes. It's Kelly," Bonnie replied instantly.

Samantha raised her eyebrows, surprised by this new information.

"And do you know Mike's last name?"

Bonnie thought for a minute, but then shook her head.

Changing the subject, Dr. K said, "Okay. Let's not talk about Carrie or Mike now. Let's just talk about you. Are you a happy little girl, Bonnie?"

"Sure. I'm happy playing with the kids at daycare, I'm happy when Mama reads to me and I'm happy when we bake chocolate chip cookies!" She gave her mother a big smile.

Dr. K smiled too, then asked, "Are you ever unhappy?"

Bonnie's smile became a pout. "I'm not happy when I dream about Mike hurting Carrie. That makes me cry."

"I understand," Dr. K said. "Does anything else make you cry?"

Bonnie looked down at her lap. When she looked up she had tears in her eyes. In a small sad voice she said, "I miss my daddy."

Dr. K said, "What do you remember about your daddy, Bonnie?"

"He loved Carrie so much! He gave her presents, he took her out for dinner, he sang with her. I really miss him."

"So the daddy you miss was Carrie's father?"

"Yes, but I am Carrie and Carrie is me."

Dr. K took a deep breath and decided that was enough for today. He invited Bonnie to go into the adjoining playroom, where his intern was waiting to amuse her.

When he returned, Samantha was on the edge of her chair. "Well? What do you think, Doctor? Is she just making all this up?" Samantha was itching for an immediate diagnosis; one that would not suggest her daughter was insane and one that could be treated, and as soon as possible!

Dr. K looked over his notes for a minute, and then asked if Samantha would like a cup of coffee.

"No thanks. I'm fine, just tell me what you think." She tapped her fingers on his desk.

"Well, I don't think I can tell you right this minute." He reviewed his notes while speaking. "Let's see, she seems to be confused about her own self-identity.   She says that she is Carrie, but then sometimes refers to Carrie in the third person. She   switches back and forth between present and past tense. She told us that Mike touched Carrie 'down there,' and than suffocated her with a pillow when she started screaming. That concept seems much too adult for a three-year-old to even think of, much less communicate. Have you noticed her using words from time to time that are beyond her years?"

Samantha started nervously circling the foot on her crossed leg. "Yes.   Sometimes she comes up with grown-up words right in the middle of baby-speak. I've just told myself she's advanced for her age.   What   do you make of all that 'daddy' talk?"

"Well she says that she's talking about Carrie's father, but that could be projection. Have you explained why her own daddy doesn't live with you?"

Samantha looked embarrassed. "Actually, the subject hasn't come up. I've been meaning to, but didn't really know what to say. I guess I should, right?"

"Yes, I think that would be a good idea. If, and I'm just saying if, she has created another identity for herself, she has also given that person a father, one who 'loves her very much.'"

"Ok, ok. I will talk to her... very soon."

Dr. K looked at her over the top of his glasses.

"Tomorrow," Samantha promised.

"Good. It's rare, extremely rare, that children have a dissociative disorder but it's not unheard of. Is there any history of mental illness in your family or your husband's?"

Samantha's eyebrows reached for the ceiling. "No, absolutely not." She paused, "at least not that I know of."

"All right. One possibility is that if Bonnie is extremely stressed out about not having a father, she may have made up another self who does have one. However, I have to tell you that I really have no idea right now if that's what's going on. Particularly with all those nightmares. I'd like to see her again, perhaps even several more times. Do you think you could come back in a week? That would give you time to talk to her and see how she reacts."

"Yes, of course Doctor." She paused before asking, "Is that dis, dis…"

"Dissociative disorder," Dr. K said.

"Yes, that thing. Is that the same as a split personality?"

"Well, yes. That's one of the conditions listed as a dissociative disorder. A split personality, also called multiple personality disorder, is extremely rare. The split results in the person confusing reality and fantasy. The person may also experience delusions and hallucinations, and their emotions may seem blunted or inappropriate." Samantha started biting her lip.

"Now before you get worried, it's true that Bonnie's emotions seem to shift quickly whenever she is talking about Carrie and she may indeed be having problems separating reality from fantasy. But, on the other hand, she could just be a very imaginative little girl. That's why I'd like you to tell her about her real father, and why I'd like to keep seeing her for a while."

"All right. I'll try not to worry, but to tell the truth, you've really spooked me!"

"Please don't get upset right now, Mrs. Mitchell. I really do not think that we are dealing with a case of dissociative disorder. Bonnie doesn't behave like a different person from time to time, does she? In cases of split personalities, the others are recognizable as entirely different

31

people. They have different voices, attitudes, ways of talking, even different physical mannerisms. Have you noticed anything like that?"

"No. Nothing like that." But then she remembered. "Except a month ago when she was playacting with her Barbie and Ken dolls. I caught her placing Ken over Barbie, and then with a lowered voice, saying, "Come on Carrie, you know you love it. You little bitch." It was her own voice, but certainly not anything she has ever said before."

"Hmm. Well, I don't know how to explain that right now. But for the time being, let's consider other more benign alternatives to explain her behavior, such as an over-active imagination. I'd like you to try and separate the things she says that could conceivably come from her imagination, and the things that seem outside her world of knowledge. It might be good if you could start keeping a journal, and then we can discuss it when you return. Please date your notes."

"I'll do that, but as far as I can tell she's saying new things every day outside her field of knowledge."

Dr. K nodded his head. "Don't get all worked up right now. I'm sure we will find an explanation soon."

They both got up and Dr. K went to retrieve Bonnie from the playroom. She skipped back in, full of smiles, and said "You have lots of nice dolls, Dr. K! Me and Julie played with them."

"I'm glad you liked them, Bonnie. And guess what? You'll be able to play with them again, since your mother has agreed to come back next week."

"Oh goodie!" Bonnie grabbed her mother's hand, and said "Bye, bye Dr. K. Till we meet again."

He seemed surprised by her terminology, but waved and gave her a big smile. "See you soon, Bonnie."

Chapter 4

*K*nowing she would have to find a way to tell Bonnie about Hank, Samantha thought back over their brief relationship which began in January of 2013.

Then, as now, she was working as a financial advisor at Charles Schwab. Although she wanted a man in her life, she had trouble finding the time to look for one. So she'd decided to give MATCH a try. She hated resorting to an online dating service, but liked the idea of being able to reject men before actually meeting them. She spent several weeks scanning photos and reading profiles that were, for the most part, discouraging. Lots of receding hairlines, bulging middles and poorly written sentences. But finally she found someone who sounded promising.

She and Hank first sent emails back and forth, then talked on the phone. She learned that he was a Business Transformation Advisor for Accenture; helping companies figure out how to become more profitable through Accenture technology. She wasn't sure how interested she was in that field, but then advising people how to invest their savings wasn't exactly dinner conversation either. Nevertheless, they finally decided to get together for a look-see, her term for a short, manageable period of time to check each other out.

They settled on having a drink after work at McMullen's on Third Avenue. She lived then on East 79th Street, just a few blocks away, so she'd rushed home from work to change. The conservative corporate look wasn't the image she'd wanted to project. Instead, she'd put on a pair of black, slim-fitting jeans, a coral silk shirt, and black boots. Then, for a bit of flair, she'd added a bright, geometric Hermes scarf, found in a consignment shop. The final touch was to release her long, wavy auburn hair from the low pony tail it had been confined to all day. With a touch of red lipstick, she was ready to meet Mr. Right, or hopefully Mr. Right.

When she'd walked into the bar she'd recognized him immediately from his profile picture. He was the Nordic type; tall and slim, with very short blonde hair, and was wearing a navy sport coat, chinos and a peach polo shirt. He must have recognized her as well since he rose from his chair immediately, his translucent blue eyes totally focussed on her.

Samantha watched the scene unfold in her mind.

"Hi. You must be Samantha. I'm Hank." They shook hands and he pulled out the chair for her. After she sat down, he scooted her chair closer to the table. She couldn't remember the last time that had happened. They bantered back and forth easily for about thirty minutes, while sipping their drinks. Then Samantha cut to the chase.

"We could go on like this, but by the time we separate we won't really know much more about each other. So I have a suggestion."

He raised his eyebrows, waved a hand and said "Proceed."

"Well, if you don't mind, let's take turns asking each other questions, no holds barred. The only rule is to answer truthfully. And it's also okay to turn around and ask the same question you just answered. Are you game?"

Hank chuckled. "Sure. Let's go for it. You first."

Samantha grinned, took a bigger sip of her wine, and stared at the ceiling for a moment. "Tell me about a moment when you were completely happy."

Now it was time for Hank to think. Within thirty seconds, however, he had it. "Okay. This isn't the happiest

34

moment, but it's certainly one of them. I was in Venice with a small group of music lovers. On this night, we had taken a few gondolas to a pink palazzo on the Grand Canal. It pulled up to the side door because the main entrance was water-logged, and we were asked to climb the stairs to the second floor. Upon entering, we were each handed a glass of Prosecco and invited to make ourselves comfortable in the living room. After about ten minutes, the lights dimmed and costumed performers entered the room, singing. It was *Traviata*, and we were right there.... in their home, nearly singing along to 'Drink, drink, drink.' Of course we didn't sing, but we did drink. And during the intermission, I walked to the tall front windows and gazed out at the canal as the sun was setting behind the Santa Maria della Salute church. It was a glorious sight, and I thought what more could one ask for?"

Samantha could see that he was lost in that beautiful memory. "That sounds so special. I would love to do that some day. I've been to Italy once, but unfortunately not to Venice."

"Well maybe we'll go some day." At that moment, Samantha thought, she'd like nothing better.

Then it was his turn. "Are you ready for my question?"

"Fire away," she said.

"In your life so far, what do you deeply regret?"

"Oh, my. Now we're really getting personal. But just give me a minute." She narrowed her eyes while she thought. "Okay, here goes. I really regret that my mother and I never became friends. She and my father were very close, but she never seemed to have a lot of time for me. We lived in Pelham Manor. Actually she still lives there. But she was a career woman when I was growing up, and commuted back and forth to Manhattan with my father. Even on the weekends she never seemed to have the time or the inclination to do 'mom' things with me; like baking cookies or throwing sleep-overs for my friends. She had her life and I had mine. I'm sure there were reasons for that, but I sure don't want to be that kind of mom."

She felt a little embarrassed at revealing that regret, so she quickly changed the topic. "Okay, enough of 'poor me.' Tell me what you're most looking forward to in the future."

Hank smiled. "That's an easy one. I'm looking forward to finding the right woman to share my life with."

"And what's the right woman like?"

"Is that a second question?"

"No. It's just a follow up. That's allowed."

Hank smiled, looked right into Samantha's eyes, and said, "she will be attractive, inside and out. She will be a good conversationalist, interested in the world, curious about what makes us tick and open to other points of view. She might be a hard worker, but will take time out to enjoy life - traveling, taking in plays and movies, going to concerts and the ballet. With me."

They fell silent for a moment. "How about you? Who would the right man be for you?"

"Pretty much the same, actually. Plus sky-diving." Hank did a double take.

"Just kidding. But if he could cook, my prayers would be answered."

"Well, darlin' that just happens to be my forté. I'll have to show you that some time too, but for now, what do you say to having some dinner here, since we've 'gotten to know each other.' "

That was how it began, and it only got better from there. They talked every day and got together on the weekends. Although they went out, he also made a point of inviting her over for dinner… just to prove that he could cook. He was not only able to cook, he was a talented one, throwing together delicious meals without ever reading a recipe. It was no surprise to family and friends that within the year, they were walking down the aisle of the Lady Chapel at St. Patrick's Cathedral. Talk about happy moments.

Then her mind skipped ahead. Despite their mutual desire to put off having children for about five years, Samantha became pregnant six months later. Much to her surprise, the news seemed to hit Hank hard. They'd been having a glass of wine before dinner when she announced what she thought was exciting news. But Hank didn't seem to share her excitement. "I thought we were going to wait a while."

"Well, so did I. But I must have skipped a pill one day. The wrong day. I'm sorry, Hank. But we'll be okay, don't you think?"

For a moment he seemed disoriented. "What? Oh, yes. We'll be okay. Of course we'll be okay." And he took her in his arms.

At about month four, they decided it would be best to move out of the City. "Why don't we try Pelham. After all, I grew up there, still have some friends in Pelham, and they have great schools. The best thing is that it's a short commute - about thirty minutes. We could go back and forth together. Oh God, this is sounding like my parents. But don't worry, once the baby comes, I will be there for her, or him, in every possible way!"

Hank had been to Pelham many times to visit Samantha's mother. He thoroughly enjoyed her and agreed that it would be nice to have a built-in baby sitter. So they found a starter home not far from her. But after they moved Hank started to behave oddly. He was quieter, less prone to laughing, more often reading than talking. He also stopped joining her for a quick drink at the Oyster Bar in Grand Central, before catching the train home. "Working late" was the excuse.

Finally, unable to cope with all this avoidance, she tried to get through to him. "What's wrong, Hank? You don't seem yourself. Can't we talk about whatever's bothering you?"

But he wouldn't talk, and when begged, wouldn't go to see a marriage counselor either. Then one day she came home and found a letter on her pillow.

My Darling,

You are right. Something is wrong with me, but I don't know what it is. And since I don't know what it is, I can't talk to you or a therapist about it. All I know is that my mind is very troubled. I have to be alone to see if I can figure out what's going on. I know you need me now and I wish I could be there for you. But, to tell you the truth, I'm afraid of what might happen if I do. I'm staying at a friend's apartment in the City while I try to work this out. Unfortunately, I have no idea how long that will take.

Believe me when I say this has nothing to do with you. It's me. Please don't try to contact me. It's best if I do this myself. I will deposit money into your account each month, so you don't have to worry.

I love you, Samantha. You are indeed that special woman I was looking for. But I just don't know when we can be together again.

Love,

Hank

After crying her eyes out for weeks, Samantha did try to contact Hank. But she didn't know which friend's apartment he was staying in, and his Accenture phone line was no longer his. The HR office told her that he no longer worked in that office, but that was all they would say. For all she knew, he could be living abroad. But since the monthly deposits continued, she knew he was alive; at least she knew that much.

Now, almost four years later, she missed him and worried about him, but had become adjusted to being a single mom. She no longer expected that he would return.

==

For two days Samantha wrestled with how to tell Bonnie about Hank. But after she picked her up from a playdate with Allison, she had an idea.

She settled Bonnie at the kitchen table with some chocolate chip cookies and a glass of milk, then sat down next to her with a photo album. "Bonnie, would you like to see some pictures of me when I was young?"

"Yes! When you were young like me?"

"Yup... now let's see." She opened the album at the beginning. "Here's a picture of me when I was just a baby. Isn't that a pretty dress?" It was her christening outfit.

"Awww! You were so cute." Bonnie ran a finger lightly over the photo, admiring it.

For the next ten minutes or so, Samantha showed Bonnie photos of herself as she grew up; from grade school class portraits, to high school and college graduation shots. Finally, they came to a photo of Samantha and Hank at the beach, looking happy and in love.

"Who's that, Mama?" asked Bonnie.

"That is Hank Mitchell, a man I loved very much." She turned the page and there was a photo of them at their wedding. "I loved him so much that we got married one year after we met. And then we had a baby!" Samantha paused and put her arm around Bonnie. She kissed her on the top of her head and whispered, "That baby was you, honey."

Bonnie's eyes widened. "So… is that man my daddy?"

"Yes, sweetheart, he is. Hank Mitchell is your daddy." Stymied about what to say next, Samantha waited for Bonnie to ask a question.

Looking at the photo again with renewed interest, Bonnie finally said, "He looks nice, but…where is he now?"

"I'm not exactly sure where he is now, honey. You know how Allison lives alone with her mother? Well, some married people decide to live apart. They love each other, but they just have trouble being together all the time. So sometimes the daddy moves away."

"But doesn't my daddy want to see me?" Bonnie looked dumbfounded.

There's the rub, Samantha thought. Doesn't he want to see her? She paused to come up with something and then decided to lie through her teeth.

"Oh I'm sure he does. But he travels a lot for his work, and I don't think he's even in this country now. But some day he'll return, and I'm sure he will come to see you then."

Bonnie looked at the wedding photo again, then turned back to the shot on the beach. Finally, she looked up at Samantha and said, "Can I show these pictures to Allison?"

After a quick moment to recall whether she had copies of those photos, which would surely be covered in fingerprints by day's end, Samantha replied, "Sure. Let me take them out of the album for you." Amazing, she thought. No histrionics, no tears. In fact she seems proud that she has such a handsome father. Whew!

Chapter 5

For the rest of the week, leading up to their visit with Dr. K, Bonnie kept the photographs by her bedside. On Friday morning, after learning that they were going into the city again for her doctor's appointment, she asked if she could take Hank's pictures to show him.

When they got there, no sooner had she climbed up into her chair, then she asked Dr. K if he'd like to see some pictures of her daddy.

"Of course I would," he replied, looking over her head at Samantha with surprise.

"Doesn't he look like a nice man?" Bonnie asked, proudly showing him the two photos.

"Yes, he certainly does. Do you know where he is now?"

"He's traveling. When he comes back he's going to come see me." She retrieved the snapshots and carefully put them in her little purse.

Samantha saw Dr. K pause a minute, before he decided to ask Bonnie the next question.

"Is this man Carrie's father too?"

"Oh no. Carrie has her own father."

"Why do you think Carrie can't see her daddy," Dr. K asked.

Bonnie sat quietly thinking about this, then said softly, "Maybe 'cause she's dead."

Dr. K decided to go along with her. "I'm sure her daddy misses her very much."

"I miss him too." Before Bonnie could get teary, Dr. K moved on.

"On another subject, Bonnie, your mother told me that Carrie used to live in the City. Do you know where she lived?"

"Yes. She lived on the top of a tall building across the street from the Zoo. I could see the animals from there." Bonnie lifted her arm up to demonstrate the height of the building, and tilted her head way back.

"Did she live alone?" Dr. K asked.

"Yes." Distracted by the lollipop bowl, she slowly moved her hand towards it. Dr. K smiled, then offered them to her while continuing with his questions.

"That must have been a very nice apartment, with a view of the Zoo. Did Carrie live there a long time?"

Bonnie thought for a minute, then said "I don't 'member. My daddy gave it to me for my birfday. I was twenty." She flashed ten fingers twice.

"Is he the man you showed me in the photographs?"

"No," Bonnie replied with a bit of impatience. That man is *my* father. Carrie's father is a different man."

"Bonnie, do you remember Carrie's father's name?"

"His name was Daddy!"

"And what about her mother? Do you remember her?"

Bonnie looked confused. "My Mama is right here," she said, pointing at Samantha.

"Yes, of course," Dr. K confirmed. "But what about Carrie's mother? Do you remember her?" Bonnie frowned as she tried to think. After a few minutes she replied "I don't 'member her. Maybe Carrie didn't have a mother."

Since Bonnie seemed to be getting fidgety, Dr. K invited her into the adjoining room to play with the dolls again.

When he returned and was alone with Samantha, he seemed to be trying to decide how much to say.

"So tell me how the week went. Did Bonnie have any more nightmares? And what did you tell her about Mr. Mitchell?"

"Yes, she had two nightmares, pretty much like all the others." Then she told him about their "daddy" conversation. "I really think it went well. Much better than I anticipated. It helps that the woman next door is divorced, so her daughter doesn't have a father around either. Bonnie was quite excited to show Hank's pictures to Allison. She seems to be proud of him and not angry that he isn't around."

"Did she continue saying 'I miss my daddy'?"

"After the nightmares, but not during the day."

"Hmm," Dr. K said. "She associates herself most with Carrie during and after her nightmares. That's when she is most upset and that's when she 'misses her daddy.' During the daytime, Carrie's name only comes up when something reminds Bonnie of her, such as the apartment building she saw across from the zoo. Or when she is asked a direct question about Carrie. Is that correct?"

Samantha sat back and thought for a minute. "Yes, I guess so. But occasionally some Carrie-related comment comes out of the blue. Like that time with the Ken and Barbie dolls."

"Last week we discussed the very rare possibility that Bonnie might be suffering from some sort of multiple personality disorder," Dr. K said. "At this point I don't think that is the case. It would be obvious to you if she switched back and forth between different personalities. Even though she says, 'I am Carrie and Carrie is me,' she knows they have different parents and that Carrie is, or was, older than she. I'm intrigued that she has described the view from Carrie's apartment, and the details of Mike's attack in a way that one wouldn't expect from a three-year-old."

In frustration, Samantha said, "So, what do you think, Dr. K. Is she just making all this up? And if so, how is that possible for a three-year old?"

"Well, this could be the result of a creative imagination," Dr. K began, "but before we go any further, there is also another explanation." He paused, sat down at his desk, and then seemed to make a decision. "It's also possible that Bonnie is remembering a different time when she was, in fact, Carrie. Mrs. Mitchell, please bear with me because this might be difficult for you to even consider. Have you ever heard of reincarnation?"

"What?" Samantha's jaw dropped open. Not in a million years could she have anticipated that question. "Of course I've heard of it. It's part of some religious belief where you get reborn in someone else's body after you die. Or maybe even in an animal. But that's not a real thing! I was raised as a Christian and taught that the soul moves on to Heaven or Hell. To tell you the truth, I'm not sure whether I even believe that now, but reincarnation is not on my radar at all." Realizing that Dr. K, as an Indian, might actually believe in reincarnation, Samantha cleared her throat and tried to temper her outburst. "But, of course, I've never been taught anything about it."

"Yes," Dr. K said, "reincarnation is a very difficult concept for Westerners to grasp. But a lot of research has been done on it, primarily in Southeast Asia, where it's a central tenet of Hinduism and Buddhism as well as a number of other religions. Actual case studies have emerged in many countries, including the United States. In fact, the University of Virginia has a whole department dedicated to the study of past lives."

Samantha tried to understand what Dr. K was suggesting. Does he really think that Bonnie lived a previous life? That's absurd! How on earth did he get on New York

Magazine's list? Trying to appear at least open-minded, despite being totally skeptical, Samantha said "Has anyone ever proved that reincarnation exists? It really seems far-fetched to me."

"Well," Dr. K began, "there are certain characteristics that most reincarnation case studies have in common. Firstly, almost all of them involve children who are between the ages of three and seven." Samantha raised her eyebrows and Dr. K nodded. "After that, any memories the child might have seem to fade away.

"Secondly, the child often has nightmares about the traumatic death of their previous personality caused by an accident or a murder. The child can be very specific about this event. They often voice a longing to see their 'parents,' even though their real parents are right in front of them, or to 'go home,' even though they are at home.

"Sometimes there is a birthmark on the child, resulting from the previous personality's death. If someone was shot, for example, the child might have a birthmark in the shape of a bullet wound. Does Bonnie have any birthmarks?"

"No, at least not like you're describing. She just has that beauty mark above her lip."

"Hmm. Well she does seem to be reliving sexual assault and murder in her nightmares. And if she was smothered there wouldn't be any wounds per se."

Now Samantha's mind focused on one of Bonnie's behaviors she had never understood. "Doctor, there is one thing. Each night, I give Bonnie a good night kiss as she nods off with her head on the pillow. But in the morning, that pillow is always under the bed."

Making a note of this on his laptop, Dr. K said, "It makes sense that if she was smothered by a pillow in her previous life, she might still be afraid of them. Phobias like that are another common sign of reincarnation. For instance, someone who drowned in a previous life might have a water phobia.

"Is there any other behavior you can think of that seems unusual for such a young child? Play behavior perhaps? Reincarnated children often play make-believe in a way that is reminiscent of their previous personalty's life or work."

Samantha sat back and tried to think, but this was a lot to take in. She stared out the window and reflected back over the past year.

"Her favorite thing to do is play dress-up with all my jewelry and scarves. She strews them all over my bed and carefully selects which to put on. Then she insists that I take her picture. That's not unusual, I suppose. But the way she poses for each shot has always seemed very grown up. She stands sideways," Samantha stood up to demonstrate, "puts one hand on a jutted out little hip, then dips her head while staring provocatively at the camera." She shook herself a bit and sat down again. "That's always made me feel a bit uncomfortable. Three year olds are not supposed to look sexy!"

"That would lead me to wonder if Carrie was involved with photography or fashion in some way. Is there anything else you can think of?" Dr. K continued his typing.

"She's never mentioned a previous mother," Samantha remarked. "If she has been," she cleared her throat nervously, "reincarnated... surely she would remember her mother!"

"Maybe she died when Carrie was too young to remember her," Dr. K suggested.

I'm glad she doesn't remember another mother, Samantha thought. I really couldn't handle that. Actually, I don't think I can handle any of this! Remembering last week's meeting, she wondered if reincarnation was better than insanity. Or at the least, the lesser of two evils? It was a toss-up.

"Mrs. Mitchell, I know this is a lot to take in. Maybe we should bring in a subject expert so you can get their opinion. Would it be okay if I contacted The Division of Perceptual Studies, at the University of Virginia, to see if someone there would be interested enough in this case to work with us? They're like past life investigators and are good at putting all the puzzle pieces together."

Samantha felt as though she were being swept away on a magic carpet, flying off to a land of make-believe. What if all this turns out to be true? Do I even want to know if it's true? If Bonnie will forget all about this by the time she's seven, maybe we should just wait. But, as she thought about the nightmares, she feared that waiting was not an option.

"All right. I guess that's okay," she said, without an ounce of certainty. "Thank you, Doctor, you've certainly given me a lot to think about. Let me know what they say." Samantha felt numb as she rose to get Bonnie.

"Before you go," Dr K said. "I am not going to discuss this with anyone other than the experts at UVA, and I would advise that you not talk about it either. Other people... well, let's just say they might not be as open as we are to exploring this possibility. I'll call as soon as I can. In the meantime," he reached into the bookcase behind his desk, "take a look at this book. It's helpful in trying to understand reincarnation." Dr. K handed Samantha a book by Jim Tucker, Director of the Division of Perceptual Studies, called *Return to Life: Extraordinary Cases of Children Who Remember Past Lives.* Samantha tentatively reached out for it as though it were a hot potato.

Chapter 6

*A*fter they returned home and changed into everyday clothes, Samantha gave Bonnie some lunch and settled her in front of the TV to watch her favorite Dora video. Then, pinning her thick hair up on top of her head with a comb, Samantha put on her red computer glasses, sat down at her desk and started to methodically consider the facts, known and unknown. In her work at Schwab, Samantha was used to analyzing facts and figures; doing research on a company's history to determine its profit potential in the future. But now she needed to do a different sort of investigation; one that would directly affect herself and her daughter's future. What do I need to find out, she asked herself, as she started to type.

1. *Exactly which building does Bonnie think Carrie lived in?*
2. *When did she live there?*
3. *Would the building management recognize the name Carrie Kelly and be able to confirm if she had been murdered?*
4. *Would the building management know the full name of Carrie's father if he bought the penthouse apartment for his daughter?*
5. *Could the police search their records for a rape/ murder victim named Carrie Kelly, who had lived on Fifth Avenue and 65th Street?*

Those are the key questions, Samantha thought, and definitely a place to start. As far-fetched as the notion of reincarnation is I'd rather be working on that hypothesis than researching mental psychoses. She was itching to get at it and decided the place to begin was back at the Central Park Zoo.

==

On Saturday, Bonnie was overjoyed to learn they were going to the Zoo. "Oh goodie! Can we see the seals Mama? And the polar bear, and the tigers and the lions and the monkeys and the… "

"Yes," Samantha laughed, "we can see them all! And I'll bring my camera so we can take pictures of you there. Would you like that?"

"Oh, yes! What will I wear?" Samantha gazed at her daughter wondering whether other 3-year-olds were always so concerned about what to wear. Somehow, she doubted it.

"How about your new red and white striped dress?" she suggested.

"I love that dress! Can I wear my Mary Janes too, since it's a special 'casion?"

"Sure," Samantha replied. And with what I have in mind it definitely will be be a special occasion. "But you might be more comfortable wearing sneakers."

"Oh no! Sneakers are not dressy." And Bonnie ran off to get dressed.

Who told her that? Samantha wondered. Or is that something that Carrie knows? Oh, God, if this reincarnation thing is real, it's going to be difficult to know who's saying what!

They took the train from Pelham into Grand Central, and a bus up Madison Avenue to 65th Street. As they hopped off the bus, Bonnie seemed to know exactly where she was going. When they reached Fifth Avenue, she cast a quick apprehensive look at the apartment building on the Northeast corner, but then kept her eyes on the traffic light so she could dash across the street to the Zoo.

While skipping from one enclosure to another, Bonnie paused to watch a tiger in his cage. As the tiger paced back and forth, she said "This tiger is from India."

Samantha walked over to the plaque on the outside of the cage, and sure enough, it was a Bengal tiger. But tigers come from other countries too.

"Bonnie, how did you know that?"

"When I was Carrie I saw one in India. I also rode on an elephant! Do they have elephants in the Zoo?"

"I don't think so, hon, but we'll look."

So Carrie went to India at some point? What on earth was she doing there? She'd already Googled Karie, Karry, Kari, Carry, and Carrie Kelly only to find that there were thousands of them in the country and hundreds in New York City. Which was why she'd come up with her next idea.

Bonnie started to flag after about two hours. "I'm hungry, Mama."

"Let's stop at the Dancing Crane Cafe and have some lunch," Samantha said. "We can get a sandwich and sit outdoors. I'm hungry too," although she felt her stomach was already full... full of butterflies. "Then maybe we can take a walk on Fifth Avenue."

As they ate, Samantha stared at her daughter. She seems just like any other kid; focused on having fun, eating and sleeping. But inside that little head lives... what? Another consciousness? Could she have two consciousnesses? Her own and Carrie's? Wouldn't that be just like having a split personality after all? She shook her head and tried to swallow her yogurt.

After her sandwich, Bonnie begged for an ice-cream and then had to go to the bathroom. Samantha tried not to show her impatience, but was itching to get started on her real mission, which had nothing to do with the Zoo. "Okay... let's go for that walk!"

Once out on Fifth Avenue, Bonnie stopped again and looked up at the top of the apartment building across the street. Following her gaze, Samantha said, "Are you sure that's the building where Carrie lived, honey?"

"Yes, Mama. I 'member it. It has two elevators. I always went in the one on this side." She stuck her hand out to the right. "...all the way up to the tippy-top."

"Let's go take a look at the lobby, hon. Would that be alright?"

"Sure! I can show you where the elevator is." Samantha held Bonnie's hand to stop her from charging across the street. There was no doorman to be seen, so they just walked in. And sure enough, there was one elevator on the far left of the lobby and another on the far right. I have never been in this building; Bonnie has never been in this building. How can she possibly know about the two elevators? Unless...

Just then, the doorman appeared. As he walked towards them, Bonnie squealed "JoJo! Hi!" And she ran over to him with a big smile on her face.

The doorman, dressed in his uniform and cap, was about fifty-five and wore a name badge that read 'Joseph.' He looked down at Bonnie with surprise and said "Well, hello little girl. What's your name? Do I know you?"

Before Bonnie could reply, potentially getting poor Joseph very confused, Samantha interjected, "Hello, Joseph. Ah, I'm trying to find a friend who I think used to live in this building about four or five years ago, on the top floor. I haven't heard from her in a long time and since we were just visiting the Zoo, I thought I'd enquire."

"What is your friend's name?" Joseph asked.

"Well, when I knew her, it was Carrie Kelly."

"I don't think I can help you without more information," Joseph hesitantly replied. "But you could always try Building Management. They might be able to look back in their records and come up with someone by that name who lived up there. There are only two penthouse apartments, one on each side."

"That's a good idea. Where is the Building Management office located?"

"Right upstairs, in Apt. 2A. Would you like me to see if someone is free to talk with you, as long as you're here?" Joseph reached for the house phone.

Despite feeling unprepared for a conversation with Building Management, Samantha nodded. "Yes, thank you Joseph. My name is Samantha Mitchell."

Once the call upstairs had been completed, Samantha and Bonnie took the elevator, the one on the left, up to the second floor. "I've never been in this elevator," Bonnie noted. "But it looks just like the other one."

Samantha squeezed Bonnie's hand and added this fact to the growing list of memories she was sharing; memories that she could not possibly have known by herself. As she tried to think of what to say to the Building Management person, she only knew that it would be something other than the truth!

Taking in the reception room of DMK Management Inc., Samantha admired the Persian oriental rug in shades of celadon and salmon. The same colors were mirrored in a glorious vase of spring flowers on top of a graceful Queen Anne reception desk. Samantha wondered if the Dutch Masters painting on the wall could possibly be an original. Greeting them from behind the desk, was an attractive woman, about 50, flawlessly made up, with blonde hair pulled back in an intricately plaited pony tail. "Hello. My name is Margaret. How may I help you?" she asked, with a welcoming smile. "Are you interested in an apartment?"

"Hello, I'm Samantha Mitchell, and this is my daughter, Bonnie. No, I'm not looking for an apartment." After repeating the story she had given Joseph, Samantha said, "I think that she lived here in 2015, but it could have been earlier."

Margaret paused, as she took an inquisitive look at Samantha. "Have a seat, both of you." As soon as they were settled, she continued. "Tell me again what your relationship is to Carrie and why you are looking for her?"

"We crossed paths in high school but lost touch over the years. You know how that is. Someone once told me that she was living in this building and since we were just visiting the Zoo, I thought I'd see if she was still here." Did that sound believable? She doubted it. "However, Joseph didn't seem to know anyone by that name. He suggested I talk to you."

"Well, we're not supposed to give out any information about our tenants, but perhaps in this case it would be all right since she isn't a tenant anymore."

"Did she move?" Samantha said, "and if so, did she leave a forwarding address?"

Margaret snuck a quick look to see if anyone else from her office was within earshot. "I'm sorry to tell you this, Mrs. Mitchell, but Carolyn Kelly, who called herself Carrie, lived in that apartment from 2008 to 2013… when she died."

"Oh my God!" Samantha said, trying not to look at Bonnie who was listening intently. "But, she was so young! Did she have an accident or something?"

Once again Margaret checked to make sure no one was listening, and then leaned in closer to Samantha. In a conspiratorial whisper she said, "Actually, she was murdered in her apartment. Since you were her friend, I think you should know the truth. But please, don't tell anyone else that I told you." Looking embarrassed, she added, "it wouldn't be good for business."

Samantha tried to act stunned, "Did the police find out who did it?"

"No. As far as I know this is still an unsolved crime." Leaning forward one last time, so that Bonnie couldn't hear, Margaret whispered, "There is a rumor that sexual assault was involved, but of course there were no witnesses. Her poor father has not been himself since."

"Oh my God. This is horrible news. I am so sorry to hear it." She took a tissue from her purse and blew her nose, as though she were trying not to cry. Not wanting to admit that she didn't know her "friend's" father, Samantha decided it was best that they go home. Her fingers were itching to get back on the computer.

As soon as they exited the building, Bonnie said "See Mama? I told you Carrie was made dead."

Samantha went down on one knee and put her arms around Bonnie. "Yes, you did honey and I believe you. But we still need to do a lot more digging to figure out how on earth you know that. It's very strange. But thankfully we have people who can help us now. Just be patient."

Straightening up, she took Bonnie's hand. "I think we should head home, pumpkin. It's been a long day." To herself she wondered if the new information she had discovered would be sufficient to narrow down her online search for Carrie Kelly.

==

After having dinner, playing I Spy, and watching another Dory video, Samantha put Bonnie to sleep. Since she

54

was now too tired to dive into her research, she settled down in bed to read *Return to Life*.

The first story was of a young boy named Patrick, born twelve years after his half-brother, Kevin, had died from metastatic neuroblastoma. As a very young boy, Patrick had a limp and blindness in one eye, as had Kevin. He also had several birthmarks identical to scars Kevin had incurred during his treatments. However, Patrick was not ill and his physical problems all disappeared by the time he was six. The story detailed exactly how Jim Tucker and his boss, Ian Stevenson, from the Division of Perceptual Studies at UVA, researched the case to determine if there were any other explanations for Patrick's recollections of Kevin's life and for those physical similarities. There were none. They ultimately concluded that Patrick appeared to be the reincarnation of Kevin.

Samantha put down the book and stared off into the distance. How extraordinary! This sounds like science fiction, yet real doctors are doing this research. She was particularly fascinated by Patrick's references to Heaven where, he said, Kevin now resided.

Why haven't we heard more about reincarnation? Why isn't everyone talking about it? If Kevin was reincarnated in Patrick, how could he also be in Heaven? As she dozed off, she had more questions than she could begin to answer.

==

The next day, while Bonnie was off playing with Allison, Samantha settled down in front of her computer again, anxious to see how much she could dig up about Carolyn Kelly.

It took no more than a minute to come up with a *New York Times* obituary for Carolyn Kelly, dated May 28, 2013.

She printed out a copy and jotted down some clues for further investigation. Well, what do you know, Samantha thought. Carrie's father is David Kelly, the New York real estate magnate, owner of DMK Management, Inc. He owns the building Carrie lived in! No wonder he could give her a penthouse for her birthday. Her mother, Sarah Barnes Kelly, was listed as deceased and no siblings were mentioned. And then Samantha's eyes opened wide. 'Appeared on covers of all the top fashion magazines for years,' she read. Oh my God! Carrie was a model. Is that why Bonnie is so comfortable being photographed? Dr. K suspected something like this.

Knowing that Carrie Kelly was a top fashion model, Samantha refined her search. She gazed at pictures of Carrie on the covers of Vogue, Harper's Bazaar and Elle, taken in exotic locations like Morocco, Thailand and India. India! And sure enough, there was a photo of Carrie on the cover of Vogue, sitting barefoot on top of an elephant, wearing a turquoise chiffon evening gown with a bevy of Indian jewelry around her neck, wrists and ankles.   Samantha printed out a copy of the shot and placed it in the journal she'd begun, right next to her notes about Bonnie's recognition of the Bengal tiger and her comments about Carrie riding an elephant in India. Of course, she thought, somewhat hopefully, *Dora The Explorer* also runs into tigers and elephants.

As she enlarged one of the other shots for a closer look, she saw something that made her feel slightly ill. Carrie had a birthmark above her lip on the right side of her face, just like Bonnie! This is so creepy! This tiny mark hit her harder than any of the other facts she'd unearthed. It seemed like visible validation of reincarnation. It also made Bonnie seem like a monstrous hybrid of herself and Carrie.

Then finally, Samantha pulled up an article from *The New York Times* titled, "Model Murder a Mystery." This is it! This is the same as Bonnie's story! But actually, as she read it,

Samantha realized that even Bonnie knew more about Carrie's murder than the police. All they knew was that perhaps someone attempted to rape her and then smothered her with a pillow. There were no fingerprints, no DNA and, of course, no witnesses. Anyone with a possible lead was invited to come forward. In fact, David Kelly had offered a one-hundred-thousand dollar reward for any information leading to the capture of Carrie's killer. Yet nothing. Until now.

==

"Over here Mama. Over here. Come and get me!" Bonnie sounded fearful and frantic. Samantha scanned the calm sea, the empty beach and then hunted in the tall, wavy grasses behind the dunes. But every time she thought she'd found her, it turned out to be another little girl, one she didn't recognize. Where's my daughter? Where is she, Samantha thought, as she swirled around frantically. Then finally, with a sigh of relief, she caught up with her. But when Bonnie turned around, it wasn't Bonnie after all. It was Carrie, posing for a photograph with a come hither look on her face and a birthmark above her lip. Samantha awoke with a jolt. Her heart was beating rapidly and she was perspiring. She ruefully realized that Bonnie was now not the only one having nightmares about a girl named Carrie.

Chapter 7

*O*n Monday, normal life resumed. Or as normal as life can be when you are consumed with your daughter's previous life. Samantha was still in a trance when she walked into her office.

"Hey there, girl! It's good to see you," said Jamie, her good friend and fellow financial analyst. "I was worried when you didn't come in on Friday. Big night out on Thursday?"

"I wish," Samantha said as she gave her friend a hug. "No, I just had to bring Bonnie into the city for another doctor's appointment."

"Is Bonnie all right?"

"She's fine. She... she just had to see her asthma doctor since she's been having some breathing problems lately." Samantha noticed how easy it was to make up stories when you were already living in a world of the unimaginable. But no sooner was the excuse out of her mouth, than she realized that it was almost true. Bonnie *was* having breathing problems after each nightmare. I wonder, she thought. Might that somehow be related to being smothered in her previous life, and have nothing to do with asthma?

Too late she realized that she had not heard Jamie's question. "What? Oh, I'm sorry Jamie, my mind was elsewhere. Did you say something?"

"I just asked what you did over the weekend."

"Oh yes. We went to the Central Park Zoo. You know how much Bonnie loves it." And then we visited the apartment where Bonnie lived in a previous life before she was murdered. She mentally shook herself. Focus, I have to stay focused.

"Do you have time for lunch today?" Jamie asked. "We have some catching up to do."

"I'm not sure I can today since I was out on Friday. But let me check my workload, and I'll let you know."

As they parted ways to go to their offices on opposite sides of the floor, Samantha realized how much she desperately needed to talk to someone. I just can't deal with this all on my own. Jamie is one of my closest friends… maybe? No! I have to have more evidence before I talk to her, or she'll think I'm crazy!"

Ultimately, she decided to pop over to Hamburger Heaven with Jamie in order to distract herself from everything else going on.

After placing their orders, Jamie leaned in and whispered, "You'll never guess who I saw yesterday."

Samantha was all ears. "Who? Anyone I know?"

"Well, I'd say yes to that. You definitely know him."

"Oh come on, tell me. I'm not going to guess."

"Hank Mitchell!"

Samantha was momentarily stunned. "What? You saw Hank? Where? Did you talk to him? How did he look?" As usual, Samantha's impatience got the better of her and she wanted to know everything all at once.

Jamie smiled, obviously pleased to have piqued Samantha's interest. "He was sitting on the steps of St. Patrick's Cathedral; no, I didn't speak to him, since I barely know him; and he looked, let's see, how can I put this… he looked sad. He wasn't watching the passersby, he was just staring straight ahead as though he were in a trance. Didn't the two of you get married in St. Patrick's?"

Samantha, still absorbing the thought that Hank might have been missing her, just mumbled "mmm." Recovering, she said "Well, what do you know. Hank's in town. As you can tell, we are not really in contact with each other." As Samantha took a bite of her burger, Jamie took the hint and changed the subject.

The rest of their lunch went by in a blur as Samantha became obsessed with the thought of Hank, obviously still here in New York City.

==

After their lunch, Dr. K called Samantha. "Good afternoon. I hope I'm not interrupting your work. How did the weekend go?"

"It was very productive." Samantha eagerly relayed what she had learned at the DMK Management office and then online.

"Excellent! That's very supportive of our case. Did Bonnie hear anything she has not already told us?"

Samantha paused to think. "No, I don't think so. She listened carefully to the manager's story of Carrie's death, but she didn't hear the sexual assault part since that was whispered to me."

"Good. Now listen, Mrs. Mitchell, because this is very important. When possible reincarnation cases are studied, they need to find out whether the child's remembrances could have come from anywhere else; a magazine, a TV show, a friend, or in particular… a family member. Although not frequent at all, there have been some reincarnation frauds reported."

"I understand, and I promise not to discuss anything with Bonnie unless she brings it up. By the way, I have started keeping that journal to record her memories and comments. For example, she recognized the doorman as soon as we entered Carrie's apartment building. Although his name tag said Joseph, she called him JoJo. Of course he didn't have a clue who she was."

"Good. Keep making those notes. It would also be great to have some kind of real-time video recording of her statements, but that's probably too difficult to do without making her self conscious."

"Wait," Samantha said. "I've been using a new baby video monitor in Bonnie's bedroom at night to be sure I wake up when she starts calling for me. I'm pretty sure I read that those tapes can be transferred to a flash drive. So I'll have videos of exactly how she looks and what she says when she's having those awful nightmares."

"That's great. The more proof we can gather the better. Did you see pictures of Carrie online?"

"Oh yes, lots. She was beautiful! And guess what? She had a birthmark above her lip just like Bonnie!"

"Hmm. That is interesting, but it could also just be a coincidence. So far, all the accountings of birthmarks in reincarnation case studies have been related to the prior personality's death, which is not the case here. Tell me, do you buy fashion magazines? Might Bonnie have seen some lying around the house? I know you told me she likes to dress up and pose."

"Oh no." Samantha laughed. "I've never been able to even imagine wearing the clothes they show in Vogue and Elle. I'm more of a Bloomingdales type."

"I ask because I'm looking for any possible sources to explain Bonnie's comments or behaviors. Who takes care of Bonnie when you are at work?"

"Mercedes. She picks up Bonnie from daycare, brings her home for lunch and then stays with her until I get home."

"If you don't mind my asking, what nationality is Mercedes? If she's from Southeast Asia she might have a head full of reincarnation stories that she's been sharing with Bonnie."

"She's an American citizen now, but she was born in Colombia and brought here as a child."

"Okay, good. Now, the reason for my call is to tell you that I did speak to someone in the Division of Perceptual Studies at UVA. They were quite excited about this case, particularly since there have only been about one hundred solved reincarnation cases in the United States. Of course there are far more in Southeast Asia where, as Jim Tucker likes to say, 'reincarnation is not merely a hope, but an expectation.' He took over the program from Ian Stevenson who began it in 1967. They've now studied over twenty five hundred cases from every continent in the world except Antarctica. You probably read about many of them in that book I gave you. Two thirds of those cases have been solved, meaning that reincarnation is the only possible explanation for the child's memories of a previous personality. And of those, 70% died from unnatural causes."

"I did read the book you gave me, and was just astounded! What can you say in the face of so much evidence supportive of reincarnation?"

As Samantha thought about having her own daughter studied though, she couldn't decide whether to be excited or scared. *Do I really want to have some researcher prove that my daughter is someone else who has been reborn? She'll be like a rat in a lab study!* Taking a deep breath to calm her anxiety, she forced herself to ask, "So, what's the next step?" As her secretary started to walk into her office, Samantha quickly waved her away and then rose to shut the door.

"I'd like to set up a time when Dr. Robert Williams, a Special Research Assistant in the Division of Perceptual Studies, could talk to you and Bonnie. He's willing to come up from Charlottesville at your convenience. We could do it at your home or in my office, whichever you prefer."

"I'll check my calendar but I'm thinking a Friday might be good, at your office. I've already established that Bonnie sees her asthma doctor in the City on Fridays when necessary. Oh, by the way, that reminds me. Do you think Bonnie's asthma may be symptomatic of Carrie's death... being smothered?"

"Very possibly. Let's ask Dr. Williams about it. Do you think that this Friday is too soon, since you've been out of the office the past two Fridays? I'm anxious to proceed as soon as possible."

Samantha tapped her foot on the floor. "I'll talk to my boss, but I don't think he'll mind. I'll call you back later today." Hanging up, she realized that no matter what her boss said, she couldn't back out now. The idea of reincarnation had been planted in her head and she had to take the next step - to prove or disprove it.

==

At dinner on Thursday evening, Samantha explained to Bonnie that they were going back to Dr. K's office to meet another man who wanted to talk with her about her nightmares. "He is a special doctor who might be able to figure out what's going on. I'm excited about meeting him."

Bonnie didn't complain. She just reached for another chocolate chip cookie. That evening she set out a pink-checked dress and, of course, her Mary Jane shoes.

Chapter 8

Dr. Bob Williams, about 35 and dressed casually in tan slacks, an open collared light blue shirt and a sports jacket, settled down on the 6 a.m. train from Charlottesville to New York. A worn briefcase spoke to his travels around the world.

Shortly after receiving his doctorate in psychology from UVA, Bob had heard Jim Tucker lecture about the subject of reincarnation. He'd become so intrigued about the concept, that he'd approached Dr. Tucker about a possible internship. After traveling with him to India to research several possible cases, Bob knew that this was to be his life's calling. The world of science had not yet acknowledged that such a thing was possible but, based on what he'd seen first hand, Bob was committed to changing that.

Now Bob reviewed the notes Dr. Karatamand had sent him. The case was definitely promising. This child, Bonnie Mitchell, seemed like a prototypical case study: memories of another life, nightmares of being murdered, and a whole list of incidental comments consistent with those he'd heard from children in India. But so far, reincarnation cases in the West were rare. Southeast Asians were, of course, much more willing to believe their children when they talked about a previous life, because it was part of their religion. But the converse was true in other parts of the world where the child in question was either ignored or just considered to have a highly active imagination.

This would be Bob's first case in the United States, and since Tucker was out of town, he'd been encouraged to check it out. It would be an understatement to say that he was excited but he cautioned himself to keep his hopes down. Even in the United States there had been cases of fraudsters trying to convince people there was life after death in all manner of ways.

After grabbing a quick bite in the train station, Bob hopped in a taxi and was amazed at how expensive it was to go from West 42nd Street to East 71st. Better take a bus the next time.... if there is a next time.

He met with Dr. Karatamand for a ten minute briefing, before Samantha and Bonnie arrived. When they were ushered in, Bob was immediately taken with Bonnie's appearance and demeanor. She looked a little bit like the pictures he'd seen of Shirley Temple, with her blond curls and impish smile.

When Dr. Karatamand introduced them, Bonnie's mother extended her hand and asked to be called Samantha. She seemed polite, but wary, as if this whole reincarnation thing might be dangerous in some way. But when Bonnie was introduced, she flashed a big bright smile, saying "Hello Dr. Bob." No wariness there.

Dr. Karatamand invited them all to sit, gesturing to the sofa for Samantha and Bonnie, the facing chairs for himself and Bob. After a little opening chatter to make everyone feel comfortable, Bob began to speak directly to Bonnie. "Do you come to the City often, Bonnie?" His voice was warm and engaging.

"No, but I love this city! I used to live here. Now I live in a white house at 435 Fowler Avenue."

"Oh really, you used to live in New York City? When was that?"

"Before. Before I was Bonnie. When I was Carrie, I lived way up on top of a building near the Zoo." Bonnie wiggled around on the couch and looked about the room as she talked.

"And how long did you live there, Bonnie. Do you remember?"

"Maybe a year? Maybe 2 years? Maybe 5 years?" She looked confused, and glanced at her mother for help, but Samantha just shrugged her shoulders. "I don't 'zactly 'member. But it was very beautiful there. My daddy gave it to me for my birfday. I really miss my daddy." This last was said very matter-of-factly.

Bob glanced at Dr. K to make sure he was getting everything down and received a reassuring nod. Continuing on, he returned his focus to Bonnie. "I'm sure you miss him. Do you remember which birthday it was?"

"Twenty, I think. I was a grown-up."

"Let's play a game, Bonnie. Can you tell me what your apartment looked like when you were Carrie? Close your eyes and tell me what you see when you open the door."

Obediently Bonnie squeezed her eyes shut. "There is a big gold doll standing in the hall. She is as tall as Mama, and is wearing a gold dress which she holds out with her hands." Bonnie jumped off the chair to imitate the position of the doll. "Her name is Boofa. Carrie always hoped that Boofa would protect her. But she didn't." Bonnie climbed back up on the chair and sat there quietly, with a somber look on her face.

Hesitant to jump into the murder story, Bob just asked Bonnie what she was thinking about.

"Boofa didn't save me," she said. "I screamed and screamed for help, but Boofa didn't save me." Samantha was about to comfort her, but Bob raised his hand just a bit to stop her.

He leaned forward to be closer to Bonnie. "What did you want Boofa to save you from? Can you tell me what happened? You don't have to be afraid. We are all here to make sure you are safe."

66

A few tears slid down Bonnie's cheek as she sat hunched up in the corner of the couch with her head down on her knees. Although Samantha's heart was breaking at the sight of her forlorn daughter, she obeyed Bob's request.

"I was sleeping. Then all of a sudden Mike was there... in my bedroom." She raised her head and spoke louder. "He was sitting right next to me on my bed. And he didn't have any clothes on! I was so scared! I told him to go away but he wouldn't. He got on top of me and..." She was starting to cry now.

"It's okay, Bonnie. You can tell us," Bob said softly.

"He was hurting me... down there. So I started kicking, fighting and screaming for help! But he just pushed me down and got on top of me." Her crying was now full force. "I kept yelling but he put a pillow on my face. I couldn't breathe, and I couldn't make him stop! Boofa," she gasped for breath, "Boofa never came to help me." Samantha pulled her inhaler out of her bag and Bonnie grabbed it. After calming down, she said in a spooky, matter-of-fact way. "That's when I died."

Bob had watched Bonnie carefully as she relived her nightmare of being sexually assaulted and smothered. He tried, but couldn't find the slightest hint of falsehood. She seemed genuinely terrified, even to the point of needing her inhaler. He was fascinated and wanted to continue, but Samantha slid closer to Bonnie, put her arms around her and murmured, "It's all right, honey. I'm here. You're safe. Take a deep breath." The look she shot Bob and Dr. K said, "No more!"

Dr. K brought Bonnie a glass of juice, and after she'd taken a few sips, he invited her to join him in the playroom.

Alone with Samantha, Bob quickly reviewed Dr. K's notes and noted her nervousness. "Mrs. Mitchell, Samantha, I'm sure this is very difficult for you, and for Bonnie as well. I admire your bravery in at least considering the possibility of reincarnation. I have to tell you, though, this is quite a case.

Bonnie is able to reveal specific details about the murder of her previous personality, which we have seen many times in reincarnated children. In fact, it is often all they can talk about. As you have noticed, Bonnie sometimes says Carrie and at other times says me. That's because in her mind they are one and the same."

Samantha stood up and started to pace.

"It's good that Bonnie has memories of where Carrie lived and a few details about her apartment. That gold doll, I'm guessing, might be a Standing Buddha. They can be found all over Southeast Asia, are about 5 feet high, sculpted from wood, and painted gold, often with bits of jewels embedded in the Buddha's robe. I wonder if Carrie ever traveled to India or Thailand."

Sighing and sitting down again, Samantha said, "She did. As Dr. K probably told you, I got information about Carolyn Kelly's life from her obituary. She was a top fashion model and travelled all over the world for shoots. I've seen magazine covers that look like they were shot in India, Thailand, Turkey. When we were in the Zoo last week, Bonnie told me that the tiger was from India. And sure enough, it was a Bengal tiger, not something that Bonnie would normally know. She also said she'd ridden an elephant, and later I saw a magazine cover with Carrie on top of one."

"Can you think of any other way Bonnie might have known about the tiger and the elephant?"

"Well, *Dora the Explorer* is her favorite video. But I'm not sure whether they say where tigers come from."

Bill nodded his head. "It sounds like Carrie might have been a collector of Asian artifacts. I wonder where those things are now. Any ideas?"

"Well, since there was no mention of immediate relatives in Carrie's obituary, other than her father, maybe he has them? His name is David Kelly."

Recognizing the name, Bob raised his eyebrows. "Yup," Samantha said, "the real estate magnate."

"So that's how Mr. Kelly could give his daughter a penthouse apartment on Fifth Avenue for her birthday. He probably owns the building." He scribbled a note on his pad.

"Right. And when I visited the management office at 980 Fifth, I had no idea who owned the building or that he was Carrie's father." She then explained how she'd researched David Kelly and his extremely successful career; building skyscrapers and hotels all over the world in cities like New York, Moscow, Bangkok and Dubai. She also told Bob about an article she'd read in Vanity Fair. It had mentioned his wife's death in childbirth, how he had never remarried and the murder of his daughter, Carolyn, in 2013. "Carrie was very beautiful, and her father is quite a handsome man. There were several photos of the two of them."

Bob took a deep breath and decided to plow straight ahead. "With your permission, Samantha, I would like to contact Mr. Kelly, tell him about Bonnie, and ask if we could visit him in his home. I'd really like Bonnie to meet him in an environment where some art or furnishings may be familiar to her and, most of all, to see if she recognizes him. According to Dr. Karatamand's notes, she often says she misses 'her daddy.' "

Samantha bent down to put her head in her hands. "Oh God." Then she looked up at Bob and said, "How do you just call someone on the phone and say 'Hi, Mr. Kelly. You don't know me, but I think I've met someone who is the reincarnation of your daughter... you know, the one who was raped and murdered?' This is crazy! He'll just hang up on you, or worse will threaten to have you arrested for harassment. That poor man has been through so much grief and loss. How can we do this to him?"

Bob was all too familiar with the feelings expressed by parents of potentially reincarnated children. Although anxious to prove that their own child wasn't crazy, they had a very difficult time with the process of proving they might really be reincarnated. "I know, it sounds like an impossible task. But what we have found in the thousands of cases we have worked on, is that the parent of a deceased child is so happy to have some connection with that person again that they are open to at least discussing it. If there are a sufficient number of corroborating facts to suggest the child's story is true, and if they can learn what actually happened, they are then at least able to have some sense of closure."

Samantha looked very doubtful. "Bob, I am so uncomfortable about all of this. What if Mr. Kelly does come to believe Bonnie? Then what? Will he want to continue seeing her? Will he think we can all be one big, happy family?" She unconsciously shuddered.

"Samantha, I completely understand your anxiety. This is an astounding idea for anyone to come to grips with. But look at it this way. Bonnie is having debilitating nightmares; she is definitely not living the life of a carefree three year old. And unless we solve this case, those dreams and fears will continue until she is six or seven. Between now and then, you and your daughter will go through a terrible amount of suffering."

Continuing on he said, "In our experience, once the child meets her previous personality's relatives and her story is validated, those nightmares start to fade away... often pretty quickly. We don't know why, but perhaps the consciousness of the previous personality finds some peace after his or her story is revealed. In this case, it's even a possibility that the police could find that man named Mike and have him arrested, tried and convicted for murder, which would certainly give Mr. Kelly some satisfaction."

Samantha gave him a skeptical look. "But we don't know anything about Mike. How on earth would the police find him?"

"Let's not worry about that just yet. Each day it seems Bonnie is revealing a little bit more. Let's just see how this all plays out." Samantha still looked doubtful.

To allay one of her other concerns, Bob said, "I also don't think Mr. Kelly will want to keep seeing Bonnie. Maybe a few times, but not much more. Think about people who communicate with a passed loved one in a seance. Now I'm not saying anything about the validity of those experiences, but once they've happened, that's usually the end."

Although still clearly unsure, Samantha relaxed a bit. "All right," she sighed. "We've come this far, we might as well see it through to the end. And anything that helps Bonnie to stop having these nightmares is worth it. So go ahead. Call Mr. Kelly, and let me know what he says."

==

In a few days, Bob Williams reached Samantha in her office. He'd thought about what she had said regarding the potential difficulty Mr. Kelly might have, hearing all this information in a phone call. "I think you're right, Samantha. This story might be too much to come out with in a single call. So I'd like to send him an explanatory letter first.

"In it, I introduce myself and tell him about the work that has been done at DOPS over the past fifty-two years. I'd like to read you the part about Bonnie to see if you approve. Okay?"

"Sure," said Samantha.

Bob cleared his throat. "I know what I am about to say will seem impossible. But we have recently been introduced to a three-year-old girl who recalls a past life as your daughter. Her name is Bonnie and she lives in Pelham Manor, a suburb of New York City. So far, Bonnie has recognized an apartment building at 980 Fifth Avenue and pointed to the penthouse which she says you gave her as a present on her twentieth birthday.

"She has described a Standing Buddha statue in the hall of her apartment, which she calls a golden doll. But more importantly, Bonnie has been having nightmares several times a week since she was two. When she wakes up, she describes, in some detail, Carrie's sexual assault and murder by a man named Mike.

"With your permission, I would like to introduce you to Bonnie and her mother, Samantha Mitchell. If it is possible, I would like that meeting to be in your home where she might recognize any art or artifacts of Carrie's which you may now have. And, most importantly, we will want to see if she recognizes you, since she keeps saying 'I miss my daddy.'

"I can't say that I know where all this will lead, Mr. Kelly. But in many of the cases we have studied, the child does recognize relatives or friends, is able to more specifically recall his or her death and then, in a relatively short period of time, the child's nightmares begin to stop. If she is able to come up with more clues to help the police identify 'Mike,' it's also possible that your daughter's murder could be solved and justice served. I imagine that's certainly something you might like to see happen.

"I am enclosing a book by Jim Tucker, called *Return to Life: Extraordinary Cases of Children who Remember Past Lives.* Please take a look at it and call to let me know if we can introduce you to Bonnie. As upsetting as all this may sound, it could very possibly lead to a sense of closure... for you, Bonnie and perhaps, Carrie. Sincerely, etc, etc.

"Does that sound okay to you?" he asked Samantha.

"Yes, it's a very provocative letter; much better than a cold call. Hopefully, he'll respond."

A month went by with no word from David Kelly. Although anxious, Bob knew that it was important to give Kelly time to get used to the idea of reincarnation and, more particularly, reincarnation of his own daughter.

From Samantha's frequent calls, he learned that Bonnie's nightmares were continuing and that she was starting to lose hope.

"Be patient," he told her. "I know this is hard on you, but hang in there. I expect we'll hear from him soon.

"One thing I worry about though, is that Kelly will suspect he is being scammed by someone out to make a quick buck, or a quick hundred-thousand bucks. That kind of thing is sure to have happened to him before. Hopefully the information I presented will persuade Mr. Kelly that this is an honest inquiry. After all, it would only take him a few minutes to go online, read about the Division's work and see my own own picture and bio to confirm I'm who I say I am. We'll just have to wait."

Chapter 9

One night, as Samantha was reading Jim Tucker's book again and wrestling with the whole notion of reincarnation, the phone rang. Who could be calling so late, she wondered, as she reached for the phone.

"Hello?"

There was a slight pause, so she said hello again.

"Sam. It's me... Hank."

This time there was a longer pause, as Samantha sat straight up in her bed.

"Samantha? Are you there?"

"Yes, yes, I'm here. But I don't really know what to say. Why are you calling me?"

She heard a sigh. "I'm calling because I need to speak with you. Preferably in person. I deserted you four years ago, and have a lot of explaining to do. Do you think it would be possible for us to get together?"

Now the sigh came from Samantha's side of the line, as she threw her head back against the pillow. "Hank. You can't just call me up at 10 p.m. after a four year disappearance and expect me to race to your side. Maybe I don't even care why you left. The fact that you could have stayed away all this time without ever contacting me is unforgivable. I gave birth all by myself, I've had to figure out how to be a good working mom all by myself and you have a daughter you have never even asked about. It took some time, but I've adjusted to life without you. No... there is absolutely no reason for us to get together." And she hung up the phone.

Although it had felt good to hang up on him, she then burst into tears. Her mind flooded with questions. Why did he leave? Where did he go? Why didn't he stay in touch? Why is he calling now? No! It doesn't matter. That man is out of my life. I'm not going to open the door just because he wants to explain. Good riddance! Nevertheless she checked her phone and jotted down his number.

==

The next day when she got home from work, there was a huge bouquet of peonies in a vase on the kitchen table, with an envelope leaning against it. As she was putting on her jacket, Mercedes said they had been delivered about an hour earlier.

Samantha was pretty sure they were from Hank since he knew peonies were her favorite flower. But even after Mercedes left she just stared at the envelope, trying to will herself to tear it up… unopened. It only took her two minutes to reject that idea. Inside was a single sheet of paper.

Dear Sam,

You have every right to be furious at me and I agree that my behavior was unforgivable. Still, I would like to explain. It's a long story, going back to my childhood. But I would really prefer to talk about it in person. Over the past two years I have had medical treatment to address my problems, and now have completely recovered.

I have thought of you every day; missed your company, your warmth and even your silly laugh. But, until now, there was no way that I could reach out to you. More than anything else, I hope that you can see your way to at least letting me explain.

I will be at our usual spot in the Oyster Bar tomorrow night at 6 p.m. If you don't show up, I will be there again for the next three nights. If you decide not to come, I will understand and not bother you again.

Sam... I love you. I have loved you ever since we met at McMullen's. Whenever I walk past that bar I remember your question: What are you most looking forward to in the future? I described the woman I wanted to spend my life with, already knowing that it might be you. And it was. I hope with all my heart that I will see you tomorrow night.

All my love,
Hank

Samantha sat down at the kitchen table. So it was a medical problem. Why didn't he tell me that? Of course I would have understood and wanted to care for him. Going back to childhood? Her mind flashed back to the conversation she'd had with Dr. K when he'd asked if there had been any mental illness in her family. With that thought, she knew she had to talk to Hank, if only for Bonnie's sake. And of course, she was very curious for personal reasons as well.

The next night, at 6 p.m. on the dot, Samantha walked into the Oyster Bar. She looked her best although, with all her worries about Bonnie, she feared her best was none too good. Hank was there ahead of her and stood up as she approached, gave her a quick kiss on the cheek and pulled out her chair.

It was awkward at first. She didn't want to plunge into interrogating him. It was his dime after all and he was the one who wanted to explain. A waiter, who looked like he had only seconds to spare, asked for their order as the place started to fill up. Samantha ordered a white wine and noticed that Hank just asked for a Perrier. They spoke of nothing meaningful for a few minutes then, after their drinks arrived, he cleared his throat.

"Okay, I think it's time for you to hear my story. Way past time really, but here it is. When you first announced that you were pregnant, something happened to me. It was like an electric shock had just zapped my brain. But in a moment I felt better and assured you that everything would be okay. When we decided to move to Pelham, I was happy to have a project to concentrate on, one that would keep my mind occupied. But after we settled in, we spent lots of time talking about baby stuff; like names, whether or not you would go back to work, wondering what kind of parents we'd be. The more we talked, the more my brain became muddled. I not only became depressed, I started to feel afraid."

Leaning forward, Samantha said "Afraid? Afraid of what?"

Shirking his shoulders, Hank said "That's just it. I didn't know. I didn't just feel uneasy, or worried, or anxious; I was downright scared out of my wits! I knew, deep in my bones, that if I stayed in that house, something terribly bad would happen to you and perhaps to our child."

"Oh my God! So what did you do? Where did you go?"

"At first I went to stay at a friend's apartment for a few weeks. As it happened, during that time Accenture asked me if I would consider moving to our office in Rome for about two years." Samantha closed her eyes. "I know, you would have loved living in Italy. Hopefully, if all goes as I hope it will, there will be another opportunity for me to take you there. But when I got the offer, it felt like a lifeline and I grabbed it. I thought a complete change of scene might help me return to my normal self. Of course I felt guilty about just going without telling you, but for some reason I couldn't pick up the phone. I know why now, but I didn't then.

"Would you like another drink? Some oysters?" asked the waiter.

"Another wine for me, please, no oysters," replied Samantha. Hank ordered another Perrier as well. The bar area of the restaurant was now packed with commuters, downing a quick one before heading out to the suburbs. Fortunately they were back in a corner, but it was still hard to hear each other above the hubbub. Samantha leaned in closer.

"Okay, so you headed off to Rome. Then what?"

"Well, things improved. I became friends with a number of folks from Accenture and with some locals as well. We frequented those charming outdoor cafes, I improved my Italian, I even took some cooking lessons. But, regardless of what I did to keep busy, I thought about you all the time and wondered if you were all right. Really, Sam. I didn't forget about you for a minute." He stared into her eyes.

"When my two year stint ended and I returned to the City, I was going to contact you right away. But almost immediately the brain fog and the fear returned. So clearly something to do with us was causing my depression. A friend gave me the name of a good psychiatrist and after hearing my story, he proposed two remedies. He gave me a prescription for a light dose of Xanax and referred me to a therapist.

Samantha was about to say just what I suggested in the first place, but thought better of it. "So, how did that go?"

"Well for a long time it went nowhere. We talked and we talked, but he couldn't find any answers for my reaction to your pregnancy or for my fears. Finally, after about a year of seeing him once a week, he tried a new tact. He had already questioned me about my childhood memories and noticed that there were few. In fact, I couldn't remember anything before the age of about eight. So he asked if I would be willing to undergo hypnosis. Sure, I replied. Anything you think might help.

"The following week when I arrived, he had a tape recorder out. He explained that he was going to take me back to when I was eight, ask questions and, if necessary, he would go back even further. Then, when he brought me out of it, we would listen to the tape together and discuss it.

"The last thing I remembered was the monotonous sound of his voice as he put me under and then all of a sudden, I was awake."

"It didn't work? I asked him, certain that only a few minutes had gone by. Oh no, he said. You went under and I think we have what we need. Since I had apparently been out for about forty-five minutes, he suggested we listen to the tape the following week. Talk about a cliff-hanger!"

"Oh, no! You had to wait a whole week?"

Hank gave her a rueful grin. "Oh, yes. Therapists run a tight ship; there's no room for improvisation. So when I went back the next week I was curious, anxious and scared. Do you want to hear the blow by blow, or should I just give you the highlights and get to the point?"

"The latter I think. I'm on the edge of my seat as it is." She took a sip of wine. "Give me the highlights with the option to ask more about the details." As the waiter approached again she waved him off.

Hank began. "I've never spoken to you much about my parents. My father, as far as I knew, had left my mother before I ever got to know him. So, as a single mom, she did her best. Does this sound familiar by the way? Anyway under hypnosis, I revealed a pertinent moment that took place when I was five. We'd had dinner together, one where my father had been complaining about everything; the food, the house, my mother's looks. She was seven months pregnant and he said she looked like a fat cow.

"After dessert I went up to my room and they soon started yelling at each other. Apparently, according to the therapist, I said this had happened many times. On this particular night, when I crept out to the top of the stairs, I could see that my father was furious. They were both standing and he shoved her up against the wall. 'What did I tell you?' he shouted. 'No more kids! That one idiot upstairs is bad enough. You never listen to me, you never obey, I don't know why we ever got married in the first place. I hate this kid you're growing.' And with that, he punched her in the stomach and she slumped to the ground."

Samantha gasped and inadvertently cradled her own stomach.

"I ran into their bedroom and called 911. My mother had drilled that into me, telling me to call that number whenever we needed help. She probably knew something like this might happen. I gave the operator my name and address and then through my tears managed to get out, 'Please come. I think my mother is dead.' When I heard my father approaching the stairs, I ran back into my room and hid under the bed.

"I listened in terror as my father climbed the stairs, went into his room and threw things around for a while. Then he went back down the stairs and out the front door, never to be seen again.

"Cutting to the chase, the police and an ambulance arrived within minutes. My mother was put on a stretcher and brought to the hospital. A female police officer stayed with me for the night." Hank mouth tightened. "Of course, she lost the baby. She returned the next day, but was never the same. The light in her eyes was gone. She did her best to take care of me, but there was no more joy in her life. She was just going through the motions."

"Oh dear. What a horrifying story. Now I see what you were afraid of. Becoming him... your father." Samantha reached out a hand to touch his.

Hank looked at her, with tears in his eyes. "That's it. That memory, and all the others of that terrible man, had been submerged in my subconscious for so long I no longer remembered anything about him." He took out a handkerchief and blew his nose.

"Over the next six months, through a combination of hypnosis and therapy, every memory was brought to the surface and discussed. Eventually, and believe me it took a long time, I came to realize that I did not have to become like my father. I am my own person and that terrible behavior he exhibited was a choice, one that could not be handed down from father to son.

"Gradually, the depression lifted. I stopped the Xanax and waited a few more months to make sure I'd become myself again. Sam... I'm back. I am no longer afraid. All I want is to be with you and to be the best father in the world to Bonnie."

Samantha wanted to cry too; tears of regret, compassion and joy. But she was also wary. "Are you sure, Hank? Are you sure that you're all better?"

He reached into his pocket and pulled out a card. "Richard Jamison is my therapist. He said it would be fine if you wanted to give him a call. I've told him that he can tell you everything. Why don't you do that, and then let me know if you think we can start again. Not exactly from scratch, since we have a daughter, but if you agree, we can try to put our lives back together."

Samantha looked down at the card, then back up at Hank. "I will call him tomorrow and get back to you, okay?"

Hank reached for her hand. "Thank you."

They agreed not to continue talking, but to wait until Samantha had made up her mind. She gathered up her stuff, and this time it was she who gave him a kiss on the cheek. "I'll be in touch."

==

When she called Dr. Jamison the next day, he agreed to meet with her for coffee at noon, in-between patients. He explained in depth the problems some people have with memories of traumatic childhood experiences, particularly those which have been submerged for years. In Hank's case, twenty-seven years. He described the therapeutic approach he had used and the progress they had made together.

Thinking back to Dr. K's question about mental illness, Samantha said "Is there any possibility that Hank's father had some sort of mental condition that caused him to behave that way?"

"No, Mrs. Mitchell. I really do not think so. My sense is that he felt trapped in a loveless marriage and used the children, Hank and the baby on the way, as an excuse to get out.

Although relieved to hear that response, Samantha was still worried. "But, Dr. Jamison, how do you know that Hank's feelings of sadness and fear won't return; perhaps in response to some stressful situation?" Like finding out that his daughter might be the reincarnation of a dead model.

"Believe me, I understand your concern. I can't say for sure that Hank won't get depressed from time to time. We all do. But I can assure you that he will not act out in the way his father did. My sense is that he loves you very much, he wants to be a good father and he is very anxious to meet his daughter. If he was anything like his father, he would not have contacted you at all."

With that comforting assurance from Dr. Jamison, Samantha called Hank that night. She told him of their conversation and said just what she knew he was hoping for.

"Let's give it a go, Hank. I honestly have never stopped loving you, and it sounds like you still feel the same about me. Why don't you come up to the house on Saturday for dinner … about six? I did ask Dr. Jamison if he had any concerns with me introducing you to Bonnie sooner rather than later and he did not. Does that sound good to you?"

Hank breathed a sigh of relief. "It sure does. In fact it's the best news I've heard in four years!

==

When Saturday came, Samantha was nervous. She decided to wear a new pair of size six jeans since she'd lost ten pounds over the past six months, a white silk shirt and a short gold chain necklace. Hank had given it to her when they got engaged, but she hadn't worn it in four years. Perhaps after today she wouldn't take it off again. On her way out of the bedroom, she paused at the head of the stairs, then slowly turned around and went back to her dresser. Taking off the necklace, she decided to be smart this time and take it slowly.

She'd already told Bonnie that someone was coming for dinner.

"Who?" Bonnie had asked.

Samantha smiled mischievously, "Well, do you want me to tell you, or would you rather have it be a surprise?"

"A surprise, a surprise," chanted Bonnie, jumping up and down.

Hank drove up from the City, and arrived on the dot of six. Since he had been habitually late when they were together, Samantha knew he was trying to put his best foot forward. Plus, he came bearing gifts. Flowers for her and something for Bonnie.

As soon as she heard the doorbell, Bonnie came running. She stopped abruptly in the foyer and stared at Hank.

"Bonnie, hon, this is Hank."

All of a sudden, Bonnie turned around and ran out of the room. Within a few seconds though she was back, Hank's picture in hand. Once again she stared at him, looking back and forth from the photo.

Then, so softly she was almost whispering, she said, "Are you my daddy?"

Hank went down on one knee and said, "Yes, I am sweetheart. I'm very sorry it has taken so long for us to meet. I have been far away. But I'm back now and I'm really happy to meet you... at last."

He opened his arms, and Bonnie nearly jumped into them. "Oh, Daddy." That was it, "Oh, Daddy." The two of them held each other a long time.

Finally, as they pulled apart, Bonnie noticed the wrapped present that was now on the floor. "Is that for me, Daddy?"

"Why, yes it is!" Hank said, with a big grin on his face. I hope you like it. A little bird told me you had a birthday recently. Aren't you four?"

"Yes, I'm a big girl now. Can I open it?"

"Sure, go for it."

"Bonnie tore the ribbon and paper off and saw the picture of a pinto horse on the cover of a jigsaw puzzle box. "Oh, I love horsies. Thank you Daddy!" As Hank was still down at her level, she gave him a kiss on the cheek and then ran off into the family room to set up the puzzle on a table.

"Oh my, she's wonderful! And the spitting image of you."

"Yeah, I think she's pretty terrific too. It was nice of you to remember her birthday. Can I get you something to drink?"

"Sparkling water would be great."

"I noticed you didn't have anything to drink the other night either. Is there a reason?" God forbid he's also become an alcoholic.

"No particular reason," Hank replied. I just want to have all my wits about me while we get to know each other again. As he followed Samantha into the kitchen, he said "Bonnie seems so well behaved and polite. Is she always like that?"

"On the whole, yes. But she has her moments, just like all kids," Samantha said, thinking, if you only knew. She poured a glass of white wine for herself, Perrier for Hank, then picked up a plate of cheese and crackers. "Let's go sit down in the living room. Dinner will be ready in about forty-five minutes."

After sitting down, they struggled with conversation for a few minutes but then fell back into their old easy banter. They got caught up on their careers, their friends and groused about the current political scene. Bonnie would run in every now and then to ask "Daddy" to check on her progress.

This is so comfortable, Samantha marveled. It feels just like old times.

Over a dinner of roast lemon chicken, bubbling potatoes au gratin, and green beans with toasted almonds, their chatter flowed on effortlessly. Bonnie seemed perfectly at home with Hank, and Samantha had to admit that she was too. After a homemade blueberry tart desert with vanilla ice cream, the three of them watched Bonnie's favorite video and then Samantha put her to bed. No sooner had she returned to the living room than Bonnie's voice could be heard, "Daddy? Come and kiss me goodnight."

Hank smiled at Samantha and, with her nod, went up to Bonnie's bedroom. When he returned, he joined Samantha on the sofa. She slid closer and put her arms around him. "Oh,

Hank," she whispered, "I've missed you so much." They held each other tight for a few minutes, warmed by a spark of hope.

After about an hour, Samantha and Hank were interrupted by piercing screams coming from Bonnie's bedroom. Hank jumped up and started to run towards the stairs, but Samantha called out to him sternly, "Hank. Stop! Bonnie is having a nightmare. I'll take care of it. You wait here." Her tone was not to be disobeyed.

Reluctantly, Hank sat down again. Samantha went up to Bonnie's room and did what she always did. She talked softly to her, and kept saying "It's all right, honey. Mike is not here. It's just you and me, and you're safe. Breathe, honey. Just breathe." Finally, after about twenty minutes, Bonnie calmed down and fell asleep again.

When Samantha returned, one look at Hank's worried face convinced her that the time had come to tell him what was going on. She poured herself another glass of wine and sat down on the couch with him, ready to share Bonnie's story. She told him everything. From the alarming nightmares to the embarrassing sexual harassment investigation, to her fears of multiple personality disorder, to now... the possibility of reincarnation. It took almost an hour.

By the time she was finished, Hank was empathetic but also extremely skeptical. "I know this is a lot to take in Hank. Believe me I have been of two minds about it every step of the way. But the nightmares are not going away. If this reincarnation stuff turns out to be true, I have to hold on to the hope that when she meets her father, I mean Carrie's father, those terrifying dreams will start to fade away. At least that's what Dr. Williams told me. Otherwise they can continue on until she is about six or seven!" Her eyes pleaded with him to support her.

"I know what you want me to say, but I really don't know enough about reincarnation to weigh in. Do you have a copy of that book Dr. Williams sent to Mr. Kelly? I'd like to read up on those case studies. Right now it just sounds like another one of those paranormal beliefs: the white light at the end of the tunnel, looking down at yourself on the operating table, psychic phenomena, ghosts, seances. I've never been able to believe in any of that stuff."

"I know how you feel, trust me. I felt the same way. But it's starting to look like it may be possible. I'll give you my copy of the book - I've already read it five times. Once you read about the memories those kids had, which turned out to be true, it's kind of hard to ignore the subject of reincarnation. Oh, Hank, I'm so glad you're back." She hugged him tight. "I haven't been able to talk to anyone about this. They'd think I'm crazy. You probably think I'm crazy too, but I hope you'll come around. You eventually reach a point when there is just no other explanation! And then you have to give in and see where that takes you." Samantha searched Hank's eyes for some sort of acknowledgment. She needed them both to be on the same side.

He held her gaze and stroked her hair. "Sam, I'm absolutely committed to you and Bonnie, and I'm going to do my best to support you both. I'll read the book tonight. Would it be all right if I talked to Dr. Williams as well?"

Relieved, Samantha assured him that it would be fine. "I know he'd be happy to talk to you." She chuckled. "We're each recommending doctors to advance our case." She tried to stifle a yawn. "Oh, God. This has been an exhausting day. if you don't mind Hank, I think you'd better go. We've made a good start on reconnecting tonight, but I feel like I've been on an emotional rollercoaster." She rose saying, "I'll be right back. Samantha stepped out of the room for a minute and then returned with the book. Dr. Williams' number was written on the title page. She put her arms around Hank's neck and rested her head on his shoulder. "Let's talk tomorrow."

At the door, Hank gently pulled Samantha to him and gave her a soft kiss which, as she responded, became long, deep and passionate. They held each other tight, and then he left... book in hand.

==

Samantha didn't hear from Hank on Sunday until 10 p.m., when she was already in bed. She had started to worry that the whole reincarnation thing was more than he could handle, and that he'd disappeared from her life once more. So when the phone rang, she snatched it up on the first ring.

"Hank?"

"Hi Sam. I'm sorry I didn't call earlier. I read the whole book, and then went on the internet to research the subject of reincarnation. I never realized how many people believe in it! And with all that case study information, it's not something one can just reject out of hand, no matter how weird it may sound. I'll call Dr. Williams tomorrow. What's your next step?"

Samantha breathed a sigh of relief. "Dr. Williams has sent David Kelly a letter explaining what's going on and asking if we might be able to introduce Bonnie to him. We've been waiting over a month, but so far no reply. If he does agree to let us come over to his home, and if Bonnie recognizes him, we'll have our answer." She paused. "Hank, I hope you don't mind, but I don't think you should come to that meeting. I want Bonnie to be focused on just one daddy at a time. You do understand, don't you?"

"Yes, of course I do. But you're going to have to replay the whole encounter for me, word for word!"

Samantha smiled, "Absolutely! I'm so glad I have someone to confide in now. You know me… keeping a secret is not my strong suit! Which reminds me, please don't tell anyone about this. No matter how it turns out, I don't want anyone to ever connect the subject of reincarnation to Bonnie!"

They spoke for about an hour more as Hank insisted on hearing about every minute of Bonnie's life so far.

"Once again, Sam, I'm so sorry I haven't been here all this time to help you. But I'm here now, and I'm going to do my best to make up for everything."

As Samantha fell asleep her mind felt lighter. No matter what happened now, at least she was not alone.

Chapter 10

*O*n Wednesday, Bob Williams called Samantha at work. Once again, she shut the door to her office and wondered if her secretary might think she was having an affair.

"Good news! Mr. Kelly has agreed to a meeting with you and Bonnie. He apologized for the delay in getting back to us, but he was out of the country when my letter arrived. Then when he read it, he had a hard time accepting the notion that Bonnie could be the reincarnation of Carrie. His first thought, in fact, was 'Hogwash!' "

"I knew that would happen. What made him come around do you suppose?"

"As I'd hoped, he read Jim's book and eventually came to the conclusion that he couldn't just completely disregard all that research. So we've been invited to come over on Sunday, at 3:00 p.m. Does that work for you? I could fly up from Charlottesville in the morning." Bob's voice sounded eager and excited.

"Oh, gosh!" Samantha didn't have quite the same eagerness. "I mean, that's great news! I just always panic a bit when we move on to the next step. Did he sound like a nice guy?"

"Well, he's going through a period of adjustment too. So, I'd say he sounded cautious."

"Where does he live?"

"Actually, he lives in the same building Carrie lived in, but his penthouse is on the other side. It's too bad Bonnie didn't mention that, but this often happens. Certain facts come out easily, and others just aren't mentioned. Has she come up with anything new lately?"

"No. She's just been having the same nightmares. But I've written down all the statements she's made, and have audio/video recordings of those nightmares... before, during and after."

"That's great. They'll support our hypothesis. But I need to warn you that Mr. Kelly could also just ask us to leave. We never know how the previous personality's relatives will react, particularly a parent."

"Oh, that reminds me, I have news. Hank and I are trying to reconnect, and he met Bonnie on Saturday. She was thrilled."

"Yes. He called me on Monday, and we had a good talk."

"Did he seem open to the possibility of reincarnation?"

"Hard to tell. We spoke for a while about our work here at UVA, how we go about solving cases and what thoughts I have so far about Bonnie's case. I told him that I was optimistic, but that I'm really looking forward to our visit with Mr. Kelly for any kind of confirmation. He seems to have an open mind, at least right now."

"Oh good. I was a bit worried that he'd find it all too woo-woo, if you know what I mean."

"Well, I'm happy for you," Bob replied. "Is he coming on Sunday?"

"No, I thought that might be too confusing."

"You're right," Bob said, "better to keep Bonnie's focus on Mr. Kelly."

"Okay, I'll see you Sunday. And again, thanks Bob. I can't tell you how much comfort it is to have you, with all your expertise, managing this process. I'd be a basket case without you!"

"Thanks. This is my life's work remember, and I'm happy to be involved."

"Oh, what should I tell Bonnie we're doing?"

"I'd suggest you not say anything. Maybe you could just take her to the Zoo again, and then pop into 980 Fifth for a surprise. Would that work?"

"Oh yes. Animals and surprises are way up there on her list of favorite things." She took a deep breath. "Okay, Bob, we'll meet you in front of the building at 3:00 p.m. on Sunday. Hopefully you won't be delayed. I certainly don't want us to go up there alone. Oh, what about Dr. K?"

"I spoke to him, and we agreed that it would be best to keep this meeting small. We don't want to overpower Mr. Kelly. I'll fill him in afterwards. And don't worry, I'll be there on time, probably early in fact. If there is any problem, I'll call your cell."

"Great, see you soon." As she hung up, Samantha leaned back in her chair. And so we move on. If Mr. Kelly comes to believe all this, it will be very difficult to back out. Not for the first time, Samantha prayed she was doing the right thing.

==

Of course Bonnie was delighted to learn they were going to the Zoo again. This time she picked out a light green and white checked dress with a matching sweater and white tights. Samantha too wanted to look her best, so she wore a new outfit; pearl gray linen pants with a matching top, and a pink and gray, floral oblong scarf. She even brushed out her wavy hair rather than resorting to her weekend pony tail. As Bonnie would say, she thought, 'it's a special 'casion.'

Samantha made sure the Zoo visit wasn't too long, so that Bonnie wouldn't be exhausted by the time they met Mr. Kelly. So she was still skipping along when they came out of the Zoo, but stopped to exclaim, "Look! There's that man we met. What's his name?"

"My, you've got a good memory! That's Dr. Bob Williams. I asked him to meet us here because we have a surprise for you. Would you like that?"

"Yes, yes, yes! What is it?"

"Well, I'm going to introduce you to someone you may know. Just come with me."

They joined Bob across the street and then went into the Lobby of 980 Fifth Avenue. Walking hand in hand, Samantha led Bonnie over to the back wall of the lobby to ostensibly look at a large, modern painting. She didn't want her to hear Bob tell the doorman, who was not Joseph this time, that they were here to see David Kelly. The doorman called up to announce them and then motioned the way to the left elevator, saying "Just go up to the penthouse."

Once in the elevator, Bonnie looked up quizzically at Samantha and Bob. "Where are we going? To see that pretty woman again?"

"No, honey. Just wait. The surprise is in the apartment at the top of the building… the penthouse."

"But wait! If we are going to my apartment, it's on the other side!" Bonnie was starting to get nervous.

Just as the elevator stopped, the door was opened by Mr. Kelly himself. He was a handsome man in his late fifties, with dark hair already flecked with silver streaks, and intelligent, hazel eyes. He was dressed in grey slacks with a pin-stripe blue and white shirt, sleeves rolled up at the cuff, and polished black loafers without socks.

As soon as he stepped back to invite them in, Bonnie ran forward, hugged his knees, and said "Daddy, Daddy! Oh

Daddy, I'm so happy to see you!" Mr. Kelly was quite taken aback and as Bonnie held on to him tightly he didn't know what to do. He lifted his arms up uncomfortably and looked around for help.

"Look Mama! This is my daddy!" Bonnie was very excited, but Mr. Kelly didn't know what to do or say.

Samantha and Bob stepped in, closed the door, and she came to his aid. "Bonnie, honey. You'll have lots of time to talk to Mr. Kelly, but let's sit down in the living room now. Okay?" She pried away Bonnie's hands, while apologizing at the same time. "I'm sorry, Mr. Kelly, but Bonnie has been wanting to see you for a long time. I'm her mother, Samantha Mitchell, and I believe you've already spoken to Dr. Williams."

David shook their hands. Although very polite, he looked quite ill at ease as he turned to lead them into the living room. On the way, they passed the entrance to the dining room where Bonnie let out a little shriek.

"Ooooh! There she is! Boofa!" A five-foot-tall, gold wooden Buddha sculpture stood serenely in the corner. Bonnie ran over to it, paused, put her palms together and slowly bowed while saying 'namaste.' Straightening up, she drummed her feet on the floor and raised her arms in excitement. "Hi Boofa. It's me, Carrie! I'm so happy to see you again. Look, Dr. Bob! This is the gold doll I was telling you about... Boofa!" She paused and then slowly turned around. "But Daddy, Boofa was in my apartment, before, before..."

David gaped in amazement. "Ahh, yes, I know. But after my daughter died, I moved him and some of her other Asian pieces of art into my apartment. I guess I feel closer to her this way."

"You are close to me now, Daddy," Bonnie said, as she reached up and took David's hand. "I am Carrie and Carrie is me. I'm sorry I died Daddy. But I couldn't fight him off and Boofa didn't save me."

Now David looked totally flummoxed, so Samantha suggested again that they go sit down. The living room was full of immaculate period furnishings, with not a single scratch or mar. As they sat on the white damask sofa and adjacent chintz club chairs, they faced a fireplace, topped by an antique gold mirror, and flanked by bookshelves on both sides. The shelves held not only fine leather-bound books, but artifacts from around the world: ceramics from China and Japan, bone sculptures from Morocco, carved African animals, and temple toys from India. In no short order, Bonnie had her eye on one of those. "Daddy, can I play with that one?"

"Of course," David replied, reaching up for a small, hand-painted, wooden elephant on four wheels. "Do you know about these toys, ahh, Bonnie?"

"Carrie found it in India. It's a toy for children to play wif in church." She started to push the elephant around on the beautiful, faded oriental rug.

"That's right!" he said, with a bit of astonishment in his voice. "That's why they're called temple toys. It's often hard for children to keep still, listening to all that preaching."

"Yes," Bob added. "I've seen many temple toys in India, but the ones I've seen in people's homes are usually a little more beat up than that one."

David started to reply, but Bonnie interrupted him. "Daddy, can you keep a secret?"

"Why, yes," he said, with a cautious smile. "I think I can."

"Okay. As long as you promise. 'Cause I don't think Carrie wanted you to see this." Then as everyone leaned in to get a closer look, Bonnie swiveled the top half of the temple toy and revealed a secret compartment inside. Nestled in that space, was a small object.

"Look! It's a secret key!" Bonnie held the key aloft for all to see.

Everyone was taken aback by this revelation. Bob was jotting down a note, but Samantha and David just looked stunned.

"I never even knew that the elephant opened," David said. Then, almost as if he were testing her, added "Do you happen to know what the key unlocks, by any chance?"

"It's the key to Carrie's book, the one she did writing in at night." There was a note of pride in Bonnie's voice for being able to share this information.

"Do you mean her diary, honey?" Samantha asked.

"Maybe. All I know is that when I was Carrie I wrote in it a lot. Do you have it, Daddy?"

"I don't know," David said. "I haven't seen it, but I do have a box in storage containing some of Carrie's personal belongings. I just haven't had the heart to go through it. I'll dig it out and search for the diary. If she really wrote in it daily, it could prove very helpful."

Now Samantha could tell David was starting to believe in Bonnie. It was just too unimaginable that she could know about the temple toy, the key, and the diary without some sort of consciousness from Carrie guiding her.

Bonnie was invited to go into the kitchen with the housekeeper for some cookies and milk while the grownups talked. "I am amazed," David said. "I really wasn't buying any of this until she found that key, which even I didn't know was there."

Bob looked up from his note taking. "Many buyers of temple toys don't even notice that they can be opened. If that key opens a diary, we could learn facts that only Carrie knew, some of which Bonnie seems to know now. But I want to reinforce that none of us should talk in front of Bonnie about any additional information we learn or the case will be compromised."

"What do you mean... the case?" David said with a frown.

"Well at DOPS, UVA's Division of Perceptual Studies, we refer to each inquiry about a potential former life as a case study. If we determine that there is no answer for what the child knows, other than the reincarnation of a previous personality, the case is considered solved. At this point we are still in the investigative stage so we don't want to plant any ideas or information in Bonnie's head. But with her recognition of you, we've certainly moved a giant step closer."

As David ran a hand through his hair, looking a bit shell-shocked, Samantha said "would you like to have a copy of all the statements Bonnie has made so far, and the video tapes I've made when she's having those awful nightmares?" Suddenly realizing how insensitive she sounded and how upsetting this would be to him, she apologized. "Oh, I'm so sorry. I wasn't thinking. They may be very difficult for you to take."

David sat up taller. "No, that's all right. I would like to see whatever you have. Carrie's murder has been the most difficult thing I've ever dealt with, after the death of her mother. But if there is even a remote possibility that we can get closer to finding her killer, I'm all in. I have no stronger wish than to find that son of a bitch and see that he gets the punishment he deserves. Excuse my language, but I have been hoping for some sort of lead on this case for six years now. I never expected one like this but if it helps us find her killer, I'm all in."

Tea was served in the living room and, after more discussion about Bob's other cases, Samantha suggested it was time for them to leave. "I'm sure this has been very hard on you, David. You're going to need some time to process it all. I certainly did."

Bob shook David's hand and added, "If you find the diary and it corroborates any of the other information we have heard from Bonnie, I would very much like to know about it. If Carrie wrote anything about a man named Mike, it might be possible for you to have her case opened up again."

"Absolutely. I'll look for it tomorrow and get back to you as soon as possible." They all shook hands again… more warmly now than when they'd arrived.

Bonnie returned and as they were leaving, she gave David another heart-felt leg-hug. "Bye-bye Daddy. 'Til we meet again!"

David's face paled. "That's what Carrie always said whenever we parted." Then he knelt down on one knee and gave Bonnie a hug. "Bye-bye, sweetheart. 'Till we meet again." As he stood, there were tears in his eyes.

Chapter 11

*A*s she had promised, Samantha called Hank on Sunday night and tried to tell him what had happened every minute they were in David's apartment; from "Hi Daddy" right up to "till we meet again." Hank was riveted.

"It was really amazing to watch, Hank. You know I feel that my whole life is changing... that everything I once believed may not be true. In a way, I think my mind is generating a whole new set of brain cells, just to accept this notion of reincarnation."

"I know what you mean," Hank said. "It really opens the door to reexamining your life and assessing what it all means, doesn't it? For instance, if reincarnation exists, what is its purpose? I've read that it's about continued growth, particularly if you've misbehaved in this life. But even with my medical excuse, I feel as though I'm guilty of that. So perhaps if I can make amends to you in this life, I'll be spared the life of a cow in the next?"

Samantha could hear the smile in his voice. "I'm looking forward to that, Hank. Amends are always welcome... particularly if they come in the form of your home-cooked dinners."

With that, they made a date for the following weekend. Samantha would have to do nothing. Hank would arrive with the food and then cook it. Perfect, Samantha thought. Perfect.

Chapter 12

*O*n Monday, Bob called Samantha at 10:00 a.m. He had already received an excited call from David. "He found Carrie's journal, and he wants to meet with us as soon as possible. Apparently it contains a real lead to Carrie's murderer!"

"Oh my goodness! That's amazing!" Samantha said, shutting the door.

"I thought it might be best if you and he could meet at his office, at 52 Central Park South. I can be included via Skype. He suggested getting together at the end of the day, around 5:30. Does that work for you?"

"Of course I can be there. I'm dying to hear what he's discovered. Maybe she wrote about Mike! I have to say this is getting exciting! Thanks Bob, see you later."

After arranging for Mercedes to stay later that night, Samantha opened the door and tried to make it seem like she cared about her work, but it wasn't easy. Somehow analyzing profit and loss calculations seemed totally worthless now.

What if the information in the journal points a finger at this 'Mike' person? Would that be sufficient evidence to convict him? If not... then what? Would Bonnie have to get involved and tell her story in court? Could a trial even proceed based on the testimony of a three-year-old professing to be the reincarnation of the victim? As the daughter of a former prosecutor, Samantha knew that would be highly unlikely. It had certainly never happened before. Moreover, she definitely did not want Bonnie to become part of a three-ring media circus. She felt as though she were in a tug-of-war game with herself. One side was excited about the possibility of finding the murderer and going to trial, while the other side was determined to protect Bonnie.

==

At 5:30, Samantha arrived at 52 Central Park South and went up to the 37th floor. Entering DMK Management, Inc., she took in the elegant lobby furnished with contemporary black leather sofas, armless chairs covered in black and white zebra skin and a bold red Rothko painting hanging behind the glass reception desk. Within seconds of announcing herself to the receptionist, a young, stylishly dressed woman appeared. "Mrs. Mitchell? Right this way. Mr. Kelly is waiting for you."

David stood up from behind his sleek desk that seemed to have no work on it and walked around to greet her. "Samantha…is it all right if I call you that?" He put out his hand. "In some eerie way, I feel as though we're family." This time David was dressed in a dark, well-tailored suit, a pink shirt with onyx cuff links and a pin dot navy tie. Very handsome, Samantha couldn't help noticing.

"Of course." Samantha said, shaking his hand. "And I know what you mean, particularly the 'eerie' part."

"Can I offer you a drink? I'm having a Scotch, and I think you may want one too after you see what I have to show you."

"No thanks. I'll just have a sparkling water if you have it." David walked over to the bar and prepared their drinks. "Has Bonnie had any more memories?"

"Not since we saw you yesterday, but she did seem very happy to have finally met her daddy. Bob has told me that when children with memories of a previous life have those remembrances validated, they begin to talk about them less frequently and then not long afterwards start to forget them."

"Ah," David said. "Well, I hope she doesn't forget everything too soon." He picked up their drinks, beckoned to the two chairs facing his desk and they sat down.

"What do you mean, too soon?"

"Think about it - with Bonnie's testimony and what I have read in Carrie's journal, we may be able to put this guy, Mike, away for the rest of his life!" Since Sunday, when he had seemed very ill at ease, confused and hesitant, David had undergone a complete character transformation. He now appeared comfortable, confident and ready to do battle.

"Look, of course I want you to have closure on your daughter's death and see that Mike, whoever he is, gets the punishment he deserves. But you also have to realize that Bonnie is my number-one priority. I do not want to put her through the traumatic experience of testifying on a witness stand. I know how upsetting that can be for an adult; for a small child, it could be devastating. I'm hoping that whatever clues she shares with us lead to enough evidence for the police to develop a solid case. But one without her testimony."

"I understand, and hopefully the diary evidence will suffice. So let's just take it one day at a time."

Samantha smiled at what was getting to be a mantra in their lives. Perhaps they were both learning to live in the moment.

"Okay, let me get Bob on Skype. I told him we'd call about now, and I emailed him the relevant pages from Carrie's journal. Here's a copy for you as well." David typed in Bob's number and turned his large screen monitor around so that he and Samantha could be facing him together.

When Bob's face came on the screen he was holding David's email in his hand. "Hi David, Samantha. These entries seem really incriminating."

David put up a hand to stop Bob from rushing on. "Samantha hasn't seen it yet so why don't I read it aloud and then we can discuss it." He took a deep breath to calm himself. "Before we begin, I have to tell you that it wasn't easy reading about my daughter's relationship with Mike. As you will hear, she made a very bad mistake that in the end probably contributed to her own death." Picking up the diary, he cleared his throat, put on his glasses and began. Bob and Samantha followed along, reading their copies of the transcript.

" 'January 4, 2013. Got a beautiful framed mandala painting for Christmas from Daddy. It's of Akshobhya, one of the Five Wisdom Buddhas... in deep forest greens, ruby reds and pearl pinks. On the back it says Akshobhya represents consciousness as an aspect of reality. I'm not sure I know what that means, and Daddy certainly doesn't, but he probably figured it would look good with all my Asian art. It's a beauty alright, but heavy! Asked JoJo to send up a maintenance guy to help me hang it.

" 'He sent a young man named Mike, and what a hottie! He must be new because I know I'd never forget him. Tall, muscular, dark curly hair, piercing blue eyes and a really sexy grin. After he hung the painting, we started talking and I offered him something to drink (after all that hard work, you know.) He has a charming Irish brogue and we talked for about an hour, but who knows what we said. I was just thinking about how much I wanted to touch him! He must have been turned on too, 'cause we ended up in the sack and had mad, passionate sex! It was great! Like having sex with a stranger, not that I've ever done that - unless you count tonight.'

David avoided their eyes and looked like he wanted to be anywhere but there, reading about his daughter's sex life.

"It's okay," Samantha assured him. "Sexual attraction is a funny thing... you never quite know when it's going to make you lose all your self control."

"Right," David said, "I guess we've all had those moments of madness." He took a sip of his drink and continued. "She then wrote, 'I have definitely been too busy traveling all over the world, because I really needed that! But now that he's gone, I'm beating myself up. What was I thinking? He's a maintenance man and I'm his boss's daughter! Definitely gonna have to put on the brakes!'

" 'January 6th. Lunch with Greta, told her about Mike. She was all ears, but agreed I have to dump him. Don't be cruel, she said, just honest. You had a one night stand. It was great... but no more!

" 'January 15th. Alone with Mike on the elevator. Bit the bullet and gave him the spiel. He just smiled, or maybe smirked, and said well, when you change your mind, you know where to find me. I hope that'll be the end of him.

" 'February 6th. Mike subbing for JoJo tonight. Came out to the taxi with an umbrella and walked me in. Felt uncomfortable being so close to him, particularly when he said... hello, lovely lady. You look scrumptious! This time his smile seemed more like a leer. And even worse, he looked like he wanted to eat me up right then and there!'

David took another sip of his drink. This was clearly painful to him.

" 'May 21st. Been out of the country several times... haven't seen Mike for a month, but today he was running the elevator again. He said, welcome home! Would you like me to stop by after my shift is over? I bet you've had a long, dry spell. I just stared straight ahead and didn't say a word, but I swear I could feel his eyes undressing me. Getting nervous. Calling Daddy tomorrow. Will have to fess up, but at least he can get rid of him. I'm so embarrassed, but what else can I do? Mike won't take no for an answer!' "

David looked up from the journal, took off his glasses and then stared at the desk for a moment. "That's the last entry in her diary. She was found dead the next day."

Samantha was at a loss for words. Finally Bob broke the silence. "David, I'm so sorry. How difficult it must be for you to read this. But how helpful that she documented all that in her diary. Have you spoken to your building manager to find out Mike's full name, and whether he still works there?"

David sat up straighter and seemed to regain his composure. "I have. His name is Michael MacShane, and he started work as a maintenance man on December 15th, 2012. Although the police questioned the entire staff, he apparently did not become a suspect. But get ready for this, he's still there! So, I'm going to call the detective who worked on the case and see if these journal entries are enough for her to take a second look."

David paused, and opened the diary to another page he had marked with a sticky. "If you don't mind, I'd like to read you one more entry from the diary so you'll get a better sense of who Carrie was. Despite our long-running disagreement about the importance of higher education, she decided after high school that she wanted to become a model and put off college. She promised me, though, that she'd pick it up again after five years of modeling. This entry was also in May, the month she died."

Putting his glasses on again, David cleared his throat and began, "I have decided to quit modeling. I've seen so many darling children in Africa who are living in poverty and don't have the chance to get an education. By a stroke of luck, I'm living this pampered life of privilege while others are struggling just to make it to the end of the day. I don't know who decides the kind of life we're born into, but shouldn't the lucky ones do something to help out the others? Thinking about going back to school to get some sort of degree to do social work and fundraising for them. I'm excited about it and think Daddy will be too." David bowed his head.

Samantha put her hand gently on David's shoulder. "Thank you for sharing that with us. It sounds like she was figuring out how to make a difference in the world. Something we should all do. I'm so sorry she wasn't able to make that dream come true. Knowing what she aspired to do though makes me really want to see her murder solved, and I know you feel the same way. Please keep me in the loop after you've spoken to that detective."

Addressing the screen, she said, "Bob, I've told David that I really don't want to involve Bonnie with a court trial. Being the center of attention in such a high-profile case would turn her life upside down."

Bob nodded, but offered up another thought. "I'm hoping the diary will do the trick too; but keep in mind that if Bonnie feels she is helping to punish Mike, it could help relieve her nightmares. One way or another, she needs to know she is a part of this retribution." His office phone started ringing so he said, "I need to go, guys. Let me know what happens, David, and if I can be of any help."

Samantha also rose to leave, but on her way out gave David a warm hug. She wasn't sure whether she wanted to help this man find the justice he deserved or simply walk out the door, never to return.

"It is not more surprising to be born twice than once; everything in nature is reincarnation."

Voltaire

Susan Burke

Part II
Searching for Answers
June - August 2019

Chapter 13

Martha Riddle, NYPD Detective Investigator in the 19th District, hung up the phone and gazed out the window. She cast her mind back five years to the investigation she had led into the sexual assault and murder of Carolyn Kelly. It had been big news at the time, especially since Carrie was a top model and the daughter of billionaire real estate developer, David Kelly. Both of them were well known in Manhattan's social elite, and since Kelly was a widower, his daughter often accompanied him to red carpet events around town, dressed to kill. They made a very handsome couple, and many people didn't realize that they were father and daughter rather than husband and wife.

Naturally, when Carrie was murdered, a lot of pressure was put on the police to find the perpetrator. Captain Fox, irritating old codger that he was, would visit her office once a day to ask about progress in the case. Following the steps that all murder investigations take, they searched for anyone who might have had a motive to kill her: building employees and residents, friends and family, work associates, and casual acquaintances, at least those they learned about. In all, they interviewed 323 people, but none of them could provide any hints to point them in the right direction. Carrie was very popular, had a lot of friends, and no one could think of someone who would have reason to do such a thing. Reluctantly, after two years, the murder was relegated to the category of Unsolved Cases. And now... this. David Kelly had called to report the discovery of a diary, or a journal, that mentioned a possible suspect.

Martha reviewed the case file, then took off for Kelly's office without telling the Captain why she was going out. She didn't want to get anyone else involved until she found out what kind of a lead this was. The pressure before had been unbearable, and she not anxious to get on that roller coaster again. But she was intrigued.

Martha Riddle was only forty, and had achieved the rank of Detective Second Grade after fifteen years in the 19th Precinct investigative unit. She was responsible for crimes on the Upper East Side, where there weren't really many rapes or murders, so most of her time was spent on robberies and burglaries. She had worked day and night to solve the Kelly murder in the hopes of achieving a promotion to First Grade Detective. But those dreams had slowly dissolved as possible tips proved to go nowhere. Now her heart started beating a little faster as she drove down to Central Park South. This time, she thought, she would go it alone. If it seemed possible to solve this case, she wanted to get the credit. And the pay raise!

Martha came from a family of policemen. Her father achieved the rank of Sergeant, and her uncle became a Private Investigator after 30 years as a policeman. She had no idea why her husband, Jimmy, had ever married her since she could never let go of a lead once she'd latched on to it. Christmas, his birthday, their anniversary or just date night, all were pushed aside. A lead was a lead, and she couldn't let it get cold. Fortunately Jimmy understood, although she wondered how he would respond when she told him the Kelly case was being reopened. But just as her mother seemed to have endless patience with her father when he was doggedly pursuing a perp, she suspected Jimmy would be the same. She was anxious to see what David had found.

==

"So what do you think?" David asked, after he'd shared Carrie's diary entries with her. Doesn't this sound like a promising lead?"

"Well, yes and no. According to Carrie's notes, she came on to him. And just because she didn't put out again, that's not proof he killed her."

David flinched, but pressed on. "Would it be a good idea for you to talk to Greta? Just to get a more complete picture of their interactions? Her last name is Neilson. I never mentioned her before because Carrie hadn't spoken of her much, and I didn't realize they were friends. Since Mike still works in the building, you should probably talk to him again. See if his alibi still holds up." David seemed ready to charge out there and interview them himself.

Martha didn't really appreciate being told how to do her job, but she knew that David would be like a dog with a bone if she didn't follow up on these clues. And, of course, she had every intention of doing so.

"Don't get your hopes up too much, Mr. Kelly. This case is now five years old; people's memories are faulty, and Mike MacShane may reasonably not have a reliable alibi after all this time. But don't worry, I'll get back to you after I've spoken with Greta and Mike."

==

It had not been hard to track down Greta Neilson. The Elite Model Management Agency, which had represented Carrie, had Greta on their roster as well. So on the following day, Martha met Greta in a Starbucks on Second Avenue, between 54 and 55th Streets. She didn't want her to come into the station house where everyone would start asking questions about who she was and why Martha was questioning her.

As Martha walked in, she immediately recognized the tall, striking blonde, despite the fact that she wore no makeup and was dressed in jeans, boots and a sloppy sweater. Why, she wondered, do models look great no matter what they do... or don't do. It's just not fair that there is such a thing as a "natural beauty." Trying not to look uncomfortable in her boxy blue uniform and white shirt, Martha sat down at Greta's table after picking up a coffee at the counter. She had decided against getting a scone since she was easily 30 pounds heavier than Greta.

"Thank you for meeting me on such short notice, Ms. Neilson." Martha put down her coffee on the table and awkwardly slid into the seat across from Greta, pleased that she had selected a booth in the back.

"No problem, Detective. I'm curious about how I may be of help to you." Greta, who still had a slight Swedish accent, looked both perplexed and worried.

"Well, as you probably remember, Carolyn Kelly was murdered about six years ago. At the time, we didn't know that you were one of her friends and therefore never spoke with you. But recently we learned about your relationship and decided to follow up."

"But that was so long ago! I just assumed that the case had dried up. Do you have new leads?"

"Ms. Neilson, did Carrie ever speak to you about a man named Mike MacShane?"

At first Greta looked a little uncomfortable, but then she slowly nodded her head. "Yes. She told me that he worked in her building and that they had a, how do you say, one night stand. She felt very guilty about it and asked for my advice on what to do."

"And what did you advise her?"

"I advised her to stay away from him and suggested she tell him the truth… that it was one night, and that was it. No more!"

"And did she tell him that?"

"Yes. But when I had lunch with her about a month later, she was still feeling very uncomfortable. She didn't like the way he looked at her and was worried that he was going to just stop by some night. I pooh-poohed her and said that he probably felt just as uncomfortable as she did. In my experience, men know when they are out of their league. And after all, he wouldn't have wanted to lose his job. Oh dear, Inspector, should I have contacted you? I wasn't even in the country when it happened, and I'd pretty much forgotten all about Mike."

"Don't beat yourself up," Martha said. "What may be important to one person is often not even remembered by another. But I appreciate your recollection now, and we will follow up with Mike. By the way, did Carrie ever talk about her love life or any other one-night stands?"

"Not unless you count moaning about not having one. You know everyone thinks it must be so easy for models; that men must be buzzing around us like flies. But nothing could be further from the truth. Sometimes I think they are just scared. Like we might break or something. Anyway, Carrie's love life was pretty much a non-event. I think that's why she allowed herself to get carried away with Mike."

"All right. Thank you Ms. Neilson. If this case should ever come to trial, can we count on you to be a witness and repeat what you have just told me?"

"Of course. Just let me know, so I can clear my calendar."

==

After lunch, Martha drove the police car over to 980 Fifth Avenue and asked to speak with Mike MacShane. When he arrived in the lobby, she noted that he still looked extremely handsome and fit, a turn-on to any young woman, including Carolyn Kelly apparently.

"Mr. MacShane, we are reopening the investigation into the murder of Carolyn Kelly due to some new information that has surfaced."

"And you think I had somethin' to do with it?" Mike said, eyebrows raised, arms crossed in a defensive stance.

"We don't know. But I'd like you to come with me to the station. Do you have a problem with that?"

"Well, I'm workin' now. I can't just walk out. Why don't I come down after my shift ends at 5:00."

"All right, that'll be fine. But don't go skipping out on me." I can't just arrest him, Martha thought. I don't have enough to go on. Let's just hope he doesn't take a flyer.

==

At 5:25, Mike walked into the station house. Martha took him into a cold, impersonal interrogation room, and turned on the tape recorder. After reading him his Miranda rights, she began to question him. "Michael MacShane, you are here today, June 5th, 2019, to answer questions related to the murder of Carolyn Kelly on May 21st, 2013. You were previously interviewed on May 23rd, 2013.

"All right, let's get started. Mike, when we last spoke you said you knew who Carolyn Kelly was, but that you had never really spoken to her." Martha read from her file, 'Sure, I know who she was. Everyone in the building knows who she was. A looker like that doesn't go unnoticed. I hung a paintin' for her once, but other than that, never had much interaction with her."

Continuing on Martha said "So, I'd like to discuss in more detail that time when you hung a painting for her. First of all, do you remember when that was?"

"From six years ago? I have trouble rememberin' what I did yesterday! One day is pretty much like another; fix this, mop that. But I think that paintin' was a Christmas gift, so I'd say it was probably in the early part of the year, or maybe at the end of 2012."

"Okay. And on that day when you hung her painting, did the two of you talk?"

"Well sure we talked. She told me where to put it, then changed her mind and moved it to another place, then changed her mind and moved it to a third place. Women!" He took a toothpick out of his pocket, smiled and started swirling it around in his mouth.

"What if I were to tell you that I have proof that you slept with Carrie on the day you hung that painting?"

The toothpick abruptly stopped swirling. Martha watched his expression change within seconds from disbelief, to chagrin, to fear, and then purposefully settle on nonchalance.

"What if I did?"

"Well, you didn't mention that in your first interview. Why is that?"

"Look Officer, Carrie came on to me. And I am not one to turn down an offer from a woman like that. But she was also the boss's daughter! I knew that if he ever found out about it, he'd kick me out pronto!"

"Did you and Carrie ever have sex again?"

"Absolutely not.   As I said… the boss's daughter? Anyway I could tell that she had no intention of allowing that to happen again. In fact she pretty much ignored me thereafter. You could say I was used and abused." Mike smirked and put the toothpick back in his mouth.

"And how did that make you feel?" Martha asked.

"Pretty shitty for a while, but I got over it. There are plenty of women out there who recognize a good thing when they see it." He leaned back in his chair and crossed his legs.

Although annoyed by his egotistical, devil-may-care attitude, Martha just said, "Do you recall where you were on the night of May 21st, 2013?"

"Right now I don't. What did I say when you asked me the last time?"

Looking at her notes, Martha read, " 'I was at my apartment with Lily Shannon. We had met up at The Trinity Pub and, you know, one thing led to another.' She corroborated your story when we spoke to her. Do you happen to know where she is now?"

"Not a clue." Mike looked a bit defiant, as though he had just said 'checkmate,' if he ever even knew how to play chess in the first place, which Martha doubted.

"Does she live in the City?"

"How do I know? That was six years ago, and I haven't seen her since that night. So again… not a clue."

Resigned that she wasn't going to be able to get any more useful information from Mike, Martha ended the interview and told him that he could leave. She did, however, advise him that, as a suspect in this case, he shouldn't leave town without giving her a call first. Mike stood up, yawned, and walked out of her office like he had not a care in the world.

==

The next day Martha gave David Kelly a call at his office. "Well, I'm afraid I don't have anything substantial to tell you." She brought him up to date on her meetings with Greta Neilson and Mike MacShane, including that Mike's alibi, Lily Shannon, no longer lived in the City and that Mike didn't know where she'd gone. "We'll try to find her, but it's highly possible that she'll just say she can't remember that night from six years ago without being reminded. So I'm afraid we don't have definitive proof, despite signs to the contrary. And as much as I'd like to pursue this, since this guy is a cocky prick, I just don't have enough to go on."

David sighed and was silent for a minute. "Detective Riddle, I may have something more for you, but I can't talk about it right now. Is it all right if I get back to you tomorrow?"

"Certainly," Martha replied, wondering what he had up his sleeve now. "You know where to reach me."

Chapter 14

*T*hat afternoon, David gave Samantha a call to tell her about Detective Riddle's investigation and her assessment that they were at a dead end.

"Darn!" Samantha said. So where does that leave us?" She'd been so sure that this Mike would turn out to be *the* Mike. Of course he still could be, but in order for the police to reopen the investigation they would need more evidence. Evidence that only Bonnie had.

David heard the worried tone in Samantha's voice. "I know you're disappointed; I am too. But let's not make any hasty decisions. I think we both need to think this over. I told Martha that I might have some more information for her, but didn't tell her what it was; just said I'd get back to her. Let's give it twenty-four hours, then talk again. Is that okay with you?"

"Yes, I guess so. I know what you want me to think about, David, but I'm pretty sure my mind is made up. I'll give it twenty-four hours though."

"Thanks. I'll call you tomorrow, and perhaps we can meet up somewhere for drinks at the end of the day. Maybe you'd like to bring Hank?"

"We'll see. Let's talk tomorrow."

==

Unable to concentrate on her work since clearly David was going to ask her if Bonnie could become a witness, Samantha considered her options. What was the right thing to do, she asked herself for the millionth time. Put Bonnie through the distress that she would undoubtedly suffer by being asked to relive her nightmare in front of strangers, or just allow the case to remain unsolved? What was right for David wasn't necessarily right for Bonnie.

Before meeting with him again, Samantha decided to give Bob Williams a call to see what he thought. Fortunately he was in his Charlottesville office and not traveling around in India or Thailand trying to solve another case. He was keenly interested in hearing Samantha's update and immediately understood her concern.

"Let's think about this for a minute. First of all, it will probably be impossible to get the DA to agree to prosecute based on Bonnie's story. But on the remote chance they do, there are steps that could be taken to protect her identify and minimize her stress."

"Oh, sure," Samantha sighed. "They'll probably come up with something, but why should we put Bonnie through all that?"

"Tell me, since she met David have you noticed any change in her? Does she still keep asking to see her daddy?"

"No, now that you mention it. She's talked about him, but hasn't asked to see him again. She is still having nightmares though."

"I suspected as much. Since she has now met Carrie's daddy, his existence has been validated. Even Mr. Kelly seemed to acknowledge that she was Carrie in that farewell hug. But, there has been no similar resolution on the Mike front.

"I've never heard about a child testifying in court to the murder of her previous personality, but it's possible that it

120

could help her recover. In my personal experience, children have stopped having nightmares after personally confronting someone who killed them in a previous life. Since we know that Bonnie would never want to confront Mike in person, perhaps you could at least explore exactly what she would need to do, should the case ever go to trial."

"Okay," Samantha said, resting her head on her hand. "That sounds fair I guess. Hank and I are going to meet with David tomorrow night to talk this over. I'll let you know how it goes."

"Fine. Should you decide to proceed, call if I can be of any help in educating the police or the DA about reincarnation. That's going to be a high hurdle for them."

"I think it's a high hurdle for all of us, Bob. But thanks, I'll give you a call tomorrow or the next day."

Feeling a bit better, Samantha called Hank, brought him up to date and asked if he would like to join her for drinks with David. He seemed pleased to be included and agreed immediately. I'm glad he wants to come, she thought. Despite all this weirdness, he isn't giving up or running away. I wonder what his point of view will be about having Bonnie testify?

==

When David called the next day there was no small talk. He just asked whether they could meet at the Carlyle Hotel at 6 p.m. She agreed and let him know that Hank would be there as well.

The luxurious Carlyle Hotel stood at 75th Street and Fifth Avenue. Samantha remembered when she and Hank had celebrated her birthday at the Cafe Carlyle and listened to Judy Collins sing "Both Sides Now." She started to hum the song and noticed how much the first line of the last refrain resonated with her. 'I've looked at life from both sides now… I really don't know life at all.' Do any of us really know life, she wondered. Because it seems that what we are taught and what we assume to be true, may not in fact be the truth. So is life totally subjective, representing only our own perceptions and not reality? Is there even such a thing as objective reality? Before she could go any further down that philosophical rabbit hole, she saw Hank striding up the avenue. He was wearing a lightweight sport coat, a polo shirt and chinos. Clearly he'd not been visiting clients today. Nevertheless, as always, her heart skipped a beat.

They hugged and Samantha said, "Do you remember when we were here last?"

"Of course I do. It was your birthday and it set me back big time! But it was worth it to see how happy you were."

"I've been thinking about Judy Collins and that song, "Both Sides Now." Have you ever stopped to think that we might not be seeing the world as it really is?"

"Not until recently. Now I can't stop thinking about it. What's real? Is what's real to me, not real to someone else? And of course today we have to wonder whether what we read in the newspaper or see on the nightly cable news is real. It drives me crazy!"

Samantha sighed. "Me too. Come on, we'd better go in. I think you'll like David. Even though he's a billionaire real-estate magnate, he has a very down to earth personality. He said he'd meet us in Bemelmans Bar.

As they walked into the Art Deco bar, they spotted David in the corner, sitting in one of the chocolate-brown leather banquettes, a glass of whiskey already in front of him on the black glass tabletop. He stood up as they approached. Samantha, admiring his stylish suit, elegant tie and crisp shirt, couldn't help comparing him to Hank and wishing that this had been a client day.

"Hi David. I'd like you to meet my husband, Hank Mitchell. Hank, David Kelly." They shook hands, and David gave Samantha a quick kiss on the cheek. She was sure that Hank had noticed the kiss but also hoped that he appreciated being introduced as her husband.

After ordering a Prosecco for Samantha and a sparkling water with lime for Hank, they started to talk. After chatting about work and politics for a while, Samantha got to the point.

"I've brought Hank up to date on the detective's meetings with Greta and Mike, but before we dive into what to do next, would you mind telling us a little more about Carrie? I feel as though she's now a major presence in my life, but I really don't know much about her except that she was a gorgeous model and wanted help poor children in Africa." She paused then quickly added, "unless, of course, you don't want to talk about her."

"No, I don't mind. Carrie was the light of my life. In the beginning it was hard for me, I must admit. Losing my wife, Sarah, when Carrie was born just about ruined me. Sarah and I had been high school sweethearts in Chicago, and it always seemed that our marriage had been preordained." Just the mention of Sarah brought a wistful smile to David's face.

"We were separated for our college years, but kept in close contact. I'm surprised we got any school work done with all that daily letter-writing. She studied at the University of Chicago and I went off to Wharton for my BA and then stayed to get my MBA in International Business and Finance.

"We couldn't stay apart for eight years, so we got married after I got my first degree and made a home together off-campus in Philadelphia. After I finished business school we moved to an apartment in the City, on the Upper West Side. Much to our surprise, Sarah got pregnant about a year later.

We were both thrilled, doubly so, when we learned that she was expecting a girl."

Samantha didn't look at Hank who must also have been thinking about how differently he and David responded to the news that they would soon be fathers.

David's tone took a dark turn as he continued on. "But then... there were complications with the birth. You may not know this, but only 1% of women die in childbirth; Sarah was one of them."

David paused and ordered another whiskey from a passing waiter. "I'm sorry. You wanted to hear about Carrie. Despite not having a mother, Carrie was a beautiful, kind, creative little girl. Of course she could be a devil when she wanted to though." He chuckled softly to himself. "I remember when I was about to take her to the pediatrician one day, she found out where we were going, stamped her foot, put her hands on her hips and said 'No, Daddy! We are not going there today. We are going to the zoo!' She refused to go out the door until I promised that we'd go to the zoo after the doctor visit. In fact the promise of a trip to the zoo always did the trick."

Samantha interrupted and said "The zoo? Bonnie loves the zoo too; she can't get enough of it. I'm sure if we lived in the City she'd be clamoring to go there every day!"

"Hmm," David said, "a coincidence or a transfer of consciousness? Better add it to the list, which seems to be getting longer by the day.

"Anyway, to continue with Carrie's story, she went to Dalton, was a good student and had lots of friends. I'd always assumed that she would go on to college but, as you've heard, Carrie had other plans. She became one of the top models at Elite Model Management within two years. And then three years later... it was all over.

"Although she had a short life, she managed to travel a lot of the world. God, I have magazine covers of her in front of the Taj Mahal, the Hagia Sophia, the Egyptian pyramids... you name it. I guess you could say that she got her education on the road.

"She was really drawn to the Asian culture... you know, respect for elders, community focus, hard work; and she embraced their religious beliefs as well. She often chided me that I needed to spend some time each day meditating and becoming more mindful. My career, and its focus on the almighty dollar, was not in sync with her desire to slow down and be present. But we loved each other and spent as much time together as possible." He reached for his drink the moment it hit the table.

"I miss her terribly; her smile, her easy laugh, her caring heart." He gazed off into the distance for a moment, almost as though he could sense her hovering... just out of sight.

Samantha reached across the table and put her hand on his. "Thank you, David. Again, I am so sorry for your loss. As we consider how to proceed, it helps me to have a clearer sense of who she was."

Hank was clearly touched by David's story as well. "I can't imagine how difficult this has been for you. I have only recently come back into my daughter's life, as you probably know, but I already feel that I would do anything to protect her. And if, God forbid, she were ever murdered, I would not be able to sleep at night until the man responsible was behind bars. Just knowing that Mike is alive and right here in town makes walking away impossible. In fact, if I were you, I'd probably kill the son of a bitch myself! But before going to that extreme, maybe we should see if this can be handled legally, assuming of course that we can protect Bonnie's identity. Right, Sam? What do you think?"

Samantha squeezed Hank's hand under the table and looked from one to the other. She'd expected Hank to be totally against getting involved, and now he was obviously connecting with David on the father/daughter front. She took a deep breath and gave in. "OK, daddies, it looks like we're going after the bad guy."

"I did not begin when I was born, nor when I was conceived. I have been growing, developing, through incalculable myriads of millenniums. All my previous selves have their voices, echoes, promptings in me. Oh, incalculable times again shall I be born."

Jack London
The Star Rover

Susan Burke

Part III
Preparing for Trial
September - October 2019

Chapter 15

*J*ack Hubbard, now sixty years old, was Executive Assistant District Attorney and Chief of the Trials Division in the Manhattan District Attorney's Office. He was a graduate of Georgetown Law and for the past thirty-five years had prosecuted all manner of homicides and violent crimes, including kidnapping, rape, assault and battery, domestic violence and murder. His success rate was so high that he could have gone over to the dark side, as he put it, become a defense attorney in the most prestigious of firms and certainly made a lot more money. But Jack Hubbard was a man of principle. He was all about putting the bad guys in jail, not finding ways to let them escape the law.

After Detective Riddle received a half-hearted go-ahead from her boss, she brought the case file to Jack, who invited David and Samantha to his office to hear their stories. He also wanted to meet with Bonnie, but had her wait outside his office with his secretary until he'd finished talking to the grown-ups. He found them both to be sincere, rational and straightforward. They were not seeking to become celebrities. Of course one of them already was, but the mother had made it very clear that she would not allow her daughter to face Mike MacShane in the courtroom, and she wanted aliases to be used for both of them so that their entire lives would not be changed forever.

When Bonnie was invited in, she was very polite and showed her winning personality. Once introduced, she shook the D.A.'s hand and said "Hello, Mr. Jack," with a big bright smile. He was instantly a fan. In some unidentifiable way she reminded him of his own daughter at that age. Juliet had lost her battle with cancer ten years ago, but as a child she'd had that same bright smile and easy-going manner. How wonderful it would be, he thought, if reincarnation really did exist and she was living another life all over again. Just thinking about that possibility eased the grief he had not yet let go of.

Returning to the moment at hand, Jack asked Bonnie a number of questions which she answered in a slightly spooky mixture of little-girl-speak and adult terminology. He was amazed by her knowledge about Carolyn Kelly, and he suspected the jury would be too. Finally, Jack assured them that that if the AG approved, he was confident they could move ahead, even though he wasn't confident they would win.

==

Jack walked into the office of Martin Radcliffe, the District Attorney General, and shut the door behind him. "Hey Marty, we need to talk. I have a case here that's come up through NYPD. It's going to be a precedent setter, and will generate a shit-load of publicity. So I think we should talk it through before I agree to take it on." For the next two hours, plus lunch, Jack took Marty through every detail of the case. Several drinks were consumed.

Martin Radcliffe came from a family of prosecutors going back three generations and was a graduate of Yale Law. He had been elected in 2011 and in eight short years had made significant inroads into cleaning up crime in New York City. From his twenty-one indictments against gun traffickers leading to the removal of over 3000 illegal guns from the City's streets, to the dismantling of nineteen street gangs, to several convictions of domestic terrorism, Marty was always breaking new ground. At age forty-nine, Marty was on a fast track to higher office. He would be up for election again in November 2020, not too long after this case would be adjudicated. "Jack Hubbard," he exclaimed, with no small amount of exasperation, "Why are you doing this to me? You know I have an election coming up next year. If you lose this case, the press will be all over me!"

"Yup. That's true," Jack said, nodding his head slowly. "But if we win," he whispered in his most tempting voice, "you might decide to run for Governor or Senator or, hell, you name it. You'll be the one calling the shots. Come on, Marty, let's go for it. You said yourself that all the evidence fits neatly together. Let the jury decide. Isn't that what our justice system is all about?"

"Let me think on it overnight, Jack. And give me that damn book! I'll read it tonight instead of taking Julia out to dinner, and I'll blame it on you!"

"Give Julia my bestMarty, and I'll see you in the morning."

By morning, Jim Tucker's book had once again done the job. Now it was full speed ahead!

==

The following day, Detective Riddle returned once again to 980 Fifth Avenue and asked for Mike MacShane to come to the lobby. Upon his arrival, she soberly announced, "Michael MacShane, you are under arrest for the murder of Carolyn Kelly." As Mike stood there, shocked, she slipped handcuffs on his wrists and led him to the waiting police car. In the backseat, Mike started to complain but was cut short. "You have the right to remain silent. Anything you say can and will be used against you in a court of law. You have the right to an attorney. If you cannot afford an attorney, one will be provided for you. Do you understand the rights I have just read to you?"

Mike shuffled around in the back seat and said "Yeah. But there's no way I can afford a lawyer."

"No problem. The court will appoint one for you, and he or she will meet with you before the arraignment."

"What's that and when will it be?"

"At your arraignment in the County Court House, a judge will read the charge against you and you will have the opportunity to plead guilty or not guilty. The arraignment has to happen within forty-eight hours of your arrest. So let's see, today is Monday, it will probably be tomorrow or Wednesday. In the meantime, you'll be held in the County Jail on Rikers Island.

Chapter 16

*H*ighly qualified, Melissa Washington had not yet secured a position in one of the criminal defense firms she had her eye on. So in the meantime, she kept busy, very busy, working for the New York Public Defenders Office. Her salary was low and her case load high, but she was getting hands on experience in every aspect of criminal law. She definitely knew her way around the Court House, and could call most of the trial prosecutors by their first names if she chose to... which she did not.

She was an attractive woman, with a very short afro, and kept her svelte figure by being run ragged day in and day out. If she had her druthers she would wear running shoes at work, but she knew enough to appear thoroughly professional at all times, which meant dark suits (most with skirts), silk shirts in varying colors, and three inch heels. At over six feet, she enjoyed being taller than most of the prosecutors. She liked to think that her height gave her that "warrior" look. And she definitely fought like a warrior. Each client, whether they were guilty or not, deserved the best possible defense and she was committed to giving it to them.

Upon meeting Michael MacShane in the courtroom, just minutes before his arraignment, she told him to plead not guilty. They'd work out the details later. The case was called at 10 a.m., and by 10:03 they were done. During that time, the arraignment judge read the charge of sexual assault and second degree murder to Michael MacShane and asked him how he pled. Melissa nudged him, and he replied "not guilty." The judge then announced "Given that you are being charged with a type A felony crime, Mr. MacShane, you will be remanded into custody without bail until the Grand Jury hearing. If they find there is sufficient evidence against you for a trial to proceed, you will remain in custody until your trial is concluded." With that, the judge banged his gavel and called out "Next." As the guards started to lead MacShane away, Melissa promised to meet with him the following morning at the prison.

==

While going through all the security checkpoints at Rikers Island, Melissa was reminded for the umpteenth time what a dreadful facility it was.

Rikers had a bad, and not unjustified, reputation of inmate neglect and abuse. It was also notorious for assaults by inmates on uniformed and civilian staff, often resulting in serious injuries. About five years ago, Mother Jones magazine had reported that Rikers Island ranked as one of the ten worst correctional facilities in the United States. Nevertheless, prisoners awaiting trial were often sent there. Perhaps it was meant to encourage them to plead guilty so that a trial could be avoided, thereby saving the State a lot of time and money.

She was escorted to a private conference room that was just one step up from a jail cell. There were no windows, one rectangular metal table about six feet long, and two opposing metal chairs. There were two bottles of water on the table, no glasses. After she waited about five minutes, Mr. MacShane was led in in handcuffs, which she asked the guard to remove.

He sat down on the opposite side of the table, stretched out his long legs in front of him and folded his arms. Despite being dressed in one of the unflattering orange uniforms of Rikers Island, he still looked ruggedly handsome, with a good physique, blue eyes and dark curly hair. The only sign of any recent upset in his routine was a five o'clock shadow at nine o'clock in the morning.

After reintroducing herself to Mike, she opened her briefcase, withdrew his thin file and a yellow legal pad. "All right, Mr. MacShane... or may I call you Mike?"

"Sure," he replied.

"Good. So Mike, as I mentioned yesterday, I have been appointed by the Judge to be your Defense Attorney, at no cost to you. All I know about you and your case is that you have been accused of murdering Carolyn Kelly in May of 2013, and that based on forensic evidence, the prosecution believes you were in the process of trying to rape her before smothering her with a pillow."

Mike uncrossed his arms and legs, leaned forward and stared right into her eyes. "Ms. Washington, that is absolutely not true."

She found the intensity of his gaze and voice to be a bit unnerving. "That's why I'm here, to represent you and prove your innocence. But, Mike, before we talk about the case, I'd like to get to know you a bit. So, if you don't mind, please tell me your story, starting with where and when you were born, the relationship you had with your parents, how you did in school, if you ever went to college, your marital history and if you've never been married, then a brief overview of your love life, and finally your employment history. I only have an hour, so just the highlights will be fine."

Leaning back in his chair again and stretching out his legs, Mike began. "All right," he sighed. "I was born on February 14th, 1990 in the Bronx. My parents both worked. Pop was a construction worker and my mom was a nurse. I have a brother, Eric, who is two years older than me. Due to my mother's weird hours, Eric and I were pretty much on our own. We went to the Christopher Columbus High School in the Pelham Parkway section of the Bronx. It's just a short walk to the zoo from there and, to tell the truth, we skipped out many a day to spend the afternoon with the gorillas. We just weren't all that   interested in learnin'. Probably because it wasn't a great school. There were over 2000 kids in grades 9 through 12! I think its only claim to fame is that Ann Bancroft and Sal Mineo went there. And, of course, David Berkowitz!" he added, with a knowing smile on his face.

Melissa did not ask who David Berkowitz, the Son of Sam serial killer, was. She just motioned for Mike to continue, and scribbled on her legal pad.

"So, my brother went into the construction business with Pop, and I just sort of kicked around after high school, waitin' to be inspired. My mom wanted me to go to a public college, but I wasn't interested, so I got a job as a bouncer at Club W for about a year. It's just a local joint with sexy girls, pole dancin'.   I knew it wasn't going to be a long term thing, so I started lookin' at the want ads for jobs in the City. Since I really didn't have any particular kind of expertise, I checked out jobs for maintenance   men.   I'm at least good at fixin' broken stuff and cleanin' up. How hard could it be I thought. At least I'll get a steady paycheck and be able move out of my parents' house. So I got hired at a few different places and sort of worked my way uptown. The further North you go, the classier the apartment buildin's are, not to mention the residents. I've been working at 980 Fifth now for a little over six years. They have six   maintenance guys, and we work in shifts on opposite sides of the building.   We keep the place clean, do work in the residents' apartments if they ask for it, sub for the elevator men or the doormen when they are on break… that kind of thing. What else did you want to know?"

Melissa wondered whether Mike's slight Irish brogue, combined with his good looks, was a come-on with the ladies. "Your love life?"

"Well I've never had too much of a problem in that department, if you know what I mean." Mike's knowing smile had returned. "But I've never gotten hitched. That costs too much money. Why get married when you can have it for free any time you want?"

What a delightful point of view, Melissa thought. "Are you involved with anyone now," she asked, pencil poised.

"Nah. Not anyone permanent. I just like to hookup when the opportunity presents itself. And you'd be surprised how often that happens!"

Okay, that's enough "cock of the walk" stuff. Let's get down to business. "Thanks for that overview Mike. I think I've got the picture. Now let's talk about your relationship with Carolyn Kelly. How long did you know her, how often did you speak to her, were you ever in her apartment, and did, as you put it, the opportunity to hookup present itself?"

"Well, she was already livin' in the buildin' when I started workin' there. She lived in Penthouse A and she was a real looker. The guys downstairs always talked about her; did you see Carrie today? Did you see Carrie's outfit last night? I wonder what Carrie's like in... uh, I wonder what her love life is like? You know, locker room talk. I can't repeat it all to you. But when you have one of the top fashion models in the world livin' in your buildin', she doesn't go unnoticed!"

"I can imagine. So when did you first meet her?"

"I never actually spoke to her until she called down for a maintenance man to come up to her apartment and hang a paintin'. Danny and I flipped a coin, and guess who won?

"When I went in, she was wearin' a pair of sweat pants, a loose-fittin' top of some kind, no make-up and her hair was clipped up on top of her head. I would have preferred that she was wearin' something slinky, with her hair down, but hey, beggars can't be choosers. She was friendly and showed me the paintin' she wanted me to hang. Some Buddhist thing, a gift from her father she said. The paintin' was kinda heavy, so I understood why she couldn't do it herself. She had a hard time makin' up her mind about where to hang it though. I held it up in the foyer, where she had a giant gold Buddha statue standing in the corner and she said 'That's great, hang it there.' Then after I hung it, she had second thoughts. Just like a woman, they never know what they really want. So I moved it a few more times before she was finally satisfied.

"She must have felt guilty or somethin' about all those changes, cuz she offered me a drink. A real drink. Not water or coke. A real drink. So I had a beer and she had a gin and tonic. She suggested I sit on the sofa, and then she sat down next to me. She asked me some questions about myself and then said somethin' about how handsome I was. She wondered if I'd ever thought about modelin'. It only took a few minutes of the back and forth to know she was comin' on to me. As I said, I've had plenty of opportunities and I'm pretty used to the signs. So I scooted a little closer to her and started telling her how beautiful she was, like she's never heard that before! Then when I reached my hand over to touch her hair, she just fell all over me. Boy, if I do say so myself, that girl was ready! So that was it. We did the deed right there on the sofa. And she wan't in any hurry to stop either, if you know what I mean. Let's just say that she kept me busy for quite a while. I was wrung out by the time I left."

Melissa noted the proud smile on Mike's face, despite the reason they were there. Rather than commenting, she prompted, "And then what?"

His proud demeanor melted just a bit. "Well, here's where it gets kinda sick. The next time I saw her was when I was on elevator duty and picked her up. On the way down, she apologized for what had happened between us and assured me that it would never happen again. She said she should have known better, that she must have felt lonely or somethin'.

"I said don't beat yourself up about it! We had fun... no harm in that. But be sure to give me a call if you ever feel that way again. And I gave her a wink. She seemed a bit put off by that, but just said goodbye and walked out the door."

"Mike," Melissa interrupted, "did you ever speak to one of the other guys in the building about your little escapade?"

"Sure. I told Danny. I mean you can't fuck, sorry, make love to the hottest woman on the East Side and not tell anyone about it. He was really pissed too. Not that it would have happened to him! No way! But I guess he was hopin'."

"And did you tell him about her comments to you in the elevator?"

"Negative! Why would I go and ruin my reputation?"

"And what kind of reputation is that?"

"All the guys think of me as a lady killer. Oops, not a real lady killer!" He laughed. "But someone who doesn't have to worry about where the next hookup is comin' from, that's for sure!"

"I see. So, what month did your hookup with Carrie happen?"

"January I think... the paintin' was a Christmas present."

"And how often did you run into her from then on?"

Now Mike sat up straighter in his chair and seemed to be thinking about how much to tell her.

"Mike, I want to remind you that I am your lawyer. Whatever you tell me is between us. By law, I cannot tell anyone else without your approval. Now, according to the police file, when you were first interviewed five years ago, you said you were with a woman named Lily Shannon all night.

And that alibi held up. On your second interview a few weeks ago, you said you have no idea where she is now. Is that true?"

Mike leaned forward again. "Ms. Washington, as I said before, I had nothing to do with Carrie's death. Yes, we had a one-night stand, yes, she put me down a few times when I tried to reconnect, but that's it. On the night of her death I was with Lily, and I don't know where she lives now. The police should be able to find her though; isn't that what they do?"

Melissa listened to his calm insistence of innocence. Alternatively, she wondered whether it was possible that this self-appointed Adonis was rejected and ended up killing the object of his desire. But all she said was "They will definitely try. Now, tell me, why didn't you go to work the next day after the murder?"

"When I woke up the next mornin', I was sick as a dog. Lily was one of the strippers from that Club W joint in the Bronx, and she could drink the best of 'em under the table.

"So I had to take the day off. No crime in that, right? When I went in to work the followin' day the buildin' was buzzin'. The police were interviewin' everyone, and takin' fingerprints. Obviously if I had done it, they'd have found my prints, right? Lily corroborated my alibi and that was it. Jesus, that was five or six years ago. What on earth could have happened to make them reopen the case?"

"According to the police file," Melissa responded, "Carrie's diary has suddenly come to light. In it she records the first encounter, pretty much as you described. But then she has many entries about how you kept coming on to her and that she was afraid of you. She also wrote about that last elevator ride and said she was petrified when she got off. She had planned to call her father the next day to get you fired. But we know what happened next."

"That bitch," Mike muttered. "I never did anything scary. I just wanted to renew our... relationship."

141

"Yes, well that didn't go too well, did it?" Noting his hostility, Melissa put her legal pad and file back in her case and rose to leave.

"But wait! That isn't enough to go on is it? I mean just because I winked at her a few times doesn't prove I killed her, does it?"

"No. It's pretty much circumstantial evidence unless they have something else. The Grand Jury is scheduled to hear this case in a few weeks. The Prosecutor will lay out the evidence they have, and the Grand Jury will decide if they think it's enough to proceed to trial. If they do, we will move on to the next step... discovery. That's when both sides share all the evidence they have.

"In the meantime, Mike, I want you to make up a list of everyone you know who can vouch for your character. People who will say, under oath, that you are a fine, upstanding citizen. Relatives, teachers, employers, friends. Try to come up with as many as possible, since we will probably need to have some of them testify in court. And Mike, they should be people who will look respectable on the stand. Probably not any of the strippers at Club W."

Chapter 17

*J*ack Hubbard was a little worried about the Grand Jury. He needed twelve of the fifteen jurors to agree that he had enough evidence to indict Michael MacShane and move forward with a trial. And, of course, this was the first time he would be presenting the reincarnation story. He brought just Samantha Mitchell, David Kelly, Bob Williams and Martha Riddle as witnesses.

Knowing that Samantha was very concerned about maintaining privacy for herself and Bonnie, he'd assured her that Grand Jury proceedings were private. No judge would be present and neither would the defendant. While the court reporter would transcribe the proceedings, the records would be sealed.

As each of his witnesses told their respective parts of the story, he could tell that the jury was not only astonished but skeptical as well. So it was going to be up to him in his summation.

"Ladies and gentlemen," he began, "I know you are probably uncertain about how to proceed. After all, I expect that many, if not all, of you do not believe in reincarnation. Let me put your minds at ease. You don't have to believe in it. You just have to agree that the child's memories of Carrie's death, which she so vividly recalls following her frequent nightmares, and her other memories which we have presented, seem to be true. You merely need to ask yourselves, is there any other possible way she could have come to know these facts? And if not, then you need to allow a trial jury to come to their own conclusion. They are the ones who have to determine beyond a reasonable doubt whether Michael MacShane is guilty, not you. We believe wholeheartedly that there is sufficient evidence to proceed. Thank you."

In the end, and much to his surprise, the Grand Jury agreed. But then he reminded himself of the old adage, "A Grand Jury would indict a ham sandwich!"

==

Before the trial could begin, both the Prosecution and the Defense had to prepare for the discovery process in which they would share whatever evidence they planned to present in court. For the Prosecution, this included all police reports, lab results, photos and physical evidence, as well as witness statements and any corroborating information. In New York, there was no law saying that their evidence had to be turned over in a timely fashion, so Jack dragged his feet.

In the beginning of October, Melissa received a box of evidence submitted by Jack Hubbard. Within five minutes of scanning the overview, she sat back in her chair and whistled. Good grief! This case is dependent upon the testimony of a child who is the reincarnation of Carolyn Kelly? No way is the jury going to buy that! But as she read transcripts of the witnesses, particularly the subject expert, listened to audio tapes of Bonnie's nightmares, and read all about the steps that had already been taken to determine the truth of the child's recollections, a chill ran up her spine. And that was before she read *Return to Life,* after which she didn't know what to think. Melissa was a Baptist, or at least that's how she'd been raised. She didn't know how much of her faith she still believed in, but she had never even considered the subject of reincarnation.

She always put that notion into the same category as ghosts and seances, where gullible people tried to communicate with the dead. And now, she thought, I'm going to have to make sure the jury does too.

When she met with Mike to tell him what the prosecution's case rested on, he laughed out loud. "Oh come on! You're tellin' me that their star witness is a kid who wasn't even born when this crime was committed? That's ridiculous! They must be hard up for cases or somethin'. Who is this kid anyway?"

"I don't know," Melissa said. "Throughout the piles of evidence, the names of the child and her mother have been redacted. Due to privacy concerns, I expect. They'll probably have aliases in the courtroom."

"Huh." Mike said, clearly skeptical. "For a while there I thought they were just going to try and pin this on me because of that diary stuff, but this will be laughed right out of the courtroom, don't you think?"

Melissa started opening up her file and removing papers. "Well, I certainly would have thought so. But let me tell you, Mike, the State does not usually prosecute cases they don't think they have a good chance of winning. Let me show you the evidence they are going to be presenting."

For the next 45 minutes, Melissa played the tapes of Bonnie's nightmares and read her comments about Carrie from Samantha's journal. She also shared the testimony they could expect from Dr. Karadamand and Dr. Williams. Was it her imagination or did Mike's face pale a bit at the repeated mention of his name.

"Now what do you think?" Melissa asked.

"I still think it's crazy! I don't know how they got that little girl to say all that stuff, but whoever she's talking about... it's not me! You're going to put me on the stand, right? I can set them straight. Just because they have a few facts right doesn't mean all this religious blarney is true."

He rose and started wandering around the room. "Well, let's talk about that." Melissa said. "Lots of defendants never take the stand because their words, tone and manner may cause some of the jury to suspect they are guilty. I'm sure OJ Simpson wanted to take the stand, but his attorneys wisely stopped him from testifying. If I call you to the stand, on cross-examination the Prosecution could get you hung up in some way. Even innocent people can sound guilty when being hammered away at by a good prosecutor. They will try to get you confused about where you were when, they'll pry into your sex life to show that you're a predator of some sort. Believe me, it's really not a good idea to take the stand."

Mike returned to his seat. "Nope. I absolutely want to take the stand. Listen, I know how to charm the birds from the trees. Don't worry, they won't get me riled up."

Despite her instincts, Melissa reluctantly agreed. "All right, but remember, we can change our minds right up to the very last minute. And as far as reincarnation is concerned, even though we may not believe in it, don't think this is going to be a slam dunk. They have an excellent subject matter expert. I will try to have the whole case dismissed, and if that doesn't work, I'll try to have the subject expert testimony withheld. But just in case I lose those motions, I'm going to start hunting for our own subject experts… the scientists!

==

Melissa did her best to throw out the reincarnation evidence at the pre-trial hearing later that month. "Your Honor, as far as the scientific world is concerned, reincarnation has never been proven. A trial of law should only allow evidence based on facts, not on religious beliefs. From my research, it appears that Ian Stevenson, the psychologist who started up the UVA Division of Perceptual Studies, and his current apostles, are practically the only people who have even studied reincarnation. How can we possibly rely on their word alone that such a thing really exists?"

Jack Hubbard replied. "Your Honor, I agree with Ms. Washington that reincarnation has not been scientifically proven. However that also means that it has not been scientifically *disproven*. Millions of people all over the world believe in it, and many of them are not Buddhists or Hindus. In fact, 30% of Catholics believe in reincarnation.

"So I would like us to put aside the question of scientific veracity and instead concentrate on the facts we can prove that have been brought to light by Bonnie Mitchell. She says that while she was Carrie Kelly, she was murdered by a man named Mike, who put a pillow over her face until she could no longer breathe. Carrie was indeed murdered by suffocation with a pillow. She identified the building where Carrie lived. She talked about Asian objects once owned by Carrie that were then found in David Kelly's apartment. She immediately recognized Mr. Kelly as her father when she first met him. She knew where to find the key to Carrie's diary. That diary revealed that Carrie was frightened by a man named Mike MacShane who worked in the building. Upon investigation, all these statements and writings were found to be undeniable facts. Although we may not understand how Bonnie knows what she knows, those facts are true. Therefore, I move that Ms. Washington's motion to dismiss the case for lack of scientific proof be denied."

Judge Brown agreed with Mr. Hubbard. He said, "Ms. Washington, I cannot deny that this is a unique, unprecedented case. And I expect that many members of the jury will have a hard time with the concept of reincarnation. But we also have to agree that the facts which have been brought to light seem to be true. Mr. Stevenson and his 'apostles,' as you put it, do not say that their case studies have been proven. They say they have been solved. Which, as I understand it, means that the facts we have learned from Bonnie could not have been known by her in any other way. If you can prove in the trial that they could have been gleaned from another source... be my guest. Motion denied. See you both in court."

==

Jack Hubbard was relieved to have cleared the second hurdle, the first being the Grand Jury. But while the Grand Jurors might have wanted to pass off the case to the trial jurors to decide, the Judge would not have allowed it to proceed if he wasn't open to the concept.

Judge Gideon Brown was a lucky draw. He was about seventy years old and had seen almost everything come before him in the courtroom, though nothing like this. Fortunately, he was known as a fair, open-minded judge. He had five children and twelve grandchildren, so perhaps he had a soft spot for youngsters. Jack was certain that Bonnie would make a good impression on him.

In fact, the next day the Judge called him and asked if he could arrange for Samantha and Bonnie to meet with him in chambers. He wanted to iron out the way their identities could be protected, as well as determine whether Bonnie could tell the difference between a truth and a lie. That would be necessary if she was going to take the oath. Of course her testimony could be taken without the oath, given her young age, but then it would be more susceptible to an appeal. Jack agreed to schedule a date with his clerk as soon as possible.

==

The next day, Jack Hubbard, Samantha Mitchell and David Kelly came together again in a very comfortable conference room at the Court House to review the testimony and evidence that they would be presenting in court. While waiting for coffee, Jack explained. "We've turned all this evidence over to the defense so there will be no surprises. Unfortunately, it's only on TV that a surprise piece of evidence is sprung on the defense at the very last minute." Jack chuckled at the notion. "If that were to happen, the judge would have to rule on its admissibility, and even if he accepted the surprise evidence, it could be cause for an appeal at a later date.

"These are copies of everything we have already turned over to them: police reports, photos, and lab results as well as your videos of Bonnie, your journal of her comments, and the relevant pages of Carrie's diary. We also included all of Bob Williams' interviews as well as that Tucker book we've all read. The police reports document in detail what you've already told them: what happens in Bonnie's nightmares, the comments she has made to you, the meeting with David, etc. As I said, no surprises."

They all dug into the box of evidence that Jack had turned over. "Do you think this is everything," he asked, "or have I missed something?"

"My, you have more than I realized," Samantha replied.

"I never saw all these lab reports and photos of the crime scene," David said, as though he wished he wasn't looking at them now either.

Samantha gently removed the photos from his hand. He looked at her, then nodded his head. "I can't imagine how they reacted to all this," she said. "Have they submitted their evidence of Mike's innocence to you?"

"Yes, but it's primarily testimony from his family, friends and co-workers. You'll notice that Lily Shannon's name is not on the list, the woman who said Mike had been with her the whole night of the murder. Apparently they found out that she moved to Los Angeles in 2014 but, a year later, was killed in a traffic accident. So although they can ask Martha Riddle to read her initial statements, she won't be there in person.

Jack alerted them to the fact that the defense might want to interview them before the trial, and in fact could ask to interview Bonnie as well.

"However, should they do that, I will refuse, and explain that she cannot be trotted out for pre-trial interviews due to her age. They already have in writing everything she has revealed. I'm sure the Judge will agree."

"I certainly hope so, because I wouldn't allow it either."

"Speaking of Bonnie... Judge Brown has asked to meet the two of you. He wants to discuss how to maintain your privacy and ensure that Bonnie can tell the difference between the truth and a lie. Can I set something up next week?"

As Samantha helped Jack put all the photos and documents back in the box, she said "Of course. Our privacy is the most important thing on my mind. In fact, Jack, you need to know that I will back right out of this entire thing if he can't guarantee that."

Jack swallowed hard and assured her that he was very confident the Judge could work out a solution to her privacy concern. "He's going to do his darndest to make sure that this case doesn't turn into a three-ring circus." To himself though he thought, and lots of luck with that!

==

When Melissa sat down with Mike to review their case, Mike noted that she had not found a scientist to debunk the notion of reincarnation.

"You're right. I've been doing quite a lot of research on the topic of science and religion. Here are some of the notes I made." She pulled out one of her ubiquitous legal pads. "We assume science and religion are totally at odds, right? And indeed they have been at certain times in history. But not so much today. In fact, the USA's National Academy of Science supports the view that science and religion are independent, but can co-exist because they are based on different aspects of the human experience. We know that scientifically based experiments or explanations must be based on evidence drawn from examining the natural world. Religious faith, however, does not depend on empirical evidence, and often involves supernatural forces or entities. Because they are not a part of nature, supernatural entities cannot be investigated by science. So rather than just ridicule religion, many scientists now say that attempts to pit one against the other just create controversy where none needs to exist."

"Sounds like a bunch of mumbo jumbo to me," said Mike. "What's the bottom line?"

"If I can find studies that say science and religion can co-exist, then the prosecution can as well. So trying to argue our case on the premise that reincarnation has never been scientifically proven won't work."

"Great. So where does that leave us?"

"Relying on your charm, I guess. That is if you still want to take the stand, which I definitely do not advise. Plus the friends and family I've spoken to who can vouch for your character. But look at it this way, even without a scientist, I still think the odds are on our side. The mere thought of a reincarnated child witness is too far out there for most people to believe… particularly beyond a reasonable doubt."

"Okay. I sure hope you're right. But just in case you're not convincin' enough on your own, I still want to take the stand."

Melissa sighed, and packed up all her papers. She hoped that he was right.

Chapter 18

*N*ow that they were definitely going to trial, Samantha reluctantly decided that the time had come to tell her daughter what was happening. So that night after dinner she sat down with Bonnie and her teddy bear on the couch. "Bonnie, dear, I need to talk to you about something. Something that, hopefully, will help make all your bad dreams go away." Bonnie was interested, but said nothing.

"I think that Mike should be punished for killing Carrie. Do you think he should too?"

"Oh, yes." Bonnie nodded her head vigorously. "He is a very bad man. Bad people should be punished. Right, Mr. Bear?" She leaned down to her teddy bear, then said "Mr. Bear agrees!"

"All right! The way grown-ups do that is they have a trial. That means that we tell our story about what happened to Carrie, and Mike will tell his story. Then twelve ordinary people, like Mrs. Cameron next door, will decide who is telling the truth. Do you understand so far?"

"Sort of." But only one person is telling the truth, right?"

"Yes. The reason we have a trial is in case the bad person isn't really bad, but just looks bad. Those twelve people, who are called a jury, will decide who they think is telling the truth. There are some other people involved too. You've met the lawyer who will help us. His name is Jack Hubbard. Mike has a lawyer too who will help him and her name is Melissa Washington. When Mr. Hubbard and Ms. Washington have an argument, the judge decides who is right.

Our judge is named Judge Brown. He's a very nice man and he wants to make sure that Mike gets punished if he killed Carrie."

Bonnie was listening really hard but it was tough to say whether she really understood. Whispering into her mother's ear, she said "Do you know where Mike is, Mama?"

"Yes, honey. He is in jail right now and he can't get out. If the jury decides he did kill Carrie, he will stay there a long time.

"What we need to talk about now is what your role will be. After all, we would never have known about Mike if you hadn't had all those nightmares and told us about him. So now you will need to tell that story, about how Mike killed Carrie, to the two lawyers and the judge."

"Will Mike be there? I don't want to see Mike, I'm afraid of Mike!" She made herself small and hid her face in the teddy bear's tummy.

"No, honey, Mike will not be there and you never have to see him again." Samantha put her arm around Bonnie and gave her a kiss on the top of her head. "I will be there of course, right next to you. I'm not exactly sure when you will need to tell your story, but before then the judge wants to meet you. It's his job to make sure that you understand the difference between the truth and a lie, so he will ask you a few questions. Are you okay with that?"

"Sure! A lie is when I say I like spinach. The truth is when I say I hate it!"

Samantha smiled, played with Bonnie's curls, and added, "One last thing. When we visit with the lawyers and the judge, we are going to have make-believe names because we don't want anyone else to know who we are. And you get to pick your name! Do you have a name you would like to have?"

Bonnie seemed to love this idea. "I like the name Rosie! There is a girl in my school with that name, and I wish it was my name."

"Okay. Then whenever we visit with the judge, your name will be Rosie. And I'd like mine to be Cynthia. Let's see.... how about Spark for a last name? Rosie and Cynthia Spark. Good?"

"Yes! Good! Can I be called Rosie now?"

Samantha smiled. Sometimes the hardest things could be so simple.

==

Only two days later, Jack Hubbard, Samantha Michell (alias Cynthia Spark) and Bonnie Mitchell (alias Rosie Spark) went down to the Court House on Foley Square to meet with Judge Brown in his chambers. When they went in, Jack Hubbard did the honors; "Judge Brown, I'd like you to meet Cynthia Spark and her daughter, Rosie."

Judge Brown was a rather heavy set man, with a warm smile. He had gray hair and wore large, black-rimmed glasses, making him look a bit like an owl... a wise old owl. He was sitting behind his desk and wearing his robes, as he was apparently due in the courtroom right after this meeting. He stood up and shook Samantha's hand, saying, "Hello, Cynthia. Thank you for coming down to meet me. And hello, Rosie. I've heard so much about you. It's nice to meet you at last. Have your ever been in a courthouse, Rosie?"

Bonnie looked up at him and replied softly, "No, Mr. Judge."

Samantha interrupted and said "No honey, we call the judge Your..."

"That's okay," the judge replied. Mr. Judge sounds good to me. Please, take a seat." Bonnie, who was wearing a blue and white checked dress with white tights, and a light blue grosgrain bow in her hair, climbed up on the chair closest to the Judge. "Rosie, how old are you?"

"Four." She cocked her head, smiled and held up four fingers. "How old are you?"

Samantha squirmed uncomfortably in her chair, but Judge Brown just said "A lot older than four, I can tell you that! Rosie, I just wanted to ask you a few questions, if you don't mind. Okay?"

"Yes, Mr. Judge."

"All right. Let's say that when I just asked you how old you were, you said five. Would that have been the truth or a lie?"

"A lie. I am four. My birthday cake had four candles."

"Very good. And if I said that you always tell the truth. Would that be the truth or a lie?"

Bonnie looked down at her shoes. Then in a low voice, she said, "Well, I usually tell the truth. But last night I said that I brushed my teeth and I didn't really. And on Saturday morning when I said that I cleaned up my room... that wasn't really true. I just put the messy stuff under the bed." She squirmed a bit. "So I guess I do lie sometimes. But they aren't big lies." Bonnie looked up at Samantha, "I'm sorry, Mama."

Samantha squeezed Bonnie's hand, and said "That's ok, hon."

Judge Brown smiled and said "Everyone tells little white lies now and then. The important thing is to know what is right and what is wrong. And it seems to me that you do! So that's all we need to talk about today. When you come back, we will meet again in this room with a nice lady named Melissa Washington and Mr. Hubbard here. I shall look forward to seeing you then." The judge shook Bonnie's hand and said "Bye Rosie. See you soon."

"Bye Mr. Judge. See ya." She climbed off the chair and took hold of her mother's hand.

"Your Honor," said Samantha. "I have one more question. I assume it's possible for the courtroom to be closed during this trial so that visitors and the press don't find out about it?"

"No, Mrs. Spark, I'm afraid it is not. Every defendant is entitled to a public trial. I can have Rosie's testimony livestreamed into the courtroom so that she will not have to face the defendant, but Mr. MacShane, the jurors, the public and the press will be able to see her. Although we could have her face blurred out, that would also reduce her believability. And, of course, when you are on the stand, you will be visible to all as well. We can only do so much. You can use your false names, but if someone recognizes you, then you and your daughter's identities will become known.

"If you have any doubts about whether to proceed, please resolve them quickly. We have already taken up time and money with the Grand Jury and I certainly do not want to go any further if you are having second thoughts."

Although this was all said calmly, it felt to Samantha like he was throwing down the gauntlet. You have to do it our way or not at all. Decide quickly and don't waste our time.

"Thank you Your Honor. I will try not to hold up the case any longer than necessary."

In the hall, Jack apologized for not having mentioned this before. "Will this be a big problem for you?"

"I'm going to have to think about it, Jack. It very well might be. I would hate to back out at the last minute, but protecting Bonnie's privacy is my number one priority. Give me a few days to mull it over, but I'm not feeling optimistic."

"Of course." Jack replied, but Samantha could tell that his heart was sinking. The case of a lifetime could be ending before it had even begun.

Chapter 19

*O*n the train to Pelham, Samantha mulled over whom to call first... Hank or David. She knew they would be on opposite ends of this seesaw, but she was not sure which side to throw her weight upon. Bonnie chatted happily with herself, asking Rosie questions and then responding with the answer.

Samantha gazed out the window as the landscape changed from the run-down tenements of Harlem, with laundry draped over the fire escapes, to the clapboard houses in the suburbs, with their manicured lawns and flowering gardens. Although not far from each other, the homes of the residents in the county of Westchester were in another world compared to those crowded apartments in Harlem.

The notion of "another world" plunged her more deeply into the subject at hand. It appears to a number of people, she thought, and to me as well, that Carrie had come back from another world. But why? The Eastern religions all have different opinions about that. Even within the Buddhist religion they don't agree. Each time I sit down to research reincarnation I just get more confused. But if Carrie, through whatever means, has been reborn, there must have been some reason for her to choose Bonnie. That is if she had a choice in the matter.

She put her head back and closed her eyes. But her mind kept spinning. If Carrie's rebirth was related to unfinished business, such as her need to see Mike punished, would she choose a host who could make that happen? Someone who was lovable and believable enough to convince others? No... she would have had no way of knowing what Bonnie might grow up to be like. More likely, she might have chosen me, someone who was open-minded, more or less, and who might pave the way for Carrie's retribution. Oh God, if you're really there, help me to make the right decision.

She lightly batted her head against the window. Why do I have to solve this problem? Why am I the one who has to decide whether or not to go forward with this trial? The odds of winning are so low, and the stakes for Bonnie and me are so high. I don't have any answers to these questions. After all, I've never studied theology or philosophy. All I have are my own instincts about what's right. It seems right to find justice for David and Carrie. But it also seems wrong to allow Bonnie to be labeled forever as a kook! With pseudonyms and a closed courtroom I'd thought the problem was solved. But now I'm a whole lot less certain.

Examining all the factors that would help her decide what to do was starting to make her dizzy. What are the odds, she wondered, that someone in the courtroom would recognize Bonnie? Practically nil. She's only four, we live in Pelham and her circle of acquaintances is tiny. But what about me? I work in the City, I have lots of clients and friends and have been knocking around this neighborhood my whole life. Of course, given the millions of people who live in or visit New York City, the odds are still pretty small that someone would recognize me. But they allow sketches to be drawn in the courtroom. Will I be recognized if one of those sketches pops up in the papers or on TV? Quite possibly! Unless...

"The station of Pelham is coming up. Pelham. Please prepare to exit and don't forget any of your belongings." That announcement jolted Samantha out of her argument with herself. She and Bonnie hustled to the door while she focused her thoughts on more present matters... what to fix for dinner.

==

The next day, Samantha bit the bullet and decided she had to tell her mother what was going on. Of course they had spoken after Billy Jo Collins had visited her, but since then, Samantha had tried to keep the temperature down. She'd agreed with her mother that the nightmares were probably just a phase. But a lot had happened since then.

Eleanor was a devout Catholic and went to mass several times a week. It was highly unlikely she would approve of this whole shebang, but there was no way Samantha could just leave her out of the loop. She'd already kept it a secret too long. So she parked Bonnie next door, gave her mother a call, and went over for a visit.

Eleanor lived alone in a three story house, now far too big for her needs. But everything she loved was there, including her memories of Dick, as they had sat in the living room each night, discussing the world and sipping gin martinis. Dinner, always by candlelight, was often put off until about 10. They were a perfect couple, without a lot of need for others. In fact, Samantha had always wanted to have a marriage like theirs.

Eleanor, a tall, stylish blonde, greeted her at the door, and gave her an air kiss. For some reason, hugging wasn't a comfortable form of expression for her. "It's so good to see you Samantha. I'd almost forgotten what you looked like! Is that a new sweater? Not one of your usual colors is it? Would you like a cup of tea?" And off she went to the kitchen without waiting for the answer.

As usual, Samantha was feeling defensive right away. Her mother had opinions about everything and was never shy about voicing them. But she was determined not to take the bait, and just stick to her agenda. So she followed her mother to the kitchen and watched as she set out teacups, a small teapot and a plate of cookies.

Rather than talk about all sorts of unimportant things, Samantha launched into her story. "Mummy, I have something important to discuss with you and I want you to have an open mind."

She recalled how her mother had suddenly insisted on being called mummy when Samantha was about ten. Up until then it had been mommy. Perhaps she'd just seen a British film, or read some Jane Austin. Whatever the case, it obviously never occurred to her, or to Samantha at the time, that 'mummy' meant only one thing in the US.

Eleanor stopped what she was doing and said, "What is it? Is everything okay at work? Has Hank left again? Is Bonnie..."

"Mummy! I obviously get my impatience from you. You're just going to have to listen and not say anything until I'm finished. Then you can let loose. Okay?"

Eleanor agreed, although she didn't like being reprimanded by her daughter. She picked up the kettle and started pouring hot water into the teapot, which already had a few spoons of Earl Gray tea inside.

Samantha tried to go in chronological order, starting with Bonnie's nightmares and odd proclamations, but by the time she got to Dr. K's suspicion about reincarnation, Eleanor spilled some of the water onto the tray. She could keep silent no longer. "Oh no, please! That's just ridiculous! Somehow you managed to find the only quack child psychologist in New York!"

"Mummy... remember what I said. Please let me finish."

Eleanor raised an eyebrow, but said nothing. She wiped up the water with unnecessary force.

Samantha then moved on to Bob Williams' assessment, the visit to David Kelly, the diary, Martha Riddle, Jack Hubbard, Judge Brown and finally announced that the trial would begin a week from Monday. She let out a big breath as though she'd just run the 500 meter hurdles.

Eleanor looked like she'd been run over by a Mack truck. She just kept shaking her head, and her lips had tightened into a thin line.

"I know this is a lot to take in, Mummy. Reincarnation isn't something we have ever considered before, but too many of Bonnie's words, actions and behaviors are similar to past cases that Dr. Williams and others have studied. There is just no other answer for how she knows what she knows."

"Nonsense! There has to be another answer, you just haven't looked for a second or third opinion. If you had, I have no doubt that you'd have an explanation. But, oh no. As usual you just jump into the first crackpot idea that you're presented with. And a trial??? That's a terrible thing to do to a small child. You are just going to ruin my granddaughter's life, and I won't agree to it!" The tea was totally forgotten.

"Mummy! I have given this a lot of thought you know. I didn't just jump into it. And I have ensured that Bonnie's name will never be known. Give me a little credit. I'm a grown-up woman, I love my daughter more than anything in the world and I would not put her in jeopardy. In fact, just the opposite. I want to do whatever it takes to make those frightening nightmares go away."

Eleanor looked at her daughter as though she'd become demented. "Is there nothing I can say to change your mind? I shudder to think what Father Riley will say. And I certainly hope that no one in Pelham ever hears about it."

Right, Samantha thought. She's more concerned with what others might think than with Bonnie's health. "Ok, Mummy, I think we'll just have to agree to disagree. I'm

Bonnie's mother and you have to let me do what I think is best. If you want, I'll keep you up to date with what's going on. If not..."

"Don't worry, I'm sure it will be well covered in the *New York Times*. It will probably be better for me to read about it than talk to you, so I don't elevate my blood pressure."

Chapter 20

*I*n the end, Bonnie was the one to make the decision about whether or not to proceed. That night she had not one, not two, but three nightmares. Each left her weaker and weaker, struggling to breathe. After the third one, at 2 a.m., Samantha stayed in bed with her for the rest of the night. She slept fitfully, and one time dreamt of a strange woman on the stand taking the oath. She swore over and over that Bonnie was her daughter.

The next morning Bonnie looked tired and depressed. She wasn't hungry and left the breakfast table to sit on the sofa, resting her head on her knees which were drawn up to her chest. Looking at her, Samantha's heart was torn in two. "Honey, let me give you a hug. Is there anything I can do?"

"Make Mike go away, Mama!" she said. "Please make him go away. I'm so scared of him!" Her eyes implored Samantha to do something. As she held her frightened daughter, Samantha knew what she had to do.

After Bonnie calmed down, Samantha took her next-door so that she could drive into the City to do a bit of shopping. Then, on the off-chance that he was home, she went over to David's apartment. When Joseph asked for her name, without an ounce of recognition, she smiled and said, "Cynthia Spark."

On the house phone, Joseph turned and said, "Mr. Kelly asks what this visit is about. He doesn't know you."

"Tell him it's about his daughter," Samantha replied.

After relaying this message, Joseph turned and said, "Okay, you can go up that elevator to the top floor," and he pointed to the left. When David met her at the door, Samantha waited a moment. "Ms. Spark? Come in." He held out his hand and said "Have we met before?"

"Well actually, we have," Samantha replied, shaking his hand. "But I had long reddish-brown hair then and didn't wear glasses."

"Oh, my God! Samantha! I thought you looked familiar but couldn't place you. What is this all about?"

She launched into the whole story, ending with Bonnie's horrific night. "So I thought I'd take a go at trying to disguise myself. And judging by your response it worked!"

As David studied the woman before him, Samantha imagined what he was seeing. She was wearing a short blond wig, with pixie-like bangs, her glasses were tinted so that it was hard to see her eyes clearly and her outfit looked more like TJ Max than Saks. She had transformed herself.

"Wow," David marveled. "That's amazing. I didn't recognize you at all and I'm standing right in front of you. I really don't think someone in the courtroom would ever know. Come on in, let's talk about this. Would you like some coffee, tea?"

"No thanks. I'm fine." They headed into the living room. "David, most people in that courtroom will know who you are, and the press won't let you alone. Do you really want to be known as the man whose daughter returned from beyond the grave to point a finger at her killer? I know that sounds crude, but you have to be prepared for it."

"I know." They both sat down on the sofa and David crossed his jean-clad legs. "Well, let me think about it for a minute. What's the worst thing that could happen? No one would do business with me anymore because they'd think I'm nuts. People who really are nuts would want to talk to me and share their stories. Not a happy picture." He wrinkled his brow and thought for a minute. "I don't care so much about the former, I certainly won't starve. Perhaps I'll try to follow Carrie's advice about finding ways to help others. And as for the publicity and the kooks, I imagine that will eventually die down. Plus, I am fortunate enough to have the means to keep it all at bay.

"You and Bonnie, on the other hand, are really vulnerable. Look, I know you want to help me find justice for Carrie, but maybe the price is too high. I really don't want you or Bonnie to become hounded for life. I think we should stop. No matter how much I miss her, this trial is not going to bring Carrie back."

They both stared at the Standing Buddha, visible through the archway into the dining room, as though he might be able to solve their problems.

"But what about Bonnie's nightmares? She's now 4. At the rate of two a week until she is six or seven, that's hundreds of more torturous dreams! And far more if she continues to have more than one dream a night. Last night she had three! I don't think either of us can go through that, physically or mentally. I really appreciate your offer to let this go, but I don't think I can."

She knew her voice sounded teary because she was so worried about Bonnie, but also because he'd been willing to back off.

"I would do anything to stop my daughter from suffering, David, and this seems to be the risk I must take." She paused. "Or one of the risks. Now I have to talk to Hank. Something tells me he won't be on my side for this one. In fact, I might as well try to pop in on him too and see if he recognizes me. Thanks so much! Your understanding and support really mean a lot to me." She stood, saying "Wish me luck!" and headed for the door.

Following her, David said "Good luck, and don't forget, I'm fine with whatever you decide. We're in this together." At the door, he gave her a hug. "By the way, I like the red hair better."

==

Hank's apartment was on East 68th Street, not far from David's, so Samantha left her car where she'd parked it and walked over. Fortunately he was home. When he opened the door he looked happy to see her but blurted out, "Samantha! My God, what have you done to your hair?"

She wasn't really surprised. In fact she would have been amazed if he hadn't recognized her. No matter how long their separation, they had been deeply in love and she knew they would remember each other's faces forever. Particularly the eyes. Somehow, no matter how much your face changes over the years, the eyes always remain the same. "Windows to the soul," they say.

He invited her in and Samantha looked around. She'd never been to Hank's apartment, but it looked like a typical bachelor pad; not really decorated per se, but comfortable enough, with a 48" TV for watching football. They sat down on the cushy Pottery Barn couch and she was pleased to see a photo of herself and Bonnie on the side table.

Once again Samantha went through her story, but the response from Hank was not at all like David's.

He was distraught about Bonnie's additional nightmares, and when he heard what the judge had said, he went ballistic. "What? It's going to be an open courtroom? I just assumed they would make an exception in this case to avoid adversarial publicity. This changes everything, right?" When Samantha didn't reply, he said, "Oh, wait. Don't tell me you think this is a disguise!"

"Well, I was hoping it would be. I went over to David's apartment and neither the doorman nor David recognized me. When I'm on the witness stand the press and the observers will be a fair distance away, and of course they can't use cameras inside the courtroom." She paused, and then in a softer voice added, "Just sketch artists. But still, don't you think this will work?"

Hank looked skeptical. "What about Bonnie? Is she going to have to take the stand in front of a packed courtroom?"

"No. She'll give her testimony in the Judge's chambers and it will be live-streamed into the courtroom. Plus we'll both be using pseudonyms, Cynthia and Rosie Spark. On the day she testifies, we'll be coming in a rear entrance where the press is not allowed. Oh, Hank, I really think this could work."

She knew she seemed to be begging, like a child wanting to be picked up, and in a way she was. She wanted him to be on her side.

Hank let out a frustrated sigh and put his head in his hands. "I think you're crazy. If just one person recognizes her or, even more likely, you... your lives will never be the same. *Our* lives will never be the same. I know I said we should proceed with a trial, but the more I think about it the more I think it's a big mistake. Take a moment, Samantha. The press will be feeding on this for years, and our daughter will be the red meat. She has her whole life ahead of her..... school, work, marriage, children of her own. All of that will be at risk if you go ahead with this. Is that what you really want?"

Samantha exploded. "No, of course I don't want to ruin her life! God, you and my mother! What I want is to improve her life... to free her of these horrific nightmares. You've heard, but you haven't seen what they're like. She cries, screams, fights and struggles.... it's like something out of *The Exorcist*! Two or three more years of that is just out of the

169

question. Bob has told us that the children they've studied, who have nightmares about a previous death, get better after confronting the murderer. That's what I want for Bonnie. I have no idea what will happen down the road. I just have to solve the immediate problem of giving my daughter some peace. Peace to sleep through the night without fear that she will be raped and murdered before she wakes up!" Samantha started to cry.

Hank took her in his arms and patted her back. "All right, all right. It's your choice and if you think this is the way to go... then do it. I can't say I agree, but you are the one to make this decision."

Half-hearted support, Samantha thought, but better than nothing at all. "Thanks. Believe me, I wouldn't do this if there were any other way to help her." She took a tissue from her bag and wiped away her tears. "On a lighter note, how do you like me as a blonde?"

"Doesn't hold a candle to the red," he replied and gave her a soft kiss on the mouth.

So much for "gentlemen prefer blondes!" Samantha thought.

==

On Monday, Samantha called Jack Hubbard and told him she was willing to proceed, with one caveat.

"So, Jack, Bonnie and I have fake names and I have somewhat of a disguise, but there's one more thing. I'm guessing that you ask most of the witnesses where they work, right?"

"Yes. It says something about their character, if they have a career and steady work. But I'm guessing you don't want to answer that question, huh?"

"No. If I say I work at Chuck Schwab, someone will put two and two together and figure out who I really am. But I also don't want to lie under oath. Can you talk to the Judge and see if it would be okay for me to just say that I'm a house-wife, or more accurately a homemaker, or whatever the right description is?"

"Sure. I'll talk to Judge Brown and Melissa Washington tomorrow morning. I don't think it will be a problem. He wants to meet with us to lay down some ground rules for the trial, so I'll bring it up then."

==

The following afternoon Jack called Samantha to debrief her on their meeting with the Judge. She closed the door to her office, thinking that it was probably time to talk to her boss about all these closed doors and days off. And of course, since she'd need to take off at least a week for the trial she'd better come up with something good.

"Hi Jack. What happened? Did Judge Brown agree to our requests?" As usual, Samantha's impatience took precedence over hello and how are you.

"Yes, he did. He's probably been mulling this over too, because he'd spent some time going over the high-profile nature of the case and the need to avoid turning the trial into a circus. He's going to sequester the jury, which is a good thing, and he told Melissa that he'd decided Bonnie's testimony would to be taken in his chambers and live streamed into the courtroom. Finally he told her that the two of you would be using aliases. He really hammered home that there would be hell to pay if either of us ever slipped up and used your real names, in or out of the courtroom. I'll prepare all our witnesses to use your new names as well. The Judge also mentioned that you'd be wearing a disguise, and that he'd agreed to the use of 'homemaker' as your stated profession.

"He explained that he had approved of having Bonnie testify because, otherwise, the rest of the evidence could not be corroborated. He said that he had interviewed her and decided that she knew the difference between a truth and a lie and could therefore be given the oath. Finally he asked Melissa to raise her hand whenever she had an objection rather than interrupt Bonnie's testimony, since he didn't want her to get confused and upset."

"How did Melissa react to that? Not well, I'm guessing."

"Well, I don't think she was thrilled, but I expect she understood the rationale. This is a first-time-round for all of us, so there are new rules. Overall, I think the meeting went well."

"All right! Thanks for the update. See you in court next Monday." Samantha hung up and buried her head in her hands.

"I know I am deathless… We have thus far exhausted trillions of winters and summers. There are trillions ahead, and trillions ahead of them."

Walt Whitman

Susan Burke

Part IV
Arguing the Case
November, 2019

Chapter 21

*W*hen Samantha arrived at the courthouse on November 4th, at 8:30 a.m., she thought about all the TV shows that had been filmed there: *The Godfather, Good Fellas, 12 Angry Men and Wall Street*. No doubt there would be another film in about five years called... what? *Born Again? Delayed Justice?* Who knows, but she had no doubt that it would happen. All she prayed was that Bonnie Mitchell would not be the leading character.

As Courtroom #9, in the New York State Supreme Court on Foley Square, began to fill up with perspective jurors, Samantha looked around from under her floppy felt hat and behind her large Jackie-O sunglasses. So far, at least, she saw no one she knew. When David walked in, she motioned to him and they sat together at the back.

Samantha and David had been on a few juries, but neither had ever heard a voir dire like this one. Instead of the usual questions for perspectives jurors, like "have you ever had an altercation with the law?" or "is anyone in your family involved with the law?" they heard "do you know anything about reincarnation?" The jurors were also asked about their religion and how strong their religious beliefs and practices were.

Samantha looked around to see if any reporters were in the room but only spotted two suspects, typing away on their laptops. They were probably assigned to courthouse duty on the chance that anything newsworthy came up. Well they'll certainly be the canaries in the coal mine, she thought. Tomorrow the joint will be jumping.

As the questioning went on, it seemed clear that the defense leaned toward the very religious types, while the prosecution preferred people who were unsure or skeptical about religion in general and were open-minded. Jack was attracted to teachers, doctors, therapists, authors; people who participated in book clubs, discussion groups or attended adult learning classes. Melissa, meanwhile, gravitated towards less intellectually curious people, laborers, blue-collared workers.

During the middle of the afternoon, while she was fishing for a candy in her purse, Samantha heard someone on the stand say her name was Michelle Masterson and that she worked for Bear Stearns. She quickly looked up, examined the woman being questioned, and then had a coughing fit. Jack Hubbard excused the juror. Only later did David find out that they had arranged this signal in case Samantha recognized someone who would most likely recognize her as well. Michelle had worked at Chuck Schwab, but left about two years ago. "We didn't work together," Samantha explained, "but it's a small world, and I didn't want to take a chance."

It took all day for twelve jurors and two alternates to be selected. As they took their seats in the jury box, the Judge made a surprising announcement.

"Ladies and gentlemen. Thank you for your willingness to sit on this jury. It will be a unique experience, not only for you, but for all of us, since this case involves the subject of reincarnation. Not something you usually come across in a court of law. In fact a potentially reincarnated witness has never been allowed to testify in a trial before. By tomorrow you can be assured that this courtroom will be packed with observers and the press. Therefore I am sorry to inform you that, starting tomorrow, it will be necessary to sequester this jury for the duration of the trial. Everyone will be talking about this case, and I don't want them talking to you. Your decision on the guilt or innocence of the defendant must be based solely on the evidence you hear over the next few days and not on the opinions of every street corner philosopher.

"Please arrive tomorrow, prepared to stay in a nearby hotel which the State will pay for. Don't forget medications and perhaps a book or two. At the hotel you will not have access to the TV or radio in your rooms. I am also asking you not to read any news reports that show up on your cell phones. I don't want to take them away from you, but if I hear that this rule has been violated, I will."

Some of the jury groaned at that news. "I'm sorry, but we have to take every possible precaution to keep your minds from being swayed by other people's opinions. Based on the witness list, I expect that we should be finished in two or three days. Does anyone have a problem with this?"

Although no one seemed to like the idea of being cooped up for several days, Samantha guessed they also didn't want to miss out on the trial of the century. And sure enough, no one raised their hand.

"Excellent," the Judge said. "And finally, please do not speak to each other or to anyone else about this case; not to your husbands, wives, parents or friends. No one. Absolutely no one. Can you do that?"

All the jurors nodded solemnly in agreement.

==

Before going home, Samantha and David went to a small bar around the corner from the courthouse. They sat in a quiet corner and reviewed the juror selections. David ordered a whiskey and Samantha a white wine.

"I like that woman who's going to be the forewoman. Susan somebody, I think. She seems to be a very

178

straightforward, no nonsense kind of woman," Samantha said, as she took out the iPad she'd been making notes in during the voir dire. "Susan Mullins."

"I liked her too." David said. "I also liked the man who works for *The New Yorker*, fact checking. He must learn about all kinds of things in his job…. perhaps even reincarnation."

Samantha looked up. "God, can you imagine being a fact checker these days? I'll bet he has to work overtime in that job. Here he is. His name is…. William Johnson." Scrolling down, she said "What did you think of the Turkish fellow, Onur Demir. Do you think he'd be open to reincarnation?"

"Who knows? He said he was Muslim, and despite what lots of people believe, that's a tolerant religion. At least it was when Mohammed was around. I've done lots of travel in the mid-East and have been very impressed by the generosity and friendliness of the Muslims I met there."

Samantha nodded. "I just hope our jury will have an open mind, put aside their own personal beliefs, and seriously consider the concept of being born again."

"On that subject," David said, while taking a sip of his drink, "I've been doing some research on reincarnation. I was surprised to learn that belief in reincarnation has been around for a really long time. I knew it was a belief of both Buddhists and Hindus, but there are many other religions who subscribe to it as well. In fact it goes back to at least 1700 BC, before the Buddha even existed."

Samantha was surprised. "Really! I didn't know that either. What does reincarnation actually mean? Being born again in a little kid's body is my scientific explanation."

David chuckled and withdrew a small notepad from his jacket pocket. Here's one of the definitions I read: 'reincarnation means the consciousness of a living being can start a new life in a different physical form or body after death.' Some refer to it as rebirth or transmigration. It's a central tenet of Indian religions, such as Jainism, Buddhism, Sikhism and Hinduism, but it's also a common belief of some ancient and modern religions such as Spiritism, Theosophy, and Eckankar. It's even an esoteric belief in many streams of Orthodox Judaism. And in case you need names, several ancient Greek philosophers such as Pythagoras, Socrates and Plato believed in rebirth."

Samantha started laughing, and motioned for him to stop. "Before you go any further, what on earth is Eckankar? I've heard about most of the others, but that one sounds like a used-car dealership!"

David laughed too. "I'd never heard of it either. "But listen to this. Their primary teaching is the belief that you can experience the soul outside of the body. The ECKists call it Soul Travel. Basically they believe that the soul can be experienced separately from the body and, in full consciousness, travel freely in other planes of reality. Doesn't that sound like fun?"

"That's cool, and lots cheaper than airfare."

"You're incorrigible!" David said. Pay attention now. We, of all people, ought to know this stuff."

"I know, forgive me. But I've been so wound up for the past eight months that I need to be able to laugh a little."

"I know what you mean. This has been exhausting. But if you'll be good, I'll tell you what I learned about karma. I looked that up too."

"Sure, lay it on me," said Samantha. "Karma is what happens to you if you've been bad, right?" She ordered another white wine from a passing waiter. The first one had disappeared too quickly.

"Well, sort of. When people say 'I have bad karma,' after they've totaled their car while driving drunk, what they mean is... 'I behaved badly so I got what I deserved.' It's sort of like a moral reckoning. Your words and deeds will have an impact on your current life as well as the next one. Not too dissimilar to the Christian notion of Heaven or Hell really. What happens next depends upon how you live your life.

"Tell me," David cocked his head and looked her in the eye. "I know you're a Catholic. Do you still believe in Heaven and Hell?"

Samantha sighed and said, "To tell you the truth, I'm not sure. My Catholic beliefs seem to have faded a bit over the years and now seem poised to disappear altogether. I didn't tell you, but I went to see Father Riley, my pastor at Our Lady of Perpetual Help, to get his advice about this reincarnation business. My mother insisted on it."

"That must have been an interesting conversation," David said, with an amused smile on his face. "What did he have to say?" He extended the bowl of peanuts to her.

Taking a handful, Samantha replied, "Well, Pelham is a pretty conservative town, and I think the priests who are sent there might be as well. He cautioned me away from even considering the possibility of reincarnation, reminding me that Catholicism is the only true religion. I really was hoping for more of an intellectual assessment and comparison of belief systems. Oh, well. Guess I should have known better. You need a Jesuit for that kind of discussion."

She reached for her new glass of wine and sheepishly added, "He gave me some holy water to sprinkle around Bonnie's room. To ward off the devil, I suppose."

"Gosh, I didn't realize they did that kind of thing any more. Did you do it?"

Samantha decided to tell him the truth. "Of course I did! You never know. I figured it couldn't hurt to give it a try."

"And… "

"She had another nightmare that night, and I tossed the rest of the holy water down the drain. Don't ever tell my mother. I didn't really believe it would work, but hope is such a powerful thing. It makes you do and believe strange things."

Samantha furrowed her brow for a minute. "David, do you think we're starting to believe in reincarnation just because we hope to find Carrie's murderer and hope to rid Bonnie of her nightmares? Like sprinkling the holy water?"

David nodded in acknowledgement, but said "No. I think we're willing to accept that reincarnation might be real because we've seen proof. And it's my hope that the jurors will see it that way as well.

After another hour of good conversation, they both decided to call it a day, go home, and get some rest. Tomorrow would be a big day.

==

Bonnie was already in bed when Samantha got home. She said goodbye to Mercedes and ate the dinner that had been left for her. Then, after making herself comfy in bed, she spent an hour on the phone with Hank, bringing him up to date on the day's events.

"We are in Courtroom #9, on the second floor. Opposite the jury box are eight tall windows casting theatrical swaths of sunlight across the room. It looks like a stage set! Very fitting, I think, for this landmark case. I was just a bundle of nerves, like an actress before the curtain goes up, and I didn't even have to go on stage today."

"How did Mike look?" Hank asked. "Nervous?"

"Oh, no. He looked cool as a cucumber. He's very handsome, clean-shaven, and well-dressed in a suit and tie. He looked just like a GQ model! There were only about fifteen other people in the spectator seats and who knows who they were… perhaps tourists, or law students, or maybe even people with nothing better to do.   But you can bet that as word gets out tonight regarding the subject of this case, the courtroom will be packed tomorrow."

"Were any reporters there today?" Hank asked.

"I'm not sure. I did see a few people with laptops, so maybe they were on courthouse duty. If so, their morning editions will alert everyone else about the excitement to come.

"David and I sat in the back of the room. I'd brought my disguise with me, but Jack was pretty sure it would take the whole day to select the jury, and it did.

"The Judge explained that since this case would deal with reincarnation, he had approved having perspective jurors asked about their religions, as well as their perceptions of reincarnation. He assured them that these questions were not meant to rule out anyone for their specific religion, but rather to ensure that they could be open-minded in their consideration of the facts presented during the trial."

"So how did that go over? Were people open about their beliefs?" Hank asked.

Samantha pulled the duvet up and adjusted the pillows. "They were, but finding just that sweet spot where a prospective juror was not biased for or against reincarnation was a challenge. Most either didn't know anything about it, which was okay, or like one outspoken elderly woman, thought it was all just a bunch of hooey, and that anyone who did believe in it was crazy. People like her tended to be more vocal in their opinions and were therefore easier to dismiss for cause.   But it was much harder to detect whether someone might have a hidden bias against a belief they knew nothing about. I'm sure Jack was worried that he would run out of his fifteen peremptory challenges.

"I feel good about the first person selected, who will be the forewoman. She's about sixty, well-dressed and attractive, retired early, and is now writing novels. When asked about her religion, she replied that she had none since she did not believe in God. She's also very well travelled and knowledgable about cultural and religious beliefs in different parts of the world."

"She sounds good. What were the others like?"

Propping the IPad on her raised knees, Samantha reviewed her notes. "The final jury consists of six women, six men and two female alternates. All are below the age of seventy-five, and most are under fifty. They cover the waterfront in terms of religious beliefs, plus there's that one atheist and an agnostic as well. Most consider themselves to be somewhat spiritual, but not necessary religious. They are very diverse, with families of Irish, English, Italian, Turkish, German, Indian, Mexican and African descent. That's New York City for you. All are American citizens and were born in the United States with the exception of Mr. Singh, the agnostic, who was born in Delhi, attended Columbia University in New York City, and then moved here for good. He might prove to be an asset on the jury, since I assume he will know more about reincarnation than the rest."

"Yes," Hank replied, "but if he is an agnostic, he may have decided it's all a bunch of hooey too. Who knows?"

Finally, Samantha told Hank about the Judge's decision to sequester the jury. "You know that's hardly ever done anymore. He must really be expecting a media frenzy. Oh God, I hope I'm doing the right thing."

"Me too," Hank agreed, with scarcely a touch of "I told you so" in his voice.

Chapter 22

*T*he next day, knowing that she would be the first witness for the prosecution, Samantha had transformed herself. Her alias, Cynthia Spark, sat in the back of the courtroom with the rest of the team: David, Dr. K and Bob.

Judge Brown welcomed the jurors. "Ladies and gentlemen. Once again, thank you for being here today. Over the course of this trial you will be performing a civil duty that is one of the most important in our judicial system. Regardless of what I may think, or what our two esteemed counselors may think about this case, you will be the ones to make the decision about whether Mr. MacShane is guilty or not guilty of murder, based on the evidence presented to you.

"It is most likely that none of you has been to law school or been involved in police work. You are average citizens who represent a cross section of this fine city. It can be a little intimidating to have such an awesome responsibility, but as we've seen time and time again, you will rise to the occasion. And you will, no doubt, make the right decision." He pulled out a lens cloth and started cleaning his glasses.

"As I said yesterday, this is a very unusual case which deals with the subject of reincarnation, and the star witness for the prosecution is a child. I have met with her and have decided that she is sufficiently aware of the difference between the truth and a lie to testify.

"Since testifying can be a traumatizing experience, even for an adult, I have decided that her testimony will be taken in my chambers with only counsel, her mother, and myself present, but it will be live-streamed into the courtroom. To save you a lot of Googling, I will also tell you that the child and her mother are both using aliases to protect their privacy.

"We will be taking periodic breaks, and lunch will be provided in the jury deliberation room. I must ask you not to go outside where you would have to fight off the hoards of journalists. And I remind you not to talk to each other or anyone else about the case.

"With that, we will begin with opening statements from Mr. Jack Hubbard, Assistant District Attorney from the Manhattan District Attorney's Office and Ms. Melissa Washington, our Public Defender. Mr. Hubbard?"

Jack stood up, buttoned his jacket and walked towards the jury box. Looking directly at them, he paused a few moments before beginning.

"At about midnight on May 21st, 2013, Carolyn Kelly was in a deep sleep. She had just returned from a photo shoot in Morocco for Vogue magazine. It was another of her many travels all over the world. Although Ms. Kelly had been a top fashion model for four and a half years, she was probably dreaming about what she was planning to do next. She had promised her father that after five years of modeling she would go back to school. And now, thanks to all her travels, she was clear about what she wanted to do with her life. In Africa, she had become inspired to get involved in the non-profit, NGO world in order to help poor, uneducated and starving children; boys and girls she herself had seen, spoken with and cared about.

"But that dream was about to become stifled. Michael MacShane, a maintenance man in her apartment building, had had a one-time hookup with Ms. Kelly. But when his many future advances were rebuffed, he decided to take matters into his own hands. Imagine how terrified she must have been to wake up with his body on top of hers; to feel his hands trying to pry her legs apart and then, as she thrashed about and screamed for help, to have a pillow clamped down over her face until she could no longer breathe. She was only twenty-two; on top of the world, with a passion to do good, and now… she was dead."

Jack walked away for a minute, giving the jury time to visualize that picture, then turned around.

"You might wonder how we know what happened in Carolyn Kelly's bedroom that night. We know thanks to a witness; the sole witness to this horrifying attempted rape and murder. That witness is Rosie Spark who, at this time, is four years old."

Samantha noted that several jurors looked totally incredulous.

"For the past two years, Rosie has suffered horrible nightmares that occur about two or three times a week, and are always the same. As you will hear from her mother, Cynthia Spark, Rosie's dreams are about a man named Mike - lying on top of her, hurting her 'down there,' and then holding a pillow over her face. No matter how much she fights, she cannot push him off, and in each and every dream… she dies."

The journalists in the room, and now there were many, were typing on their laptops as fast as their fingers could fly.

"You will hear how Rosie started referring to herself as Carrie, describing Carrie's apartment, her collectibles brought back from South East Asia, and begging to see her daddy. You will learn about Cynthia's desperate search within the medical community to find out what was wrong with her daughter.

After several dead ends, she met with Dr. Karadamand, a specialist in children's psychological disorders, who will tell you why he came to suspect that Rosie was displaying signs of a previous personality. Despite Cynthia's skepticism, he asked for her permission to invite someone from UVA's Division of Perceptual Studies to meet Rosie.

"Dr. Bob Williams, a Researcher at DOPs (as the Division of Perceptual Studies is called) will explain how they have investigated possible reincarnation cases for over fifty years, not only in Asia, but in the United States as well. And he will explain why he has come to believe that Rosie is the reincarnation of Carolyn Kelly.

"You will meet David Kelly, Carolyn's father, whom Rosie immediately recognized as Daddy when she was brought to meet him. He will tell you about that visit and how amazed he was by what little Rosie knew about his daughter's life.

"You will also see pages from Carolyn Kelly's diary which corroborate her growing discomfort due to Mike MacShane's inappropriate advances. Her nearly hysterical fear of him will be vouched for by Greta Neilson, a close friend of hers.

"And finally, you will hear from Rosie herself. Although she is only four, we are confident you will find her testimony not only compelling, but completely believable."

He paused again. The jurors were paying close attention.

"Before I close, I would like to ask you some questions, which you do not need to answer aloud. This jury represents a broad cross-section of religions. Some of you practice regularly, others do not. And a few of you do not subscribe to any religion. Wherever you fall on that spectrum, ask yourself this. What do you think happens after you die? I expect some of you might say that you go on to Heaven or Hell, depending on your behavior in this life. Others might say that you've been taught about a hereafter, but aren't sure whether you believe in it or not. And still others might say that you won't go anywhere; once your life is over, it's over. When your bones or ashes are buried in the ground, they will become part of our ecosystem and support the growth of other life... be it flora or fauna. Another kind of rebirth, if you will."

Several heads were nodding in acknowledgement.

"Assuming you agree with me so far, my next question to the Christians on the jury would be... why do you believe in Heaven and Hell? Or, if you are Muslim, why do you believe in Jannah and Jahannam? Or if you're Baptist or Jewish, why do you believe in Salvation? After some discussion, I think we might all agree that it comes down to faith. Though we may have different beliefs about the hereafter, none of them has been scientifically proven. And for many of you that doesn't matter. You believe what you believe, regardless. I want you to hold on to that thought. Reincarnation may not be what you believe, but millions of people do. And who can prove that it doesn't exist? Apparently not the scientists." And with that, Jack Hubbard sat down.

Samantha nodded her head. He's proactively countering the argument that he expects from the defense... that reincarnation is not a proven theory. Very good. Now let's see how the defense responds.

Melissa rose to address the jury. She was dressed in a white pantsuit with a bold, red silk shirt and red shoes with three inch heels. "Good Morning, Ladies and Gentlemen. I am Melissa Washington, the Defense Attorney for Michael McShane. We didn't hear too much about him from Mr. Hubbard. Perhaps that's because his 'eye witness' only saw someone with his first name in her dreams. So therefore, let me introduce you to him.

"Michael MacShane, whose friends call him Mike, is thirty years old and has worked as a maintenance man in 980 Fifth Avenue for the past six years. Mike does not come from an elite family, as Carolyn Kelly did. While her father bought and sold buildings, Mike's father built them with his own hands. His mother was a nurse, working double shifts to bring home a bit more money. Pearl MacShane will tell you about her son's adolescent years and how he had to mostly fend for himself. Neither she, nor her husband, had the time to encourage him in his studies or even notice when he and his brother played hooky from Cardinal Cook High School in the Bronx. She worries that the poor quality of the school, and her inability to provide strong parental guidance, contributed to her son's limited climb up the ladder of success. But she will also tell you about the kind and caring young man he is now.

"His boss, Burt Robinson, will testify to the fact that Mike is a good worker and is rarely out sick. Danny O'Hara another maintenance man in that Fifth Avenue apartment building, will tell us how well-liked Mike is by the other employees; someone who can always be counted on for a good laugh. Both of them are of Irish descent, and like to have a beer every now and then with their mates at the Trinity Pub on East 84th Street. Mike is always the center of attention at those gatherings, due to his charismatic personality. He readily admits that he's had lots of girlfriends. As Mr. MacShane said to Danny, 'he has no problem in that department.' "

Mike turned to face the jury and gave them a handsome smile.

"You will hear how Mike has been somewhat of a magnet, attracting beautiful women wherever he goes. So when the prosecution tells you that Carolyn Kelly came on to him after he had hung a painting in her apartment, you can imagine that he was not surprised. That's just what women do, in his experience. And if they are as attractive as she was, he is more than happy to oblige. But that experience was a one-off, a hookup, an impulse of the moment. He did not expect, given Ms. Kelly's social status, that it would ever happen again. And it did not.

"Mr. Hubbard touched on the role of science vis a vis religion… or I should say the non-role of science in religion. We believe what we believe, he said. And that is true. But in this case, whatever you believe is the truth must be the truth beyond a reasonable doubt. You cannot convict Mr. MacShane on a hunch or on a child's nightmares. You must know in your heart, beyond a reasonable doubt, that he is guilty. We intend to show you that he is not."

"Not bad," Samantha whispered to David. "She's right too! Who on earth can believe in reincarnation beyond a reasonable doubt? Who can believe in any religion beyond a reasonable doubt?"

David patted her hand. "Yes, but remember that reincarnation is not a religion. It's a belief and, as we discussed yesterday, it's not limited to one religion or any religion for that matter. It's been a belief for centuries, all over the world."

"We will take a ten minute recess," Judge Brown said, "and when you return, Mr. Hubbard may call his first witness for the prosecution." He banged his gavel and everyone stood up, stretched and headed out of the courtroom.

Chapter 23

"*W*elcome back ladies and gentlemen. We are going to spend the next hour or so hearing from some of Mr. Hubbard's witnesses and then we will break for lunch. Mr. Hubbard, the floor is yours." Judge Brown settled back in his chair.

Jack Hubbard stood, and buttoned his coat. "Thank you, Your Honor. For our first witness, the state calls Mrs. Cynthia Spark."

Although she was nervous, Cynthia Spark, a plainly dressed blonde, with tinted glasses, did her best to speak in smooth, even tones. Guided by Jack's questions, she spoke of Rosie's nightmares, her odd statements, such as "Carrie is me before I is Rosie," her playacting with Barbie and Ken, her knowledge about the location of Carrie's apartment, her aggravated nighttime asthma, the pillow under the bed, and how she posed seductively for photos. Then she took the jurors through her search for a medical answer to Rosie's behavior, even considering sexual abuse and mental illness. She explained how she reluctantly began to consider reincarnation only after she and Rosie had met with Dr. Karadamand and then with Dr. Williams from The Division of Perceptual Studies.

She was on the stand for about an hour and a half and had the rapt attention of the jurors and everyone else. When Bonnie's screams were heard on the videos of her nightmares, you could hear a pin drop in the courtroom.

When Samantha happened to glance at Mike, as the tapes were being played, she couldn't get over how relaxed he looked. His long legs were stretched out in front of him, his arms were crossed, and he shook his head slowly from side to side as though he couldn't believe what he was hearing. Samantha worried he wasn't the only one.

In response to Jack's further questioning, she explained how she'd had her mind opened to the subject of reincarnation after reading Jim Tucker's book, *Return to Life: Extraordinary Cases of Children Who Remember Past Lives*. Unfortunately when Jack asked for the book to be introduced into evidence, the Judge sided with the Defense's objection. He noted that there are thousands of books out there, pro and con reincarnation, but that the jury would have to rely only upon the evidence introduced in the courtroom.

Darn, Samantha thought, that's a real setback. But then she noticed that a number of jurors were jotting something down. Probably the name of the book, she thought. Maybe they'll find a way to get their hands on it, thanks to Kindle. I know I sure would, no matter what the Judge said.

Melissa Washington did not take Samantha through everything again, but did ask a few questions. "Mrs. Spark, did you ever take your daughter to see a psychiatrist or a neurologist?"

"No, I did not. I took her to her pediatrician and then to Dr. Karadamand, a very well respected child psychologist."

"I see." Melissa replied, as though she thought Samantha had not been thorough enough in seeking a medical explanation for her daughter's nightmares.

"And, Mrs. Spark, what does Rosie say Mike's last name is?" Reluctantly, Samantha had to admit that she had never mentioned that. "Hmmm." Melissa replied, as she turned to face the jury. "There are an awful lot of guys named Mike out there."

Chapter 24

*J*ack smiled at Samantha as she stepped down from the witness stand, as if to say don't worry, you were great!

Then he moved on to his second witness, Billie Jo Collins. She told everyone that she was a social worker for Child Protective Services and that she'd been called by Rosie's pediatrician to investigate a possible sexual assault.

Jack looked down at his pad. "I know that you did a thorough investigation of the people who spend private time with Rosie: her nanny, Mercedes Rodriguez, her next-door neighbor, Elaine Cameron, her daycare teacher, Patricia Henderson, and her grandmother, Eleanor Murray. Since you received no evidence of possible sexual abuse from these people, with the Defense's concurrence, I would like Ms. Collins' report to be stipulated and entered into evidence."

"So stipulated," said Melissa.

"The one thing I would like to talk to you about, Mrs. Collins, is your discussion with Rosie which I believe was private. Is that correct?"

"Yes. With her mother's approval, I asked her to show me her bedroom. As we became comfortable with each other, I asked about her nightmares. She told me that in her dreams a man named Mike hurt her 'down there.' She used air quotes so the jury would know those were her exact words. "I asked who Mike was, and she said he was a friend of Carrie's. Then, of course, I asked who Carrie was. Her reply stunned me. She said, 'I am Carrie and Carrie is me.' She used air quotes again.

"Did you follow up further on that comment?" Jack asked.

"No. I am not a psychologist, and I didn't feel qualified to question her about that statement."

"Did you tell her mother about it?"

"Not that day. I decided that while interviewing the other contacts, I would see if they had ever heard Rosie mention Carrie or Mike. None had. When my investigation was complete, I met again with Cynthia and told her about it. Hearing the name Carrie reminded her of a day when her daughter pointed out a penthouse apartment opposite the Central Park Zoo, and talked about how Carrie used to love looking at the animals from there. When Cynthia asked Rosie who Carrie was, she received the same answer - 'I am Carrie and Carrie is me.' "

Jack nodded his head. "What did you advise Cynthia to do since you didn't feel qualified to handle the situation?"

"I suggested that she see a child psychologist because I knew something was wrong. I just didn't know what."

"Thank you Mrs. Collins. No further questions."

Melissa rose and said, "No questions Your Honor."

Chapter 25

Jack's next witness was Dr. Karadamand. After the oath was administered, Jack asked him to state his name, occupation and connection to this case.

"My name is Dr. Abdul Karadamand, I am a child psychologist, and Cynthia Spark brought her daughter to me for assessment."

"Please tell us where you studied, and how long you have been in this field."

"I attended Princeton for my undergraduate degree in psychology, and then Harvard for my Masters and PHD in child psychology. During my time at Harvard I spent two years of a supervised internship at Massachusetts General Hospital. I have been a practicing, board certified psychologist for twenty years and am now associated with New York Hospital."

In his testimony, Dr. Karadamand corroborated everything Cynthia Spark had said about their meetings. He explained why he had discarded the possibility that Rosie had a dissociative disorder, and then began to seriously consider reincarnation.

"Dr. Karadamand, I understand you were born in Delhi, India, and lived there for eighteen years. Can you tell us a little bit about how people there relate to stories about reincarnation?"

Dr. K crossed his legs and settled in to talk about one of his favorite subjects. "Reincarnation is a core belief for Buddhists and Hindus. So when we hear of a story about a child remembering a previous life, we think nothing of it. It's an expectation, not a surprise."

"And tell me, Doctor, now that you have lived here for the better part of thirty years, do you still believe in reincarnation?"

"Yes, most definitely. That's why I was so excited to meet Rosie, who reminded me so much of the children I had heard about in India. She is a very special child. But since you could say that I might be predisposed to think she had been reincarnated, I wanted to have her seen by an expert. That is why I suggested we call in Dr. Williams."

"Thank you, Dr. Karadamand. We will be speaking with Dr. Williams next, so no further questions."

When Melissa stood for her cross, she said "Tell me, Doctor, have you ever met a child who recalled a previous life before?"

"No, I have not. I heard about several of them when I lived in India but never met them personally. I was a teenager after all. And though I have heard there are reincarnation cases in the United States, I have not personally met any of the subjects of those cases. That is why I was so excited to hear Rosie's story."

"Dr. Karadamand, did it even occur to you to refer Rosie Spark to a psychiatrist or a neurologist? Or did you just leap to the conclusion that reincarnation was the answer because you happen to come from India?"

Dr. K was starting to look a little uncomfortable in the face of this hostile questioning, but remained cool in his response. "Of course I considered that, Ms. Washington. But as I'm sure you know, psychologists receive a lot of education in mental disorders, and it was not my opinion that Rosie was suffering from such a thing. She did not show any of the signs of multiple personality disorder; such as speaking in different voices and exhibiting different behaviors. When Rosie speaks as if she were Carrie, she still sounds like the young child that she is. In order words, her personality doesn't change."

"Do you suppose your participation in this reincarnation case might advance your career, Doctor?"

"Perhaps," Dr. Karadamand said, "but that is certainly not the reason I am here today."

"Of course not. Tell me, Dr. Karadamand, when you talked with Rosie, did she ever mention Mike's last name?"

"No, she did not."

"No further questions, your Honor."

Samantha leaned in to David. "She has some nerve implying that he's making all this up! And she's really pressing on the fact that no one knows Mike's last name. How could it be that important? Mike worked in the building, Mike slept with her, Mike kept coming on to her, Mike terrified her, and , according to Bonnie's dreams, Mike killed her." She slapped her hand on her knee in frustration.

"Ladies and Gentlemen," said the Judge, "it has been a full morning. I am going to give you a sixty minute recess for lunch in the deliberation room. Do not speak with any of the reporters in the building and do not go outside. Please return promptly by 1:00 p.m. We are adjourned until then." The gavel came down.

Chapter 26

*A*t 1:00 p.m., with everyone present and accounted for, the clerk called the court to order, and Judge Brown resumed his seat. Samantha was looking forward to the Prosecution's next witness... Bob Williams. It was going to be up to him to convince the jury that reincarnation might be possible. Jack was looking forward to his testimony as well, and they had gone over it several times.

"Your Honor, the prosecution calls Dr. Robert Williams to the stand." Bob was wearing a dark suit and tie for the occasion and, with his briefcase by his side, looked very professional.

"Dr. Williams, please state your name, occupation and connection to this case," Jack said.

"Dr. Robert Williams. I am a Senior Research Specialist at the University of Virginia's Division of Perceptual Studies. My specialty is the study of children who recall past lives. I have been working with Jim Tucker, the Director of the Division, for eight years. I was called in by Dr. Karadamand to assess Rosie Stark as a possible reincarnation of a previous personality."

"And what is your educational background Dr. Williams?"

"I have a PhD in General Psychiatry from UVA and I am board certified by the American Board of Psychiatry and Neurology in general psychiatry, as well as child and adolescent psychology. In fact, if I could just interject, I do have the qualifications to assess mental disorders." He looked directly at Melissa.

"Thank you for closing that loop, Dr. Williams." Jack gave him a slight smile. "Tell me, what attracted you to the Division of Perceptual Studies?"

"Actually, I heard Jim Tucker give a lecture at UVA. I was so intrigued with the real-life experiences he'd had, researching possible cases of reincarnation, that I asked him for a job. I haven't been sorry for a single day."

"How long has the Division of Perceptual Studies been around?"

Bob settled into his chair and looked at the jury. "Ian Stevenson was the founder of DOPS in 1967. He traveled extensively over a period of forty years, investigating three thousand cases of children who claimed to remember past lives. He became known internationally for his research into reincarnation; the premise that emotions, memories and even physical bodily features can be transferred from one life to another."

Jack was facing the jury when Bob defined reincarnation and noticed all the jurors leaning forward and rapidly taking notes on their pads.

Turning back to his witness, he said "Can you walk us through the steps that you, and others at DOPS, take to assess whether a child is really remembering a past life?"

"Certainly. Since Dr. Stevenson became so well known, we no longer have to search out cases. They come to us. We have a website and invite people with questions to contact us. If their story sounds promising, we visit with the child and his or her family. Because so many of the cases we have studied are similar, we seek answers to four key questions:

First: Does the child speak about memories of places, events and family members that he or she couldn't have known about?

Second: Does the child have nightmares about a violent death?

Third: Does the child have any birthmarks or scars that match up with the death of their previous personality?

Fourth: Does the child have any unexplained illnesses or phobias that do not correspond to his or her genetic family tree or environmental surroundings?"

"And is that what you looked for when you interviewed Rosie and her mother?" Jack asked.

"Yes. Rosie definitely has memories of a specific place... her apartment on Fifth Avenue, and a family member... her daddy. Since Mrs. Spark and her husband separated before Rosie was born, Rosie could not have been referring to her real father. She was also able to recall special artifacts in Carrie's apartment, such as a Standing Buddha sculpture which Rosie calls 'Boofa.' She told me about her frequent nightmares of a violent death, which you have heard described. Since her previous personality died from smothering, there were no birthmarks or scars related to that, but she does have a pillow phobia and stows her pillow under the bed every night. Her recently diagnosed asthma causes her to have trouble breathing, but only at night after one of her nightmares. So I suspect that problem could be related to her memory of being smothered in a previous life."

"So, were you convinced that Rosie met your qualifications for being the reincarnation of a previous personality?" Jack looked directly at the jury, as Dr. Williams answered.

"Very much so. But I believed that we should investigate further, so I set up a meeting with Carolyn Kelly's father, David Kelly."

"Was Mr. Kelly open to that?" Jack asked.

"Probably not at first. With Cynthia's permission, I sent him a long letter, citing our research over the years, and my perceptions of Rosie's case. I asked him to think about whether he would be willing to let us meet with him, and I included a copy of Jim Tucker's book, *Return to Life*. I thought if he read that book or was inspired to read any of the research published on our website, he might agree to meet with us. After about a month, he called. I can't say that he was enthusiastic but he was at least willing to be open-minded and agree to a meeting."

Before Bob could go further, Jack said, "I will be asking Mr. Kelly about that meeting next, but do you have any particular recollections that you want to mention now?"

"Yes. There was no doubt in my mind that Rosie recognized Mr. Kelly, as well as those Asian artifacts I mentioned. And had it not been for one of her recollections, which I'm sure he will tell you about, we wouldn't be here today. And finally, I could tell that by the time we left, Mr. Kelly recognized his daughter, Carrie, in little Rosie."

"Thank you Dr. Williams. Oh, another question, how long can we expect Rosie to have these nightmares?"

"In our experience, these children can often have disturbed sleep as infants. Their dreams aren't articulated, of course, until the child has learned to speak - sometime between two and three. Then between the ages of five and seven, all their memories usually start to fade away. But if someone is able to validate the child's memories and/or fears, those memories usually dissipate earlier. Now that Rosie has met her 'Daddy,' she has not mentioned him as often. It is our hope that if Mr. MacShane is found guilty and punished, as Rosie might say, her nightmares will stop, without her having to wait several more years.

"Objection, Your Honor." Melissa was on her feet. "Conjecture."

Jack said, "Your Honor, the witness is using fifty years of research, done by the Division of Perceptual Studies, to make this assertion. It is not conjecture."

"Overruled. The witness's statement stands."

Mike let out a disbelieving sigh and shook his head again, while Jack smiled inwardly at the impression Bob had made on the jury.

"Thank you, Dr. Williams. Your Honor, we reserve the right to recall this witness at a later time if needed." With that, Jack took his seat, and Samantha took a look at the jury. Most of them seemed fascinated, as though they were watching a good sci-fi flick, which might just prove to be true.

As Melissa rose for her cross, Jack folded his arms. "Dr. Williams, it's a pleasure to meet you. Knowing that we would have the benefit of your expertise on the subject of reincarnation, I took the liberty of doing a little research of my own. Tell me, Dr. Williams, wasn't reaction to Dr. Stevenson's assertions decidedly mixed? In fact, didn't some critics find fault with even the way he conducted his research?"

"Yes, he did have his share of critics, as one might expect."

"In fact, wasn't there some concern that the children or their parents, interviewed by Dr. Stevenson, had deceived him?"

"Yes, but…"

Melissa pressed on. "And wasn't there concern that Dr. Stevenson asked them leading questions?"

"Yes, but…"

Melissa interrupted again. "Didn't he, in fact, often work through translators who were predisposed to believe what the interviewees were saying, and that therefore his conclusions might have been undermined by their confirmation bias?"

"Yes, that is true. In response to that, I can only say that it's necessary for a sceptic to read the many books and scholarly articles written by both Dr. Stevenson and Dr. Tucker before agreeing or disagreeing with their work."

Melissa then asked, "Did Dr. Stevenson himself believe in reincarnation?"

Dr. Williams paused a moment before responding, "Dr. Stevenson did not take a position on reincarnation. He argued only that his case studies could not, in his view, be explained by environment or heredity and that reincarnation was the best, although not the only, explanation for the stronger cases he had investigated. In interviewing witnesses, Dr. Stevenson also searched for alternate ways to account for their testimony: that the child might have come upon the information in some normal way, that the witnesses were engaged in fraud or self delusion, or that the correlations were the result of coincidence or misunderstanding."

"And did you do that as well, in Rosie's case?"

"Yes. I sought an explanation for how Rosie could know what she did, but could find none. I'm sure that Mr. Kelly was concerned that someone might be trying to extort money from him. But, of course, that was not the case and he too came to believe that, in some mysterious way, Carrie's consciousness had been reborn in Rosie."

Melissa tried again. "Dr. Williams, have you or the others in your organization ever proven that reincarnation exists?"

"We never use the word proven. Instead, if we can find no other possible explanation for the child's assertions and memories, we describe the case as solved. Reincarnation is one explanation, but we have never proven that to be true."

"Thank you, Dr. Williams, that will be all." Satisfied that she had at least weakened believability in reincarnation, Melissa sat down.

Samantha whispered to David, "What do you think?"

David looked concerned. "I think she made a good dent in Bob's testimony by raising all those concerns about

Stevenson.   Well, I'm next." He patted her knee. "Wish me luck."

Chapter 27

*A*s David Kelly's name was called, Samantha watched him approach the stand, wearing a three piece, dark pin-striped suit, white shirt, and a lavender striped tie. He did not appear at all nervous, perhaps because he was accustomed to giving presentations and persuading his audience. Although this was a very different kind of audience, she knew that he was up to the task.

Under Jack's carefully planned questioning, David's testimony was poignant, compelling and provocative. As he described Rosie's visit, the jury hung on every word. They looked amazed when he told them about how she pulled the key out of its hiding place. As he read the pertinent excerpts from Carrie's diary, Jack entered them into evidence. Samantha knew that they needed the diary testimony but also worried that, for some jurors, it might cast aspersions on Carrie's character.

She was pleased to see, however, that when David spoke of that farewell 'til we meet again scene, a few of the female jurors wiped away a tear or two.

When it was Melissa's turn, she wasted no time getting back to the writings in Carrie's diary. "Mr. Kelly, please forgive me for asking, but do you know if your daughter slept around with a lot of men? Perhaps even someone else named Mike?"

David stiffened in his chair. "No, Ms. Washington. To the best of my knowledge she did not."

Melissa smiled and turned toward the jury. "Of course that's the problem, isn't it? What father really knows the answer to that question? You can only say 'to the best of my knowledge,' which of course means that Carolyn Kelly might have had quite a promiscuous sex life and...."

"Objection, Your Honor. Conjecture."

"Sustained. Mrs. Washington, please stick to the facts and don't hypothesize."

Although the jurors were glued to David's testimony, Samantha noticed Mike yawning, seemingly without a care in the world. I've never seen a defendant look so relaxed, she thought. His behavior is sending signals that he's innocent and is just waiting for this whole farce to be over.

==

After a ten minute break, Greta Neilson was called to the stand. She looked every bit the top model she was; tall, blonde and slender, wearing a pair of palomino-colored suede slacks with a matching jacket and silk blouse. Three gold chain necklaces swung from her neck and she walked easily on stiletto heals. Under Jack's questioning, she corroborated everything that Carrie had written in her diary for the prosecution.

When the defense asked her about Carrie's love-life, she replied, "I guess you could say models have their pick. Whether we choose to go home with someone more or less depends on whether we have an early call the next morning." Samantha stopped breathing for a minute, until she added, "But Carrie and I didn't do that often."

==

Greta was the last witness of the day, so the jurors were excused to be driven to their hotel. Samantha and David returned to the neighborhood bar, sat in the same dimly lit corner and spent about two hours reviewing everyone's testimony. They both agreed that it had gone about as well as could be expected, but were worried about the doubts the defense had planted regarding the legitimization of DOP's work, and the problem of not having Mike's last name.

"You did really well though," David assured Samantha. You've kept such meticulous records; I think the jury was very impressed. As am I." He added warmly.

She smiled, a little bit self-consciously. "You were remarkable. A few of the jurors shed a tear or two when you described that touching farewell scene."

"You know, I think about that every day. It was almost as though Carrie was speaking to me directly, using words that she knew I would recognize in order to make me believe that she was inside Bonnie. And it worked! But as much as I want to see justice done on Carrie's behalf, all this focus on her for months on end has been draining. I miss her so much."

"Of course you do," Samantha said, as she laid her hand on his. "You're having to grieve all over again. Not that you will ever stop grieving, but you know what I mean." Then noticing that she was still holding his hand, she withdrew it to pick up her wine glass. David just looked at her and didn't speak. Something had just happened, but neither one of them wanted to acknowledge it.

==

Samantha was not surprised when Hank called at about 10 p.m. She was already in bed, but couldn't sleep. Too much had happened that day, right up to David kissing her on the cheek when they separated. Hank was on a week-long business trip in San Francisco, but had obviously been tuned in to the news.

"Hi Sam. It already looks like a carnival there. I'm so sorry I'm not with you to provide some moral support. How are you managing? Did you testify today?"

"Yes. It wasn't bad, but I was really happy to get it over with. That disguise sort of makes me feel as though I'm hiding in plain sight. David and I are sitting way in the back of the courtroom in order to be out of the spotlight. God, there were tons of reporters and cameras there today."

"Really? I thought cameras weren't allowed in the courtroom."

"Media in New York trials are usually allowed to use audio and video, but a judge can waive that right if he thinks it's necessary. Fortunately, Judge Brown did. But anything outside the courtroom is fair game. The reporters and cameramen are all over the front steps and in the hall. In addition to my disguise, I was wearing my floppy hat and sunglasses so I don't think anyone took my picture, but I can't really be sure. Bonnie's testimony will be live-streamed into the courtroom tomorrow, and I'm hoping the sketch artists won't be able to capture a good likeness of her from the screen."

"From your lips to God's ears, but as you know, I have a very bad feeling about this trial and how it will effect our lives going forward... primarily Bonnie's, but yours and mine as well."

Samantha took a deep breath before answering in as calm a voice as she could muster. "Hank... I am just as concerned as you are and am doing my best to ensure Bonnie's

209

anonymity. There is a reason we agreed to go ahead with this trial, remember? To see that justice is carried out. Not only on behalf of David, but for Bonnie as well. She knows about the trial and is looking forward to testifying because she wants the 'bad man' punished. And hopefully when he is, her nightmares will cease.

"I have to hang up now, Hank. I'm just exhausted. We'll talk again soon." After a hurried "good night," she fell back on the bed and prayed for an uninterrupted night of sleep.

Chapter 28

*T*he next morning there was a crowd on the front stone steps of the courthouse, with several people holding up covers of the morning papers bearing headlines like: "Reincarnation on Trial," and "Carolyn Kelly comes Back from the Dead." Samantha and David, however, with Judge Brown's approval, went in the back door to avoid being mobbed by the press. Samantha was still wearing her disguise, but with a different top.

The proceedings began at 9:00 a.m. sharp. The Judge welcomed the large crowd and requested that they be silent during everyone's testimony. He also informed the press and visitors once more that they were not, under any circumstances, to use audio or video devices inside the courtroom.

Samantha knew that with the ubiquity of cell phones, it might be impossible to ensure the Judge's orders were carried out. She guessed that Jack was probably nervous about today's witnesses, which would include Bonnie. As he called Martha Riddle to the stand, she thought okay, now we'll get into the nitty-gritty of this crime.

Martha was wearing her police uniform and carried a file. "Detective Riddle," Jack began, "please state your full name, occupation and connection to this case."

"My name is Martha Louise Riddle and I am a Detective Investigator for the NYPD in the 19th Precinct. I was the investigator on the Kelly case five years ago and am today as well."

"Thank you Detective Riddle. Let's start at the beginning. When were you called to go over to 980 Fifth Avenue to investigate a possible homicide?"

Martha opened her file and consulted some notes. "On May 22nd at 5:30 p.m., I was called by Ms. Anne Hendricks and notified that Carolyn Kelly was dead in her apartment. I arrived at her residence, at 980 Fifth Avenue, with a forensics investigator, a photographer and an evidence investigator at 6:15 p.m."

"Please tell us what you discovered and what your next steps were."

"First, we interviewed Ms. Hendricks who told us that she had been invited to come over for a special Moroccan dinner at 6:00 o'clock. Apparently Ms. Kelly had just returned from Marrakech and was anxious to try out a recipe. Ms. Hendricks found it suspicious that Ms. Kelly was not at home, and that there were no smells of food being cooked. So she went down to see the doorman." Martha paused as she referred to her notes, "The doorman, Mr. Joseph Langley, said that he had not seen Ms. Kelly since the previous day at about 4:00 p.m. He also said that she'd had no visitors while he had been on duty that day, right up until his shift ended at midnight.

"Responding to Ms. Hendrick's concern, the doorman called a maintenance man, Mr. Danny O'Hara, who opened the door to Ms. Kelly's apartment with the pass key. Inside, Ms. Hendricks and Mr. O'Hara found Ms. Kelly in her bedroom, obviously dead, and immediately called 911.

"After taking their statements, we asked them to leave and sealed off the apartment. The two witnesses had told us they had touched nothing in the apartment, with the exception of the elevator door handle. The front entry to the Penthouse is the elevator door," she explained.

"So when you went into the bedroom, what did you see?" Samantha could sense that the entire room was hushed in anticipation of the murder scene details.

"We saw a nude Caucasian woman, with long, wavy blonde hair, about twenty-five years of age, lying on her back in the bed. She was wearing a silky, black nightgown which was pulled up above her hips. Next to her body was a pillow and the bedcovers had all been pulled back."

"What were you able to deduce from the scene?" Jack asked.

"Rigor mortis showed that the woman, who was indeed Carolyn Kelly, had been dead for about seventeen hours. Her mouth was frozen open and her eyes were shut tight. She looked as though she might have been screaming. The forensics investigator checked her entire body for any cursory indication of a struggle. She found slight bruising on the inside of her thighs, and on the inside of her upper arms and wrists."

Samantha could feel David stiffening at her side.

Interrupting at this point, Jack said "Your Honor, the State would like to enter Exhibit 6 into evidence. It is a number of photographs of Ms. Kelly as she was discovered, as well as close ups of the bruises on her thighs and arms."

Melissa was on her feet in a flash. "Objection, Your Honor. This is just sensationalism."

"It supports the verbal testimony, Your Honor." Jack said.

"Overruled," Judge Brown decided. "A murdered victim is not a pretty thing to see, Ms. Washington, but it is why we are here today. The jury may see the photographs."

As the photographs were passed from one juror to another, they were also projected onto a large screen in the courtroom. There were several gasps from the jurors and the spectators. David buried his face in his hands, and Samantha ran her hand back and forth across his back.

"Detective... what might the photos of bruises on her thighs and wrists indicate?"

"Well, it's possible that the bruises on her thighs could indicate an attempt at sexual assault, but not definitively; particularly since there was no sign of vaginal penetration. Those on her wrists might indicate that they were tied together or held very tightly."

"Thank you. Now please continue with your report."

"So continuing in our examination of the body: there were small red and purple splotches in her eyes and on her face and neck, indicative of asphyxiation. My evidence investigator dusted the room and the apartment but found no fingerprints, other than those of Ms. Kelly, on her body or in the apartment. Additionally, neither the front nor back door had been tampered with, so whoever did it had a key or had been let in. There was a half empty glass of wine on the kitchen counter, but just one. We later determined that the DNA on the glass matched Ms. Kelly's. No one else's DNA was found in the apartment.

"Our initial suspicion was that someone she knew had entered the apartment with the intention of raping her perhaps, but had ended up having to smother her."

Melissa rose again, "Objection, Your Honor. Speculation."

"Sustained. Detective Riddle, please state only the facts, not any assumptions," Judge Brown requested.

"Yes, your Honor. I apologize. We do not really know whether the perpetrator planned to rape or murder her. Asphyxiation was proven to be the cause of death later in the autopsy, where they found the same red and purple splotches in her lungs. These are called petechial hemorrhages."

This time Jack interrupted. "Your Honor, the State would like to enter the autopsy report into evidence, which confirms suffocation. My apologies, continue Detective Riddle."

"Only Ms. Kelly's DNA was found on the pillow case, on a lipstick smudge in the center which appeared to be an imprint made from having the pillow held firmly over her face."

Jack requested that a photograph of the pillow, with its eerie farewell kiss, be entered into evidence. The jurors seemed moved as the photo was passed from one to the other and projected for all to see.

David only glanced at the projections, then looked down into his lap as though something more interesting had just materialized there.

"What were your next steps, Detective?"

"Well, of course we called Mr. Kelly first so he could came down to the morgue and identify his daughter. He was surprised and completely distraught. He had not spoken to her for two weeks, but they'd made plans for dinner together on the weekend. He had no idea who the perpetrator might be. He himself had an alibi for the evening her death occurred, which was later corroborated. So then, over the next two weeks we interviewed every employee in the building, all of the residents, and many of Ms. Kelly's friends and work acquaintances. In all we spoke with 323 people."

"Did you interview Michael MacShane?"

"Yes. We interviewed him on May 23rd. His alibi for his whereabouts on the night of the murder was that he had spent the entire night with... " the detective checked her note pad, "a Miss Lily Shannon."

"And did you check his alibi with Miss Shannon?"

"Yes, we did. She vouched that Mr. MacShane had invited her over to his apartment after they'd had several drinks at the Trinity Pub, and that she'd spent the night at his place."

215

Mike leaned back in his chair and smiled. Melissa leaned in to his ear, no doubt telling him to sit up straight and stop grinning.

"So, were you ever able to come up with any leads?" Jack asked.

"No. Unfortunately not. We did our best, but we could find nothing. The investigation was officially labeled a cold case about one year later."

"All right. Now let's move on to June 2019. What caused you to reopen the case?"

"Mr. Kelly came to see me with excerpts from Carrie's diary which he had just discovered in storage. In it, as you have heard, she wrote about her one night stand with Mr. MacShane and her escalating fear of him thereafter. Mr. Kelly suggested that we find Greta Neilson who was mentioned in the diary as someone whom Carrie confided in about her concern.

"We did, and she confirmed everything written in the diary." Reading from her notebook, Martha added, "When I enquired about Carrie's love life, Greta said that 'models are put on pedestals, and that most men are afraid to come on to them for fear they'll break.' "

"Did you speak to Lily Shannon again, to confirm Mike's alibi?"

"We tried to, but she no longer lived in the City. Our investigator found that she had moved to California about a year after this incident. But then a few years later, died as the result of a traffic accident.

"When Lily Shannon lived in New York City, where did she work?

"She worked as a stripper..."

Melissa rose. "Objection your Honor. Ms. Shannon's occupation is not relevant to this case."

"Goes to character of the defendant, Your Honor," Jack interjected.

"Sustained. The jury is instructed to disregard the profession of Ms. Shannon. Continue Mr. Hubbard."

Samantha assumed that the jurors had already heard the important information because Jack moved on.

"When you met with Mr. MacShane to go over the new evidence from Carrie's diary, how did he respond to the part about their hookup?"

"At first, he didn't mention it. But when I told him I had evidence of his sexual relations with Ms. Kelly, he acknowledged it. He said he hadn't spoken of it the first time around because he was afraid he'd get fired, seeing as how Mr. Kelly owns the building."

"And did he seem worried at all, Detective Riddle?"

"No, not at all. In fact he seemed quite relaxed. He even seemed somewhat proud that Ms. Kelly had actually seduced him." Jack turned around to look at Mike who still did not look embarrassed and merely smiled.

"Moving on, did Mr. Kelly come to see you again with even more evidence?"

"Yes. About a week after I told him that I feared the diary would be insufficient to convict Mr. MacShane, he returned with Mrs. Spark. They showed me the video tapes of Rosie's nightmares that have been presented here, and read the transcripts of her memories. Mr. Kelly told me about his meeting with Rosie as well. In addition, they provided me with an affidavit from Dr. Williams, laying out the research done at DOPS and why he believed Rosie was the reincarnation of Carrie."

"And did you decide that information was sufficient to proceed to a trial?" Jack asked.

"Well, not immediately. But after I read the book they gave me, *Return to Life,* I found the research done in this field to to be compelling as, ultimately, did my supervisor, Captain Fox."

"No further questions, Your Honor." Samantha checked the jury and saw that Riddle's evidence had impressed them.

Today Melissa was wearing a black pantsuit, nipped in at the waist, with a turquoise silk shirt and a short pearl necklace. Once again she wore her three inch heels, this time in black. "Detective, in your experience does a rapist or murderer usually leave fingerprints or DNA?"

"Yes, semen DNA if there has been intercourse and fingerprints or DNA resulting from a struggle. Without fingerprints, we must assume that the murderer wore plastic gloves or wiped off hard surfaces upon departure. It is, however, nearly impossible to lift fingerprints from fabric, such as sheets or a pillowcase. Since Ms. Kelly had no DNA under her fingernails, we can also assume that she wasn't able to attack him with her hands. While holding a pillow over her face, he would have had to restrain her hands as well. That could account for the bruises on her arms and wrists."

"Is it unusual for a murderer to seem relaxed during their interrogation?"

"Well, yes and no. The really experienced ones learn to mask their emotions entirely."

"And is Mr. MacShane an experienced murderer to your knowledge?" She turned to face the jury, waiting for the answer she knew would be given.

"No, he is not and he has no criminal record."

"So, Detective Riddle," Melissa said, turning quickly to face the witness and spreading her arms wide, "isn't it a possibility then that someone else committed this crime?"

"Well, I suppose that it is hypothetically possible, but the evidence does seem to point to Mr. MacShane.

"Nevertheless, Detective" Melissa pressed, "in a murder trial where the prosecution must prove the guilt of the defendant beyond a reasonable doubt, is it possible that someone else committed this crime, particularly since Mr. MacShane did have a confirmed alibi?"

"Yes," Detective Riddle replied reluctantly, "I suppose it is possible."

"One more question. Detective Riddle, do you believe in reincarnation?"

"To be honest," Martha said, "I didn't before this case. Now, I'm not so sure."

"No more questions, Your Honor."

The Judge took over. "Let's take a fifteen minute recess. Jurors... please do not go out on the front steps or speak to anyone about the case."

During the recess, Samantha and David walked up to another floor and sat on a bench. "So what do you think?" Samantha said.

"Well, we got all the details of the murder scene, complete with photographs and lab tests, but she told us that without Rosie's testimony, the diary evidence would be circumstantial. So it's all going to come down to whether the jury believes a four year old child. We're just going to have to wait and see."

"God!" Samantha stood up and started to pace, her heels clicking on the parquet floor. "This is so nerve-wracking! I used to love courtroom dramas... this one, not so much."

Chapter 29

*A*t 10:45 a.m., Samantha and David were back in their seats as Jack called Danny O'Hara to the stand. He was a short fellow in his twenties with an impish grin and a buzz-cut. He wore jeans, a tee shirt and a slightly crumpled sports jacket. "Mr. O'Hara, please state your full name, occupation and connection to this trial."

"My name is Daniel William O'Hara, but everyone calls me Danny." His Irish brogue was engaging. "I'm a maintenance man at 980 Fifth Avenue and a friend of Mike MacShane." He smiled at Mike, who returned it with a wink.

"Mr. O'Hara, did Mr. MacShane tell you about his liaison with Carolyn Kelly?"

"His ___?"

"Excuse me. His one-night stand."

"Oh sure!" Danny replied. "He was quite proud of it. Said she was all over him. Usually he has to warm 'em up, but not this time."

"Danny, did Mike ever talk to you about other liaisons he'd had with women who lived in the building?" This was a fishing expedition, but something about Danny's previous response made Jack decide to give it a try.

"Objection, Your Honor, relevance."

"Goes to pattern of behavior, Your Honor, " Jack replied.

"I'll allow it," the Judge replied. "Overruled."

"So, Danny, did Mike ever talk about having hookups with other women at 980 Fifth Avenue?"

"A few, yes, but he'd never tell me who they were. And he didn't give me any details. He'd just say something like 'I got another one!' I think he thought of his sexual conquests as notches on his belt. But he also believed that he was making these women happy. At least, that's what he said."

"So he was sort of the Don Juan of 980?"

"The what?"

A few of the jurors chuckled. "No more questions." Jack smiled and walked back to his seat.

"Ms. Washington?" the Judge said.

"Good morning, Mr. O' Hara. Tell me, would you say that Mike had his pick of women?"

"He sure did." Danny looked a little jealous.

"Did you ever think of Mike as a rapist or a murderer?"

"No. Never."

"No further questions." Melissa returned to her chair.

"Redirect Your Honor?" With a nod from the judge, Jack said, "Did Mike ever tell you any stories about being rejected by a woman?"

Danny thought for a minute. "Let's see. Oh, yeah, there was one woman he was with for several months who left him. He was really pissed about that. But they resolved their differences eventually. Agreed to be 'friends without benefits' I think he said."

"No further questions, Your Honor."

Danny looked a little chagrined as he exited the stand, concerned that he might have said something to cast suspicion on his mate.

Jack's next witness was Joseph Donovan, the doorman at 980 Fifth Avenue, who was dressed in his uniform.

"Mr. Donovan, thank you for taking time off from work to be here today. I'll be quick. We have learned from Cynthia Spark that her daughter, Rosie, recognized you when they went there to enquire about Carolyn Kelly. Do you recall that visit? And if so, did you find anything unusual?"

"Yes, I do recall that visit. In particular because the little girl called me JoJo."

"Does anyone else call you by that name?" Jack said.

"The only person who ever called me JoJo was Carolyn Kelly."

Jack smiled, and said "Thank you, Mr. Donovan. No more questions."

Melissa, stunned by that answer, tried to divert the attention of the jury by quickly beginning her questioning.

"Mr. Donovan. How long have you know Mr. MacShane?"

"Oh, by now, I'd say it's been about six years."

"And, what is your perception of Mr. MacShane?"

"Well he's very friendly, a hard worker, and always willing to help me out at the door when I need to be away for a few minutes. I like him."

"Were you aware of him being sexually involved with any of the women in the building?"

"Absolutely not. Nor was anyone else. Word would have spread and that would have been grounds for firing."

"Danny O'Hara testified that Mr. MacShane implied he'd had hookups with other women in the building."

Joseph chuckled. "Well, I suspect that was just bragging. Mike is a good looking guy who likes to come off as a romantic lover-boy."

"Mr. Donovan. Can you tell us please if Carolyn Kelly had many male friends?"

"Oh, sure. When she was in town she liked to entertain, so there were plenty of dinner parties up in her penthouse. I figured some of them were theme parties based on the country she'd just been to, cause guys would show up in Arab or African-looking clothes. I don't know what they're called, but

I've seen them in the movies. Those parties went on till the wee hours."

Jack was starting to wonder if he should have brought Joseph to the stand in the first place.

Melissa continued on. "Did you notice her going out on dates with men, or coming back with them after evenings out?"

"Yes to that as well. Carrie, sorry, Ms. Kelly, was very popular."

"And when she returned from those evenings out, did her date usually go up to her apartment with her?"

"Well, I'm not on duty after midnight, so I didn't usually see her come home. But doesn't a polite man take his date to her door?"

"Thank you, Mr. Donovan. No further questions."

Chapter 30

At noon, Samantha joined Bonnie and Mercedes in the Judge's chambers, where they had been brought by one of the Judge's aides. Mercedes had packed some peanut butter and jelly sandwiches, chips and cokes so that they could eat lunch there. Samantha hoped their small-talk over lunch would help to alleviate any nervousness Bonnie might have. The video recording equipment had been set up and would be streamed onto the screen in the courtroom.

At 12:45 p.m., when the Judge arrived, he greeted everyone and said "Hello, Rosie. It's nice to see you again. Did you have a nice lunch?"

"Yes, Mr. Judge. Peanut butter and jelly is my favorite." As she spoke, she dusted off any lingering breadcrumbs from her blue corduroy jumper and, at the judge's invitation, took the seat right next to his desk. Samantha pulled over a chair to sit next to her and Mercedes remained on the opposite side of the room. Jack and Melissa had now joined them and were seated on two chairs opposite the Judge's desk.

"All right, Rosie. Mr. Hubbard and Ms. Washington are now going to ask you some questions. All you have to do is answer them truthfully and to the best of your ability. If you don't know the answer to something, just say 'I don't know.' Do you understand?"

Bonnie looked a little jumpy, and just nodded her head.

"Please say yes or no, Rosie."

"Yes, Mr. Judge." Samantha patted her hand.

Only a close-up of Bonnie could be seen on the monitor as the camera man started taping and Judge Brown began. "We are gathered in my chambers to hear the testimony of Rosie Spark in the homicide case of the State vs MacShane. I will administer the oath to this witness. "Rosie, remember when we spoke about the difference between the truth and a lie?"

Rosie nodded and said "Yes, Mr. Judge."

Judge Brown smiled and said, "All right, I am going to ask you a question. Do you, Rosie Spark, promise to tell the whole truth and nothing but the truth?"

"Yes, Mr. Judge." She sat up straight, her little legs sticking out straight from her dress. She looked around nervously, wondering what would happen next. Samantha was nervous too, about exactly the same thing.

The video operator kept his camera trained on Rosie so, although the jury could hear Jack Hubbard, they could only see the child. "Hello Rosie. It's nice to see you again. You look very pretty today."

"Thank you, Mr. Jack."

"Rosie, before we begin, I want to show you a picture of six women. If you can, please point out which one is Carrie."

He passed her a composite of six model headshots. Without a moment's hesitation, Rosie pointed at the fourth face. "This is me!"

"Thank you, Rosie. Let the record show that Rosie selected Carolyn Kelly's photo. I'd like to enter this photo into evidence.

"Now, Rosie, I am going to ask you a number of questions about your dreams. First of all, we have heard that you have a lot of nightmares. Is that true?" Jack's voice was warm and friendly.

"Yes."

"Are they always the same?"

"Yes."

"Can you tell us what they are about?"

Samantha nodded as Bonnie looked up at her. Then taking a deep breath, she began. "In my dream I am sleeping in a big bed. I wake up and there is a man on top of me, and he is pulling up my nightie. Then he touches me… down there." She pointed between her legs. "It hurts. I start screaming and try to get up. He pushes me down. I kick and scream for help, but nobody comes. Then the man holds my arms up." she crossed her hands at the wrists and held them over head. I try to keep screaming but he puts a pillow on my facc. I can't breathe and I can't hit him with my hands. I keep kicking, but I get really tired. Then I die." This entire recitation was done in a matter of fact voice, nothing like the video tapes made directly following one of her nightmares.

After a moment, while Samantha patted her daughter's hand, Jack continued on. "Rosie, in your dreams, are you Rosie?"

"No. I am Carrie. And I am a grown up."

"I see," Jack said, "and who is the man? Do you know?"

"He is Mike, and he is a bad man! He put a pillow on my face and made me dead!"

"Do you mean he put a pillow on Carrie's face? And made her dead?"

"I am Carrie and Carrie is me." Jack paused to give the jury a chance to absorb that statement.

Jack continued on. "OK, Rosie. Let's talk about something else. I hear you like to go to the Central Park Zoo."

"Oh, yes. I love to see the monkeys and the lions and the tigers…"

"I'm sure you do." Jack said with a smile on his face. "That reminds me, didn't you see a Bengal tiger there?"

"Yes, I did. He was a very pretty tiger."

"How did you know that tiger was from India.?"

"Carrie saw one when she was in India. It was in a park just for animals. When she was there she also had her picture taken on top of an elephant."

"Excuse me a moment, Your Honor." Jack quickly walked over to his table and pulled something out of a file. Upon his return, he continued. "I would like to enter this photograph into evidence, which shows Carrie on top of an elephant in India. It appeared in Vogue magazine four years before Rosie was born."

Focusing again on his witness, Jack said, "Now tell me, Rosie, have you ever been in the building across the street from the Zoo?"

She responded quickly. "Yes! I used to live on the top floor before... before I was Rosie. But I have been there too with my Mama. I went to see my Daddy."

"Do you mean Carrie's Daddy?"

"Yes." Bonnie seemed to be getting used to the questioning.

"What did you see in your father's apartment?"

"As soon as the door opened I saw Daddy. I was so happy to see him again! I miss my Daddy a lot. I gave him a big hug."

"Rosie, did you see anything in the apartment that belonged to Carrie?"

"I saw Boofa! I miss him too, even though he didn't save me when I needed him. And Daddy let me play with an elephant toy that Carrie got in India. I made him promise not to tell, and then I showed him how it opened so he could see the surprise inside."

"What was the surprise inside?"

"It was a key. It opens Carrie's book, the one she wrote in every night."

"Thank you, Rosie. I don't have any more questions for you right now. Your Honor, photos of the Standing Buddha statue, the elephant temple toy described by Rosie, as well as the relevant pages from Carrie's diary, were submitted earlier during Mr. Kelly's testimony."

Judge Brown asked Ms. Washington if she had any questions.

Melissa gave Rosie a warm smile. "Hello Rosie. My name is Melissa Washington, and I would like to ask you a few questions too. Is that all right?"

"Yes Miss Miss…?

That's okay," she replied, "Ms. Melissa can be a mouthful. Tell me, Rosie, do you know what Mike's last name is?"

Rosie shook her head. "I don't 'member."

"Did you or Carrie ever see Mike before that terrible night?"

"I don't know. I can't 'member."

"Rosie, I have a photo of six male faces here. Can you tell me which one is the man you see in your nightmares?"

Rosie stared at the photos. "I don't 'zactly 'member what he looked like. Maybe he is this one?" She pointed at a photo of a dark haired, handsome man.

"Are you sure, Rosie?" Melissa asked.

"No," she said quietly. "I'm not. It was dark."

Melissa, with a small smile on her face said, "Let the record show that Rosie did not select Mike MacShane's photo."

Bonnie looked anxiously at her mother. "I can't tell, Mama."

"It's okay honey," Samantha whispered, "Don't worry."

"And finally," Melissa said, "I know you couldn't pick out his photo, but can you just tell us what Mike looked like?"

Rosie screwed up her face in frustration. "I think he was tall, with brown hair?"

Melissa paused while everyone absorbed the fact that Rosie could not identify or describe Carrie's killer. She had a slight smile on her face and was just about to say no further questions, when Rosie jumped up and said "I do 'member that he had a snake on his arm! It was very scary!" She pointed high up on her own right arm. Samantha did a double-take.

For a moment no one spoke, then Melissa said, "Permission to approach, Your Honor." As the camera followed them, the jurors could see the backs of Ms. Washington and Mr. Hubbard as they walked up to the Judge's desk. They could not, however, hear their back and forth whispering.

Judge Brown then said "Mrs. Spark, I am going to ask you a question, and I remind you that you are still under oath. Has Rosie mentioned the existence of a snake tattoo on Mr. MacShane's arm before?"

Samantha stood and said "No, Your Honor. This is the first that I have heard of it. But it's important to know that she has been remembering more and more things lately. That's why I started a journal so that I could keep a record of her memories. This one, however, is new to me."

Judge Brown said "I will allow the child's testimony to stand. If you are finished, Ms. Washington, we can return to the courtroom."

Before leaving the Judge's chambers, Samantha gave Bonnie a big hug. "You were wonderful, honey! You were a very big girl today, and I am so proud of you! I'm sorry that I can't come home with you now, but I will hopefully be there before you go to sleep. Now you run along with Mercedes, and I'll see you soon."

As they reentered the courtroom, Melissa sat down and whispered into Mike's ear. "Do you happen to have a snake tattoo on your right arm?"

This time, Mike leaned into Melissa's ear. "I do not have a tattoo of any kind on my right arm."

Something about the specificity of his response put Melissa on alert. "Your Honor, could we please have a short recess so that I can confer with my client?"

"Jurors, we will now have a fifteen minute break. Please do not stray far, and do not discuss the case with each other. And, need I say, do not go outside."

==

When everyone had resumed their seats, all eyes were on Mike. Jack stood up and said "Your Honor, before we proceed with the Defense's case, I would like to ask the Court to have Mr. MacShane show the jury his right arm."

There was no objection from the Defense, to Samantha's surprise, so the judge approved the request. "Mr. MacShane, please remove your jacket and shirt so that the jury can see your right arm."

Mike stood up, removed his jacket and carefully hung it on his chair. He then slowly took off his tie. As he walked over to face the jury and started to unbutton his shirt, he stared directly at an attractive female juror, perhaps in her 20's. She blushed. He was not wearing an undershirt. As he withdrew his right arm, Melissa said in a tired voice "As you can see, Your Honor, Mr. MacShane does not have the tattoo described by Rosie."

Jack stood up just as Mike was starting to re-button his shirt. "Your Honor, we request that Mr. MacShane also show the jury his left arm."

"Objection," Melissa said, with frustration in her voice. The witness specified the right arm. Are you going to allow the Prosecution to hunt all over his body?"

The Judge said, "Overruled. I will allow Mr. MacShane to uncover his left arm, but that will be it."

Mike stopped buttoning his shirt, and smiled directly at another young woman on the jury, who smiled back. Samantha rolled her eyes. Really? He's coming on to the female jurors?

As Mike removed his shirt again he turned slowly so that everyone could see his great physique: buff shoulders, biceps, pecs... all in peak condition. But they could also see that he had a snake tattoo in blue and green on his left upper arm. The snake was all coiled up with the exception of its head, which was raised and poised to strike. Several jurors gasped.

Jack said "Let the record show that Mr. MacShane has a snake tattoo on his left arm."

Before Mike could put his shirt on again, Jack received permission from the Judge to photograph the tattoo and enter it into evidence. He took it with his cell phone, and sent it to the court reporter to print. Jack had only a few minutes to consider his next move, but he was obviously used to making decisions quickly. "Your Honor. In light of this new evidence about the tattoo, I am requesting a recess until tomorrow. I would prefer not to rest our case until I am more familiar with the subject. I expect Ms. Washington might benefit from the extra time as well."

"Ms. Washington?" The Judge asked. "Would a recess until tomorrow morning be all right with you?"

"Yes, Your Honor. That's fine." This would give her time to figure out how to counter this evidence, which on its face looked quite damming.

The Judge said "At the request of both councils, we are adjourned until tomorrow morning at 9:00 a.m." And his gavel came down.

Chapter 31

*"W*ell that does it," David said to Samantha. "He's nailed!" But much to their surprise, Mike didn't seem at all uncomfortable on his way out of the courtroom. In fact, he even flashed another engaging smile at the jury and gave one of the women a wink. "What's with this guy?" David said. "He's either mental or has a serious ego-inflation problem!"

Before leaving, reporters were typing fast and using their cell phones. They wanted to be sure to get their stories in before the deadline for the evening papers.

"What did you think of Bonnie's testimony?" Samantha asked as they gathered up their belongings to leave. "Was it believable?"

"It sure was. It didn't seem rehearsed or anything. She just honestly told her story. But oh my God, that snake reveal was the kicker. Did you really not know about that?"

"No, I swear I didn't! I don't think the defense has a leg to stand on now, do you?"

"I don't think so, but both lawyers wanted to have some time to figure out how to deal with the tattoo news. Can't wait to hear what they come up with tomorrow.

"Say… now that we have the afternoon off, let's do something fun. Something to take our minds off this trial for at least a few hours. After all, you can't dash off to work looking like Miss Prim!"

"No, that would certainly not be a good idea. And they think I'm on vacation this week anyway. What did you have in mind?"

"Well, I don't know about you, but I'm tired of sitting. Let's go down to Battery Park, wander around until we get hungry, and then have an early dinner."

As David helped her on with her coat, Samantha had to acknowledge how much she was enjoying her time with him. "That sounds like a good idea. I could use a walk as well. But I can't promise that I'll be able to set the trial aside. It's occupying too much of my brain at the moment."

They went out the rear door and were met by Jersey, David's driver. He held the rear door for her and Samantha settled back in one of the black leather bucket seats of the silver Jaguar XJ. Not bad, she thought. I could get used to this.

David had Jersey take them down to the end of Battery Park closest to the Statue of Liberty, then asked him to pick them up there again in two hours.

As they strolled along the Hudson River, David offered Samantha his arm. She took it saying, "You're such a gentleman. Do you know how this custom got started?"

"It was originally meant as a way for the lady to be steadied when walking across uneven ground. Now I think it's just a way for the gentleman to walk closer to the lady." He gave her a warm smile, and she continued to hold on to his arm.

Hmm, she wondered, is that a hint?

After a while they came across a statue called *The Immigrants*, built in 1973. They read the plaque and learned that the sculptor, Luis Sanguino, had depicted the struggle of immigrants in his larger-than-life bronze grouping. It included an Eastern European Jew, a freed African slave, a priest, and a worker. Their poses were meant to emphasize the hardship that immigrants underwent to escape oppression, taking a perilous journey to a new land that offered hope.

"Look at their faces," Samantha said, "you can see weariness, anxiety and relief. You know, this part of town, with

Ellis Island, the Statue of Liberty, and this sculpture, makes me wish we were still a country that welcomed immigrants with open arms. Now we seem to have nearly closed the door on all those 'tired, poor, huddled masses, yearning to be free.' I know that immigration is a huge problem, but surely we can do better. It's what this country was founded on!"

"I agree," said David. "And to think... in another life we might have been, or could yet become, one of those immigrants. Maybe if everyone just thought of it that way, they'd work harder on coming up with a caring solution."

They walked on, stopping to sit on a park bench every now and then to gaze out at the river. On one of their rests, Samantha suddenly remembered something. "Oh, I forgot to tell you what I learned on Saturday!"

"Do tell," David replied with an inquiring smile.

"Well, I was having a manicure at the nail salon and realized that my Thai manicurist was probably Buddhist, so I thought I'd ask her a few questions. I told her I was writing a book about a three-year old child who appeared to be the reincarnation of a model, murdered five years previously.

"Christine, that's the manicurist's name, nodded her head. English is a second language for her, but she tried to answer my questions as best she could. She acknowledged that she had grown up in a Buddhist household, but wasn't sure she believed in reincarnation.

"Even so, I asked her if she knew how it worked. She told me that when you die, you don't get reincarnated right away. If you have anything bad on your record, you have to go to Hell for a while and be punished. Then, after you've been punished enough, you are reborn.

"I told her that I'd never heard that before, and then asked why so few children remember their past lives. Her explanation was that if you give him soup your past life memories are wiped away." David's eyebrows came together.

"Right. I had no idea what she was talking about either. Soup? And I asked, who is him? Since she looked up, I assumed that she meant God. I tried to clarify…you're saying that if you give God soup after you die, your past life memories will be wiped away? When she nodded, I was incredulous to say the least. And practical. So I asked her how someone who had died would be able to make soup!

"At this point, the male manicurist at the adjacent table cut in and said …no, no, no. God gives *you* the soup. You don't give God the soup.

"I tried to be polite and acknowledged that that made much more sense. As if any of it made sense. So there you have it… reincarnation explained by a Buddhist! Good thing we don't have Christine on the witness stand!"

David had a good laugh. "Good grief! What a hoot. It does make you wonder though how these beliefs get started in the first place, before they're passed on from generation to generation. As we discussed the other day, most religions appeal to people because they offer hope. Hope that this life is not the end, that there will be another life to come, be it heaven, hell, or another turn on *this* merry-go-round. There are billions of religious people who may disagree on the specifics, like what heaven or hell looks like, what is or isn't a sin, but all agree there will be another life somewhere. And where that somewhere is depends upon how well you live this life."

"What about you, David?" Samantha asked. "Do you believe in God and a hereafter of some sort?"

"I did when I was young. My parents were Catholic and saw to it that I went to church each Sunday and attended religious education classes on Wednesdays after school. I was even an alter boy. But sometime during my college years, I started to question my beliefs. Philosophy classes might have had something to do with that, or just reaching an age where I questioned everything, including what the church said I could or couldn't do. Up until a few months ago, I'd have said I was an atheist. Now... I'm not so sure."

They both sat quietly for a few minutes, gazing at the river and pondering one of the greatest unsolved mysteries of all time. Deep red horizontal rays stretched across the horizon as the sun dipped below the New Jersey skyline. A chilly breeze started blowing in off the river. As Samantha shivered a bit, David offered her his cashmere neck scarf, which she gratefully accepted. They rose to head back and continued their discussion.

"You know," Samantha began, "I wonder if there might be a scientific, rather than a religious, explanation for reincarnation. Something to do with energy, time and matter. It was probably next on Stephen Hawking's list.

"I too am a fallen-away Catholic," she said, "and after I die I want my ashes to be fertilizer for a newly planted tree. In that way I will become part of the environment and contribute to climate control as well. But as for my consciousness? Who knows where that will go."

After meandering around for a little longer, they met up with Jersey again, and David suggested that they head up to Riverpark, over on East 29th Street. "They've got great food and it's relatively quiet, so we can talk."

"Sure." Samantha replied. "I've never been there but have always wanted to go. It will do us both good to have a nice dry martini!"

As Samantha leaned back in her seat, she thought how enjoyable this was... a handsome man, easy conversation and a bit of flirtation. But aloud she said "This is so nice of you. The past few days have been so action packed that I haven't had time to think about anything but the case. That walk in the park helped clear my mind, at least a little bit. Listening to each witness testify makes me tense, and watching the press make frantic notes raises my blood pressure. What about you? Aren't you nervous at all? You never look like you are."

"More angry than nervous. I keep looking at that smug rat, Mike. He looks like he doesn't have a care in the world. Is that all an act do you think?"

"Nope. I think he just falls into that category of men who are so confident in themselves that they can't acknowledge anyone else might think differently. They sincerely believe that their charm and good looks can get them through life. They've always driven me crazy!"

"So you've met men like that before, have you?"

She turned to look at him and replied, "Oh, yes! Maybe good looking boys are cursed. Everyone fawns over them and they learn to expect being the center of attention. If their parents don't teach them some humility and the need to care for others, they just grow up to be narcissistic men, expecting the world to revolve around them."

"I hope I haven't turned out to be like that," David said, looking at Samantha with an innocent look on his face.

"Oh, no. You seem to be a well grounded, compassionate person... despite your good looks!" And she thought, yup, something's definitely going on.

==

Riverpark was located on the campus of the Alexandria Center for Life Sciences. "How fitting," Samantha said as they pulled up to the entrance on East 29th St. "The study of life. Just what we've been wondering about."

"It's owned by Alexandria Real Estate Equities, and they lease out space to all sorts of renowned academic and medical institutions; top-notch scientific talent, powerful investment capital firms, and a broad and diverse commercial life-science industry. The building offers shared space for labs, offices, even restaurants, in order to motivate collaboration between those groups," David said.

"How did you hear about them?"

"Well, as a real estate developer myself, I'm a huge fan of the concept, the architecture, and certainly the food! Let's go in."

David gave Samantha his hand, while she was getting out of the car, and asked Jersey to return in two hours.

Riverpark was on the second floor and after taking their coats, the Maitre D' brought them to a table in the corner that had a lovely view of the East River. They each placed an order for a martini. Hers: Bombay Sapphire Gin, on the rocks, with three olives. His: Grey Goose vodka, straight up, with a twist. Both: extra dry. When the drinks arrived David raised his glass and toasted "To justice."

"I'll drink to that." Samantha said, and they clinked glasses. "Ah," she said after a sip, "I needed this."

Samantha didn't realize how hungry she was until they were given their menus. She'd only had half a peanut butter sandwich when Mercedes arrived with Bonnie. Now, after that long walk, she was ready to dive into a delicious meal. As they perused the menu, everything looked good. In the end they decided to share a dozen oysters on the half shell, and an order of white asparagus panna cotta followed by roasted diver scallops for her and steamed black bass for him. They also ordered a few sides; sugar snap peas and roasted radishes in anchovy butter, also to share. Each dish was prepared in a unique manner that Samantha had never come across before; most with herbs grown in Riverpark's own garden. She tried to think of the last time she'd been out to such a fine restaurant. Not in a long time. Mexican and Chinese takeout were more like it.

"Do you have a preference in wine?" David asked, while reading the wine menu.

"Something dry and white. Beyond that, you pick," Samantha said. They followed the sommelier's recommendation and ordered a delightful bottle of Viognier. For the next hour they discussed the case, reviewing each person's testimony in detail. So far, they agreed, it was looking good.

"I wonder if the defense will call any scientists to refute reincarnation."

"Probably," David guessed, "but even if they do, the jury has already heard an awful lot of facts that are difficult to overlook, no matter how they came to light. I got a little nervous when Bonnie couldn't identify Mike's photo, but her recollection of the snake tattoo was like manna from Heaven!"

"You know," David said, as he reached for a slice of French bread, warm from the oven. "I was thinking about that arm thing. From Bonnie's perspective, or Carrie's if you will, Mike was on top of her and the tattoo was on his left arm, so that would have been on her right! It all makes sense now, and it definitely makes our case stronger." He dipped his bread in a small dish of olive oil, then tried to get it to his mouth without dripping.

"I know how nervous you were about Bonnie testifying. How do you think she's holding up?"

"Actually, she seems to be fine. Oh, she got a little fidgety today, but I really think she wanted to do this. When I told her we would have made-up names during the trial, she got really excited. Now it's going to be hard to get her to give up 'Rosie' and return to Bonnie. She also wanted to have a wig like mine. Kids have an uncanny ability to take things in their stride."

Over dinner, David tried to learn more about Samantha. Perhaps due to the martini, the wine, and feeling so relaxed

Susan Burke

with him, she found herself revealing more than she ordinarily would; her years growing up in Westchester County with mostly absent parents, who both worked in the City; her hard work at Cornell, which paid off with her current job as a Senior Analyst at Charles Schwab; and even the story of how she'd met Hank and why their marriage had gone off the rails for four years. The Hank story went on for longer than she had intended.

"You and Hank have really been through a difficult time," David responded. "I hadn't realized.   How is your relationship working out now? I mean, now that he's back in the picture. He seems like a really nice guy."

Samantha took another sip of wine, thought of Hank's phone call and opted not to tell David about it. "Well, its still too early to tell. I've really not had the chance to spend too much time with him since this whole thing began. But we're trying, and I guess that's the important part. I really do want Bonnie to get to know her father... her real father," she said softly. David nodded his head and said "Of course."

Talking about Hank seemed to be making both of them uncomfortable. So she switched the topic. "Now that we've had time to absorb all this reincarnation stuff, what do you think? Do you believe that our consciousness can be reborn? And if so does everyone get reborn? Why have so few cases, relatively speaking, been discovered?"

Appreciating the shift in conversation, David replied "Well, it's pretty hard not to believe, don't you think? But I have the same questions." He took a bite of fish. "If Carrie's consciousness lived on after her death, where was it for the two years before Bonnie was born?   They say that Bonnie will probably forget all about this very soon, if we're lucky. But will Carrie's consciousness still be within her? And if not... where will it go? One question just seems to lead to another."

Samantha offered one hypothesis. "I have a thought. Hear me out. Maybe our consciousnesses, or souls if you will, live forever... moving from one living host to another. But they only rise to the surface of the host's perception when the previous personality died a violent death. I kind of like that idea because it seems to play into the idea of evolution. If our consciousness lives forever and moves around, it can inform each new body of what it has learned so far, and then continue to grow again. A continually expanding consciousness, hopefully improving the human race. What do you think of that idea?"

"I like it," David said. "I just wish that, after all this time, we might have evolved more than we have. Judging by what's going on today, not just in our country, but all over the world, we seem to be going backwards. Hate crimes are rising at an alarming rate, racism is increasing, and there's an ever broadening gap between the haves and the have-nots."

"Well, maybe evolution works like a pendulum." Samantha said. "One step forward, two steps back? And in our own measly little lifetime, the change is not apparent."

"I can see that you're more of an optimist than I am," David replied. Their conversation continued on through dinner, ranging from one controversial subject to another, but they found they were nearly always on the same side.

"Dessert?" The waiter enquired, as he cleared their totally clean plates.

"Oh no." Samantha said. "This was delicious, but I don't think I could possibly eat another bite."

"Oh let's just look at the menu. Come on, you only live once." David grinned and said "Guess that's the wrong line for the moment. How about, live it up!"

Giving in to temptation, they checked out the menu and decided to share something called Cereal & Milk, a chocolate ganache cake with caramelized rice puffs and vanilla malt. "It

241

just sounds too intriguing to pass up," Samantha said and David agreed. By the time they finished their dessert and after-dinner coffee, they had spent three hours together, without tiring of each other's company in the least.

In the car, David had a suggestion. "Listen, I think Jersey should let me off at 65th and York and then drive you home. It's not a long walk over to Fifth, and I could use the fresh air."

"Oh no, really. I can take the train. I'm not sure when the next one is, but it's still early." Samantha could hear a slight slur in her voice, but she didn't want David to think she wasn't capable of managing her trip home.

"Nope. I've made up my mind. You're going with Jersey. Then I won't have to worry about whether you'll fall asleep on the train and end up in Connecticut somewhere!"

At 65th Street, David opened the car door, then turned back and gave Samantha a soft kiss on the cheek. "Thank you. This has been a lovely evening. One that I will long remember." Then he stepped out, closed the door and strode off. On the trip home, Samantha gazed out at the twinkling lights of the Queensboro Bridge, stretching out over the East River. After a few minutes, she rested her head on the seat -back and closed her eyes. As she thought about David, she wondered whether the two of them… but she nodded off before that thought could go any further.

Chapter 32

*A*s Samantha started to open her eyes the next morning, she realized two things: Bonnie had not dreamt of Carolyn Kelly's death, but *she* had dreamt of David Kelly. In her dream he was stroking her hair and whispering in her ear, "It's all right, everything is going to be all right." The same words she used when Bonnie was having a nightmare. What was that all about, she wondered, even though she had a pretty good idea. But then she caught a glimpse of the clock. Damn! She needed to get a move-on to catch the 7:05 train.

In the kitchen she gave Bonnie a big hug and told her how proud she was of her. "You were wonderful yesterday! You did such a good job!"

"Really, Mama? But I didn't 'member what Mike looked like."

"I know, but you remembered enough. That snake drawing for instance. In the courtroom, after you left, Mike had to show his arm to the jury, and they all saw it. Thanks to you, we have a strong chance of winning!"

"Oh, goodie!" Bonnie was smiling from ear to ear, as she hopped up and ran around the kitchen.

When she returned to her seat, Samantha said, "Today I'm going back to the courthouse, and it's going to be an important day. The Defense will talk to people who know Mike really well, and then each side will make their closing arguments. That's when they sum up everything that has been said over the past few days. Then the jury will go to a room all by themselves and talk about everything they heard. If they decide that Mike is really bad, he will be punished.   If they have trouble making up their minds though, it may be a late night." As she spoke, she downed a glass of juice, buttered some toast and drank her coffee standing up.

"Mercedes, thanks so much for staying here last night. I'll give you a call if I can't get home tonight." Where did that idea come from, she wondered.   And where do I think I'm going to stay? Rather than probe her unconscious any more, she gave Bonnie a kiss on the head and waved goodbye.

==

Without her wig, wearing her own clothes and dark glasses, Samantha merged with the others walking up the courthouse steps. There were even more people here today, if that was possible. Many held placards saying things like "Jesus did not believe in Reincarnation," "Heaven Yes. Reincarnation No." She hoped the jury hasn't been exposed to all that, but she knew they probably had. As she hurried into the courtroom at 8:55, she realized nearly everyone who had been involved with the trial was there: Martha Riddle was sitting next to an older man, perhaps her boss, Captain Fox; Greta Neilson, Dr. Karadamand and Dr. Williams, a woman who might be Mitch's mother, and someone who looked familiar but she couldn't quite place. Oh, yes, she thought, Martin Radcliffe, the District Attorney. Apparently everyone thinks we'll wrap this up today and wants to be here for the verdict. She spied David, who waved and pointed to the seat next to him which he'd saved for her. It's all right, she told herself, everything is going to be all right.

==

After the Judge opened the session, he asked Jack Hubbard if he had any more witnesses for the prosecution.

Yesterday, when Jack had asked for a recess, he was feeling pretty good about the snake tattoo but knew that he needed to consider what the Defense would come up with before proceeding. It didn't take him long to figure out what he would do, were he in Melissa's shoes; claim that the tattoo was put on after Carrie was killed. Sometime between 2013 and 2019. So he'd sent his assistant out to find a subject expert, one who could refute that claim.

"Yes, Your Honor. The prosecution calls Hector Hidalio to the stand."

Melissa was quick to rise. "Objection, Your Honor. There is no one by that name on the witness list."

"That is correct, Your Honor. Since we learned new evidence yesterday, the Prosecution has taken the liberty to do some quick hunting for a subject expert to educate us all."

"And about which subject are we to be educated?" Judge Brown asked.

"Tattoos, your Honor." There was an audible buzz in the courtroom.

The Judge looked at Melissa, who didn't object, so they proceeded. Mr. Hidalio was quite an impressive looking man. He had the height and weight of a linebacker, and was about 60 years old. His dark hair had receded so far back it was almost off the map, but Mr. Hidalio made up for that loss with an impressive handlebar mustache. He was dressed in a black T-shirt, black jeans and black sneakers drawing everyone's attention to his trade. Both arms were completely covered in colorful tattoos, and one might assume that there were plenty more to be found elsewhere on his body. Although Mr. Hidalgo needed no additional ornamentation, he also sported one silver pierced earring.

"Mr. Hidalio, thank you for coming here today on such short notice. My name is Jack Hubbard, and I am the Prosecuting Attorney in this case. Please give us your full name, your occupation, and how long you have been working in your field."

"My name is Hector Miguel Hidalio. I own a tattoo parlor in Greenwich Village and have been crafting tattoos for twenty years."

"That's a long time. I'm guessing your business is quite successful?"

"Absolutely. I've been written up in The Village Voice and have lots of repeat customers."

"Excellent. With your many years of experience, I'm hoping that you can help us with something. Can you tell, Mr. Hidalio, how old a tattoo is by looking at it?"

"Not precisely, but there are some tell-tale signs of age in a tattoo, such as fading."

"And when would you expect to see signs of fading?"

"I'd say after ten years, give or take a few, particularly if an inferior ink was used, or if the tattoo was done in bright colors."

Pulling the photograph of Mike's tattoo out of his file, Jack said, "Mr. Hidalio, what can you tell us about this tattoo?" Simultaneously the photo was projected onto the large screen.

Even though he had seen it already, Mr. Hidalio took his time and peered closely at the photograph.

"The snake tattoo is very popular because it represents all the traits of the snake: secretive, sneaky and seductive. It has both positive and negative meanings. Not only patience, healing and rebirth, but also evil, death, darkness and power. So no matter what type of person you are.... the snake is a good choice."

"And can you tell us how long ago this tattoo was crafted?" asked Jack.

"Well, not exactly. But if I had to guess, I would say at least ten years ago, based on the blurring of the inks around the edges. Bright colors were used originally, but you can see that they have faded, perhaps from being out in the sun."

"Mr. Hidalio, please take a moment before you answer this question. Might this tattoo have been acquired less than six years ago?"

He took another look at the photo. "No. In my professional opinion... no. In fact, if you like, I can show you the difference between a four-year old tattoo and one that is about ten."

"By all means," replied Jack.

When Mr. Hidalio started to show everyone a cheetah tattoo on his right arm, members of the jury were craning to see, so Jack suggested that he stand in front of them.

Mr. Hidalio walked over and was truly in his element as he explained that the cheetah tattoo had been put on about three or four years ago. "As you can see," Mr Hidalio said, automatically flexing his muscles, "the jungle has a variety of green inks, clearly differentiating the leaves on the trees. You can actually see the strands of the cheetah's golden fur, and the black dots are bold... no bleeding. Even the whites of the cat's eyes are visible."

Jack noticed that Ricky, the musician on the jury, looked like he might be in the market for a cheetah tattoo.

"Is it okay if I pull my T-shirt up just a bit, to show the jury an older tattoo on my back?"

Jack turned to the Judge. "Your Honor?"

Judge Brown sighed, and said "Oh, sure. Why not?"

Mr. Hidalio turned around so that his back was facing the jury, and lifted up his t-shirt. Lo and behold, there was a snake, very similar to the one that Mike had.

"I really wanted you to see this one because I think you'll be able to see the aging. Notice that the greens in the snake are no longer bright. And the yellow flecks on his skin seem to be fading into the green. Even though his position is different from the photograph you showed me, the fading and blurring are the same."

Jack pretended to be impressed though, of course, he'd already learned the science of tattoo fading. "So, Mr. Hidalio, how old is this tattoo?"

Still holding up his t-shirt for the jury, Mr. Hidalio replied, "about ten years, give or take."

"Thank you Mr. Hidalio. Your testimony has been very helpful. No further questions."

While Mr. Hidalio was being questioned and was exhibiting his tattoos for the jury, Melissa considered her options. Mike had told her that he'd gotten his tattoo about five years ago. Even if he'd been telling the truth, that statement would now be a tough sell. Calling Danny to the stand, to vouch that he got it then, seemed risky as well. She couldn't ask him to lie, and somehow she doubted that his answer would agree with Mike's. She decided she'd just have to wing it.

"Mr. Hidalio, my name is Melissa Washington, and I am the Defense Attorney. I just have two questions. "Is there anyway at all that this tattoo could have been inked about five years ago?"

"Not unless he went to the worst tattoo parlor in the city and they used really crummy inks. But the snake design is very intricate, so I have a hard time believing that's what happened."

"But, nevertheless sir, it is possible, correct?"

"Well, as they say, anything is possible."

"And secondly, how popular is the snake tattoo?

"Very popular. Even women like to tattoo cute little snakes on the back of their necks, or on their ankles. But if I had to wager a guess, I'd say that nearly fifty percent of men choose the snake as their first tattoo. They think it's macho and sexy, if you know what I mean."

"Thank you," said Melissa. "No further questions, Your Honor."

Jack rose and said, "I have no further questions either, Your Honor. The Prosecution rests." As Melissa returned to her seat, she told herself she'd done her best. At least she'd planted a seed of doubt.

Chapter 33

*I*t was now Melissa's turn to offer up the case for the Defense, beginning with character witnesses to talk about what a great guy Mike was. First up was Pearl MacShane, Mike's mother.

As Pearl took the stand, she seemed gray... in every possible way. She was a woman totally lacking in color, which is hard to find. Her skin, her hair, her clothes, all various shades of gray. She carried a small gray bag and took out a tissue as soon as she had taken the oath.

"Mrs. MacShane, thank you for being here today. I know how upsetting this must be for you. To begin, I'd like you to tell us a little about Mike, what he was like as a child, where he went to school, when he moved out, and how close you two are today."

"Well, Mikey was born on February 14th, 1990... my Valentine's Day gift. He was a beautiful child, with curly dark hair, a twinklin' smile and a very engagin' manner. In fact he's still that way, twenty-nine years later. Everyone who knows him loves him. I just can't believe that he's bein' accused of murder. Mikey wouldn't hurt a fly."

"Is Mike an only child, Ms. MacShane?"

"No. His brother, Eric, is five years younger than him, and they were inseparable. Always kiddin' around, cuttin' classes at Christopher Columbus High School in the Bronx. Neither one of them got very good grades, but I blame myself really. I'm a nurse and worked lots of extra shifts to bring in some more income. My husband is in the construction business, but somehow, between the two of us, there never seemed to be enough money to go around. So I think that Mikey, and Eric too, got the short end of the stick."

Samantha thought Pearl's Irish accent was endearing and wondered if 'Mikey' had one as well.

"What did Mike do after high school? Did he go to college?"

Pearl looked a little embarrassed. "He really had no interest in goin' to college. So he started lookin' for work to help us out financially in runnin' the house. As I said, he's a beautiful boy, inside and out. I'm always tellin' him that. I hope I haven't given him a swelled head, but that's just what I think."

Oh, no. Samantha thought. How could anyone think that Mike had a swelled head.

"Once Mike started working in the City as a maintenance man, did you two keep in touch often?"

"Well, not as much as when he was livin' at home, of course. But he still comes home for dinner about once a month, and calls every week."

"Does he have any girlfriends, Mrs. MacShane?"

"He sure does. I'd have to say that he's never without a girlfriend. In fact it's hard keepin' up with 'em."

Melissa smiled. "Mrs. MacShane, did Mike ever tell you about a woman named Carolyn Kelly?"

"No, he did not. I'm guessin' that she didn't mean that much to him, since he told us about so many other women in his life."

"Thank you, Mrs. MacShane. No further questions."

Jack stood up and buttoned his jacket. "Hello, Mrs. MacShane, my name is Jack Hubbard, the Prosecuting Attorney. I just have a few questions for you. If Mike has such an easy time with women and has so many girlfriends, why do you think he's never gotten married?"

"Well, to tell you the truth, I think he likes variety. He's just not ready to settle down. And he's still young yet, isn't he?"

"Has he ever complained about any of his girlfriends to you?" Jack asked.

"Oh sure, from time to time. Sometimes he'd fall head over heals for a lass, and then she'd drop him. That always drove him crazy." She chuckled a bit. "I don't think he really knows how women work. He just doesn't understand that a woman has a right to change her mind."

Samantha admired how Jack managed to get quiet Pearl to offer up that some women, the ones like Carrie who had dropped him, drove him crazy.

"One last question, Mrs. MacShane. Did Mike ever show you the snake tattoo on his arm?"

"No, he did not. Probably because he knew I wouldn't approve. Tattoos not only defile your body, they are forever. I'm sure God doesn't approve of them either."

"Thank you Mrs. MacShane. No further questions."

==

The next Defense witness was Veronica Shadwell, one of the women who had dropped Mike. She spoke very highly of him, however, saying how well he'd treated her, what a gentleman he was, and how close they became over their six-month relationship. But during cross, when Jack asked why they split up, she said that she'd felt a bit smothered by him and needed some space.

"And how did Mike take that request for more space?" Jack asked.

"Not too well, to be honest. He kept trying to woo me back. Sort of couldn't take no for an answer." Veronica than amended that remark, saying, "It was very flattering actually, but eventually I had to tell him that I no longer loved him and just wanted to be friends, friends without benefits," and she smiled.

"And did he agree to that?" Jack smiled too.

"Not at first, but eventually he came around. After he'd found someone else I expect."

"No further questions. Thank you Ms. Shadwell." And Jack sat down.

Samantha was starting to get itchy. So he loves lots of women and just can't accept it if they don't love him back. God, does it all boil down to that? One handsome, charismatic guy who can't accept that a woman would turn him down?

Since it was now 10:15, the Judge announced a fifteen minute break.

==

Next up was Burt Robinson, Mike's boss; a heavy-set man in his sixties, whose jacket was held barely closed by one button. He testified that Mike was a very responsible employee, and that no one ever complained about him. He also said that he was never out sick.

During his cross examination, Jack said "Mr. Robinson, you mentioned that Mike is never out sick. Really, never?"

"Well, not that I can remember."

"But wasn't Mike out sick on May 22nd, the day after Carolyn Kelly's murder?"

Mr. Robinson took a file out of his bag and checked Mike's attendance record. "Well, that's true. He was out that day, but I don't know why. Sorry, I hadn't even realized that."

After Melissa called a few more character witnesses, she surprised everyone by calling Michael MacShane to the stand.

"What?" Samantha whispered. "Even after we saw that snake tattoo on his arm, he's going to testify? I thought an attorney couldn't call a witness to testify if they knew he was going to lie."

David looked stumped too. He crossed one leg over the other, leaned forward and rested his chin on his hand. "You're right. They can't. So does she really think he's innocent? What does she know that we don't? Regardless, I'm glad we're going to hear from that snake. No pun intended."

Jack was just as surprised and picked up his pen.

"Mr. MacShane. I expect that everyone in the room knows who you are by now, but please state your name, your occupation, and why you are here today, for the record."

Mike smiled at her and at the jury as well. "My name is Michael MacShane, but you can call me Mike. I'm a maintenance man at 980 Fifth Avenue and have worked there for six years. Apparently I am here today because a four-year old kid thinks I killed Carolyn Kelly before the kid was born."

Melissa nodded her head as if to say "Yes, can you believe that?" "Mr. MacShane, Mike, I am not going to ask you to tell us all about your life since we have already heard testimony from your mother and a number of your friends, as well as your boss at work. Do you, however, want to correct or change anything we heard?"

Mike sat back, as if he was giving this some thought, and then said, "Nope. They were pretty much on target. I'm just a nice guy who happens to love women, and they usually love me back. What more can I say?"

Melissa took a stroll around the area between the witness stand and the jury box. "All right, on that front, please tell us about your relationship with Carolyn Kelly. You heard David Kelly, Greta Nielson and Detective Riddle provide testimony about the entries Carrie made in her diary regarding that one night stand, and what followed over the next several months. But I'd like you to tell us what happened, in your words, rather than hers."

Mike sat back and said "I'd be happy to. As you heard, Carrie wanted help hangin' a heavy paintin', after which she offered me a drink. Not many of the residents in that buildin' offer the maintenance man a drink, but I was happy to oblige. At her invitation, I sat down on the sofa where she joined me with our drinks. Pretty soon I discovered that wasn't all she had to offer. Now I don't want to sound crude or anythin', but that woman was hot to trot! Within about fifteen minutes of warm-up chit-chat, she was all over me. She had her hands in my hair and started unbuttonin' my shirt while kissin' me as though I was her long-lost husband, home from the war."

"I see," Melissa said. "then what happened?" The jury was all ears.

"Well, at first I tried to pull back. I knew that her father owned the buildin' and I was afraid that if I played along it could backfire on me, big time. But it's awfully hard to turn down one of the most beautiful women in the world, and as I said... I love women. I love to make 'em happy. And, if I do say so myself, I made that woman very happy!"

"How long would you say you were making her happy?"

"Oh, at least an hour. I think she was makin' up for lost time, havin' been out of the country for a few months. Eventually, though I had to pull away. After all, I was supposed to be workin'. How long can it take to hang a paintin'?" He chuckled at this memory.

Samantha could tell that David was steaming. She reached out and put a hand on his knee, as if to prevent him from jumping up and tearing Mike apart from limb to limb.

Melissa thought, so far, so good. "Now, Mike, would you please tell us what happened from then on, whenever you saw Carrie in the halls or on the elevator."

"Well, I was nice as could be. Did I want to see her again? Of course I did. But she made it clear that there would not be a repeat performance. She was polite, but I could tell that she was a little embarrassed to have seduced a maintenance man. But hey, such is life. There are lots of other women out there, ready and waitin'. "

"In her diary, Carrie wrote that you kept coming on to her and didn't seem to want to take no for an answer."

Mike gave her a knowing grin. "Well, Ms. Washington, I don't know if women are always entirely truthful in their diaries. Perhaps she was exaggeratin' just a bit? Or maybe she just wasn't used to my kind of flirtin'."

"All right, Mike. I am going to ask you a question, and I want to remind you that you are under oath. Did you go to Carolyn Kelly's apartment on the night of May 21st, 2013 with the intent of having sexual relations with her?"

"No m'am. I did not."

"And did you, on that night, murder her in her bed?"

"No m'am. I absolutely did not, so help me God." As he said this, Mike made a quick sign of the cross. He was no longer smiling, but looking intently at Melissa.

"Thank you, Mike. Now before we conclude, I have to ask you about your snake tattoo. Could you tell me, please, when you got that tattoo?"

The knowing smile had returned. "Five years ago. I remember it well since I was three sheets to the wind that night. As I was staggerin' home, I passed this tattoo parlor. My eye caught a picture of this snake, the one you saw, and I just had to have it! I get a little impulsive after too many beers. So I went in and had them do it right then and there! The women love it. You know the snake is a sign of masculinity."

"If you were inebriated that night, how do you know it was five years ago?"

"Cause the next night was my birthday, when I turned 24. I was lookin' forward to showin' it off, but there was so much bruisin' that I had to keep it covered up. Pissed me off!"

Melissa decided to quit while she was ahead and before Mike could start talking about his sex life again. "Thank you Mike, I think that about covers it. The Defense rests.

Jack stood up and approached the stand. "Mr. MacShane, you've said that you were unable to show your friends the tattoo on your birthday due to bruising. Do you remember who was there to celebrate your birthday with you?"

Mike narrowed his eyes, considering how to reply. "No one. My arm was so uncomfortable that I just stayed in."

Jack looked down at his notes. "One other question. Have you had sexual relations with any other female residents at 908 Fifth Avenue?"

Mike sighed. "A few, yes. But at their signal, not mine! The life of a maintenance man can be quite unpredictable." He smiled. "It's one of the reasons I like it. You just never know."

"No further questions, Your Honor."

"Ladies and gentlemen, after a quick ten minute break, we will will hear closing arguments.

==

Out in the hall, David and Samantha discussed the morning. "I'm not feeling quite as good as I did last night." Samantha said. "I loved the tattoo guy, and he seemed very believable to me. But Melissa got him to admit that the tattoo could possibly be just five years old, and that tons of men are walking around with snakes on their arms!"

"Yeah, she did," said David. "but I still think his professional opinion outweighed the concession she wormed out of him. Did you believe Mike? That's the big question. "

Samantha took a swig of her Coke. "That's a hard one. My heart tells me he's lying, but he's such a charming liar that the jury might believe him."

"My thoughts exactly."

Chapter 34

*A*fter the break, Judge Brown took his seat and explained what the rest of the day would include.

"Now we are going to hear the closing statements from the Prosecution and the Defense. After that I will be giving instructions for you to follow in the jury deliberation room, as you consider the facts you have heard. All the exhibits are in there for you to reference. If you need to have any of the testimony read back, just send me a note via the bailiff. You will then be brought back to the courtroom to hear it. We have also arranged for you to have lunch in the jury room since you will not be able to go out. If you cannot reach consensus today, we will resume tomorrow, same time, same place. All right, Mr. Hubbard, the floor is yours."

Jack rose, straightened his tie and buttoned his jacket.

"Ladies and gentlemen. Carl Sagan, the eminent scientist, once asked the Dalai Lama, 'What would you do if I could prove that reincarnation does not exist?' The Dalai Lama replied 'I would tell the Buddhists all over the world to stop believing in it. But tell me, how are you going to prove it doesn't exist?' He went on to say, 'What science finds to be nonexistent, we should all accept as nonexistent, but what science merely does not find, is a different matter.'

"As we discussed a few days ago, there is no way to prove or disprove our religious beliefs. So therefore, I am not going to ask you to believe in Buddhism or Hinduism or any of the many other religions that subscribe to reincarnation. But I am going to ask you to consider the facts you have learned."

Jack then proceeded to remind the jury of all the testimony they had heard: from Martha Riddle's description of Carolyn Kelly's death, to Carrie's own words from her diary about her fear of Mike MacShane, to each astounding revelation made by Rosie, culminating in her description of the snake tattoo.

"All of these facts keep adding up until we are unable to look away. We may not be able to explain them, but that does not mean they aren't true.

"Two people have attempted to explain them: Dr. Williams and Dr. Karadamand. They believe that Carrie's consciousness was reincarnated in Rosie, two years after she was murdered. Dr. Williams has spoken of all the research done by UVA's Division of Perceptual Studies. Although we may not understand reincarnation, he and his organization have seen similar signs thousands of times over. Ask yourselves this... do you understand how to do heart surgery? No. Do you know how to fly an airplane. Probably not. But other people, who have become experts in those fields, do and we put our trust in them. Several jurors were making notes, but most were just listening intently.

"Albert Einstein, whom we all respect as a world-renowned physicist, proved... let me say that again.... proved that our concept of a linear past, present and future is all an illusion. It has to do with his theory on space and time and is certainly far too complicated for me to understand, much less explain. I mention it only to demonstrate that in the world of science there are many proven ideas that are also too difficult for most of us to conceptualize or believe.

"So I'd like to suggest that the idea of reincarnation, which has not *yet* been proven by scientists, is the same. It might exist, but we are unable to explain it. Perhaps one of the stumbling blocks we have is that it is associated with particular religions. So, put the religious context aside and just consider the concept of reincarnation as we have come to understand it, a consciousness being born again. It would seem to be the only explanation for how a child can know and articulate something only known to another human being who is no longer alive. For our purposes here today, we are assuming that it is due to a process called 'reincarnation.' Even if you don't understand it, the rebirth of a consciousness could still be true, just as it is true that a linear past, present and future can all coexist at the same time.

"So, as I see it, you have two choices. You can decide this case with or without Rosie's input. Either way, you cannot escape the fact that Mike MacShane is the man who couldn't allow a woman to walk away from him, who couldn't believe her when she said no, and who was convinced that his sexual attraction could not be denied. Using his passkey to Carrie's apartment, he snuck in the servants entrance on the night of May 21st 'to make her happy,' as he would say. But she was not happy to be awakened by him. As Rosie told us, she fought him off as best she could, even after he put a pillow over her face. But, in the end, she was no match for his strength. No, Michael MacShane did not make Carrie happy. He made her… dead."

As Melissa stood up to make her closing statement, Samantha wondered whether she could counter what sounded like a very persuasive argument.

"Ladies and gentlemen. We've heard lots of conjectures strung together over the past few days. Such as, Carolyn Kelly slept with Mike MacShane one night, so he must be the guy who killed her. Conjecture. Mike thought she was very beautiful and wanted to have sex with her again, but since she said no… he killed her. Conjecture. Mike MacShane has a snake tattoo on his arm, so no one else could have killed her. Conjecture.

"We do know that when David Kelly showed the diary to Martha Riddle at NYPD, she told him that it was insufficient proof of Mike MacShane's guilt.   After all, none of his fingerprints or DNA was left at the scene, and he had an alibi when they first questioned him six years ago. We can imagine that Mr. Kelly was very disappointed. Now what if, and this is just a what if, David and Cynthia Spark knew each other. They talked over this latest disappointment and perhaps fantasized about how convenient it would be if Carrie could come back to life and point her finger at Mike. Then one idea led to another and they concocted this reincarnation story. All they needed was a creative, playful little girl to act the part, and precocious little Rosie fit the bill. To her, it all became a game. All she had to do was tell people about this one nightmare. The rest could be left to Cynthia and David.

"As Dr. Williams himself has said, some of the cases they investigate turn out to be frauds. And perhaps, just perhaps, this is one.

"You've been told to just look at the facts. Well, a fact is only a fact if it is believable beyond a reasonable doubt. Now I don't really expect you to accept my little hypothesis, but it does go to show that a creative story can become believable if it contains a few indisputable truths. So, for example, once we start down the road of believing what Carrie wrote in her diary, we just naturally want to take the next step of convicting that man she knew named Mike.

We don't know why Rosie kept having that nightmare, but if it really is about Carolyn Kelly and a man named Mike, then it must be *this* Mike. Right? Wrong! This is what we call circumstantial evidence. It is not undisputed truth.

If the average man or woman can't reasonably believe that Michael MacShane killed Carolyn Kelly, then you can not render a guilty verdict. If the average man or woman can not reasonably believe that Carrie was reborn in Rosie's body, than you cannot assume it is true.

"From where I stand, this case is built on a tower of 'what ifs.' What if there was only one man Carrie knew by the name of Mike? What if Rosie has Carolyn Kelly's consciousness mysteriously speaking out from within her? What if, what if, what if? It is not my job to prove the innocence of Michael MacShane. It is the Prosecution's job to prove his guilt. And that guilt cannot be based on a number of hypothetical ifs." She closed her file and returned to her seat.

Jack stood up. "Rebuttal, your Honor?"

The Judge nodded his head and Jack began. "I agree that if you decide Mike MacShane is guilty then it must be beyond a reasonable doubt. But you notice that we do not say beyond all doubt. And why don't we say that? Because very little in life is provable beyond all doubt. Another way of saying reasonable doubt is to say I just can't think of how else this could have happened. I don't know about you, but Ms. Washington's hypothetical story seems totally implausible to me, particularly since Rosie would have had to be taught about a lot more than just the nightmare. Ask yourselves this. Why would Cynthia make up a story like this, and not only lie on the stand herself, but have her four-year old daughter lie as well? As she herself told us, she didn't want to come to court. She did it only to relieve her daughter of those terrifying nightmares by having Mike punished for being, as Rosie described him, 'a bad man.'

"Finally, did Cynthia Spark, David Kelly, Martha Riddle or anyone else know about the snake tattoo? No, only Rosie knew about it, and that is because Carolyn Kelly saw it. The snake tattoo, and its existence on Michael MacShane, is the glue that holds our case together.

"You will have to decide whether to believe the murder suspect when he says that it was not put on until after Carrie's death, or Mr. Hidalio, who has been in the tattoo business for over twenty years and who has absolutely no reason to lie. He says it is at least ten years old, and therefore would have been on Mike's arm as he lay on top of Carolyn Kelly, trying to have sex with her. In fact it could have been the very last thing she saw before a pillow snuffed out her life. Perhaps that is why Rosie recalls it now. And the fact that she does, supports our belief in everything else she told us. If you believe her about the tattoo, then everything else falls into place… the key, the diary, the one-night stand, the constant innuendo from Mike, and then finally Carrie's death. When you talk about this case in your deliberations, just put one foot in front of the other, and the road will lead to Mr. MacShane's conviction… beyond a reasonable doubt."

As Jack took his seat, Judge Brown took over to give the jury their instructions.

Samantha wondered how many of the jurors had already made up their minds. She suspected very few, and that their deliberations would take some time.

Judge Brown began the speech he made at every criminal trial. "You must decide whether the State has proved, beyond a reasonable doubt, the specific facts necessary to find Michael MacShane guilty of one or more of the crimes charged in his indictment. I will review the descriptions of the charges at the end of my statement.

"You must make your decision only on the evidence presented here during the trial; and you must not be swayed by bias or favor toward the defendant or the State.

"The indictment against this defendant is not evidence of guilt. The law presumes that every defendant is innocent. The defendant did not have to prove his innocence or produce any evidence at all.

"The State must prove guilt beyond a reasonable doubt, and if it fails to do so, you must find the defendant not guilty. A reasonable doubt is a real doubt, based upon your reason and common sense. Proof beyond a reasonable doubt is proof that leaves you with an abiding conviction that the charge is true. If you are convinced that the defendant has been proven guilty beyond a reasonable doubt, say so. If you are not convinced, say so."

The Judge took a moment to fish around under his robe for a tissue and blew his nose.

"Excuse me for the interruption," he said with a little smile. "All right, continuing on. While you should consider only the evidence in the case, you are permitted to draw such reasonable inferences from the testimony and exhibits as you feel are justified in the light of common experience. In other words, you may make deductions and reach conclusions that reason and common sense lead you to draw from the facts which have been established by the testimony and evidence. But do not speculate about possibilities that were not fairly proved.

"When I say you must consider all of the evidence, I do not mean that you must accept all the evidence as true or accurate. You should decide whether you believe what each witness had to say, and the importance of that testimony. In making that decision you may believe or disbelieve any witness, in whole or in part.

"To decide whether you should believe any witness I suggest you ask yourself a few questions," He paused a moment, noticing that several jurors were taking notes. "Don't worry about taking notes during these directions. You will each be provided a copy of them.

"Now, back to the questions you should ask yourselves:

1. Did the witness impress you as one who was telling the truth?

2. Did the witness have any particular reason not to tell the truth?

3.   Did the witness have a bias or prejudice?

4.   Did the witness seem to have a good memory?

5.   Did the witness appear to understand the questions clearly and answer them directly?

6.   Did the witness's testimony differ from other testimony or other evidence?

"Expert testimony was admitted in this case. This does not mean that you must accept the expert witness's opinion. As with any other witness, you must decide the extent to which, if any, to rely upon the opinion offered.

"The indictment charges three separate crimes, called counts, against the defendant. You will be given a copy of this indictment to refer to during your deliberation. If you find him guilty, you must select one or more of the following charges:

"If you believe that Mr. MacShane willfully murdered Carolyn Kelly, with malice aforethought, you must find him guilty of murder in the second degree. The sentence is fifteen years to life in prison.

"If you believe that Mr. MacShane killed Ms. Kelly without malice aforethought, but with intent to seriously harm or kill, or had extreme, reckless disregard for life, than you must find him guilty of manslaughter in the 1st degree. The sentence is five to twenty-five years in prison.

"If you believe that Mr. MacShane killed Ms. Kelly by committing a reckless act that he was aware of committing, and that he disregarded the potential fatal risk, a risk that any reasonable person would not ignore, than you must find him guilty of manslaughter in the 2nd degree. Although this count lacks the intention to do harm, there is within it the knowledge that the activity being engaged in could cause serious or fatal injury to another. The sentence is five to fifteen years in prison.

"If you believe that Mr. MacShane tried, but failed, to have sex with Carolyn Kelly, that is considered forcible touching which is a Class A misdemeanor, punishable by up to one year in prison and/or a $1,000 fine.

"And now, with that, you may proceed to your deliberation. Lunch will be waiting for you. Thank you and good luck."

Samantha watched the jurors file out and thought... good luck indeed! Leaning over to David she said "I wish I could be a fly on the wall for that deliberation!"

Susan Burke

"The virtues we acquire, which develop slowly within us, are the invisible links that bind each one of our existences to the others – existences which the spirit alone remembers, for Matter has no memory for spiritual things."

Honore Balzac

Susan Burke

Part V
Deciding the Verdict
November, 2019

Chapter 35

*J*ury deliberation rooms are never comfortable, Susan Mullins thought. They seem to say "Don't even think about staying here too long. Everyone is waiting for you to finish. Hurry, hurry, hurry!" This jury room had a long rectangular table, surrounded by folding plastic chairs. The side table now held coffee, tea, sugar, fake cream pods, napkins and paper cups. All the comforts of a prison rec room, she thought. There was even a bathroom, so they would never need to leave until they had come to a decision.

Since it was now 12:30, the bailiff had brought in a box of sandwiches: turkey, ham & cheese, tuna salad, chicken salad, bags of chips and sodas. Not a feast, but they were all ready to dig in.

In anticipation of her duties, Susan dressed in a professional manor and wore a dark green pantsuit, with a taupe silk shirt. After everyone had filled their lunch plates and was seated, she explained that, in New York, the first juror selected becomes the forewoman. "I hope that's okay with all of you." The other jurors were not only okay with it, they seemed relieved.

"While we're having this scrumptious lunch, I suggest we get to know each other a bit. Why don't we start by going around the table so that each person can introduce themselves. Give us your name, and a short introduction. I'll start. My name is Susan Mullins. As you may recall, I am the atheist of the group. I am a writer by profession and have written two novels, which," she assured everyone, "have nothing to do with murder. Who wants to go next?"

A casually dressed man in his 30's, sitting to Susan's right, jumped in. "Hi everyone. I'm William Johnson, but you can call me Bill. I'm a researcher for *The New Yorker* magazine, checking stories to make sure all the facts are correct. And let me tell you, I'm kept pretty busy these days. I'm an Episcopalian, at least during the holidays." Several others smiled in acknowledgment.

Sanjay Singh, obviously Indian or of Indian descent, explained what he did in the cyber-tech field. From their puzzled faces, Susan assumed that no one really knew what he was talking about, but suspected they should. "I am married, and we have two young kids, who so far haven't spoken of any past lives. I'm an agnostic."

George Meyer was about sixty, and was dressed in a nondescript suit and tie. Looking like he already wanted out, he quickly introduced himself as a Chase banker. "I'm hoping we can get this done today. I have to get back to work. Oh, and I'm Jewish, not that I know what that has to do with anything."

Next was Onur Demir, who had black hair with graying sideburns and a charming smile. "Hello everyone. My name is Onur Demir, and I invite you all to come to my Turkish restaurant, Sultan Kebab, whenever you're over in SoHo. I'm a Muslim, but don't really go to the mosque all that much. However, I do restrain from eating pork and, on most days, from drinking alcohol... just in case."

"Hello. I'm a nurse at Mount Sinai," Juanita Lopez offered. "I'm Baptist and go to church every Sunday. I love the music, and our pastor gives beautiful sermons." Susan guessed that Juanita was perhaps the oldest in the group, about seventy, of Latin descent and obviously an American citizen since she was a juror.

"Hey. I'm Richie Roberts. Nice to meet you all finally. I'm a musician and live in the Village. I was raised as a Methodist, but I don't believe in subscribing to one particular

273

church. Just be a good person, I say, and it will all work out. This is my first time as a juror and man, this is one cool case!" Richie was dressed informally, in jeans with a crew-neck sweater over a t-shirt. He was probably the youngest juror, around twenty.

"Hello. My name is Sandra Romney, no relation to the one in Utah. I'm a secretary and work for MasterCard International. They say once a Catholic, always a Catholic, but it seems like the older I get, the less sure I am about it all. I'm married too, and have a twenty-year-old daughter who lives in California."

And on it went. Daniel Louis, along with Richie Roberts, was one of the two African Americans. He was a stockbroker, an Episcopalian, and was married with three children aged three, seven, and nine. He was also on the Vestry of St. Bartholomew's Church, on 50th and Park. He looked very buttoned up; wearing a well-tailored suit with a crisp white shirt and a paisley, Windsor knot tie.

Beatrice Garcia was a young, divorced fashion designer and looked quite stylish, with a multi-colored, woven shawl and drop earrings. She described herself as a recovered Catholic, living on the Upper West Side.

Finally, we come to the two attractive young women Mike has been smiling at, Susan thought.

"Hi, I'm Mary Ann Townsend. I recently graduated from RISD and am now a struggling artist, sharing a studio in SoHo. I was raised as a Mormon. We don't believe in rebirth but we do believe in three Heavens and one Hell. Go figure." This got a few chuckles.

"Last, but not least, my name is Alice MacGregor. I work for Saatchi & Saatchi Advertising, as a copy writer. I'm Catholic, sort of, and live in midtown on the East Side."

"Thanks everyone," Susan said. "It looks like this jury represents the diversity of New York City, with many religions and nationalities represented. None of us is Buddhist or Hindu, but I'd say that's probably a good thing. We'll all be equally unbiased about the existence of reincarnation.

"It looks like most of you have finished your lunch, so why don't we begin. To start, I suggest we take the lay of the land and see where each of us stands right now. We can always change our minds later." While the jurors threw their plates and napkins in the trash, Susan moved the whiteboard closer to the table. She picked up one of the erasable magic markers to record their initial votes.

"Leaving aside for the moment the choice between murder or manslaughter, how many of you believe that Michael McShane is guilty?"

Susan raised her hand, and slowly but surely so did Sanjay, Bill, Onur, and Beatrice. "And how many of you think right now that he is innocent?" Mary Ann and Alice put their hands up. "All right, at the moment we have five voting guilty, two not guilty and five undecided."

For hours they reviewed all the testimony, listened to the tapes and looked at the exhibits. It was clear that the notion of reincarnation was a real sticking point for some.

Bill addressed it head on. "I totally understand how hard reincarnation is to believe, particularly when we hardly ever hear about it here in this country. But you know, I think I read that book they keep talking about. It was several years ago, but one of the stories has really stuck with me. Maybe because it was also presented in an interview of Jim Tucker by Chris Cuomo on ABC's Primetime.

"It was about this little kid down South who loved toy airplanes. He was always making them crash into the coffee table. But when he was about three years old, he started having nightmares of being in a plane crash. He'd have the same dream, maybe three or four times a week, in which he'd kick around in the bed, and say 'airplane crash on fire, little man

275

can't get out,' or something like that. The parents tried to dismiss it and assumed the dreams would stop. But when the kid was around three and a half, he started talking during the daytime about how he used to be a pilot who was shot down in World War II. He said his name was… John? James? Jack? One of those. His father started questioning him, and this little kid told him that he'd been on a specific aircraft carrier. Sorry, I can't remember the name of the carrier, but the kid said he'd been shot down by the Japanese at Iwo Jima! Isn't that amazing?

"As Jim Tucker explained in the interview, this case was originally written up by the boy's father, who spent years researching it on his own. He was a Christian and didn't want to believe in reincarnation, so he went out of his way to disprove it. During his investigation, he attended a reunion of veterans who had been stationed on that aircraft carrier. Much to his amazement, he met several elderly veterans who corroborated the child's story. There had only been one pilot shot down at Iwo Jima, and he had the same name!

"Ultimately, the father had to acknowledge that his son's remembrances of a prior life, as this pilot, were all true."

Everyone started to talk, but Susan interrupted them. "Since the Judge wouldn't allow that book into evidence, does anyone feel that we shouldn't have heard this story?"

"As far as I'm concerned," George said, "every single person involved in this trial has read that damn book! So I see no problem. And it's not as though we read it. Bill just remembered it."

No one else seemed bothered, so Susan let it drop. After all, it was also on Primetime, and people are allowed to share their memories.

"Wow!" Richie said. "That's a pretty compelling story. Plus it happened right here in the good ole US of A."

"And it involved a child having recurring nightmares about his own death," Juanita said. "When my daughter was little she had nightmares from time to time. But as terrified about them as she was, she was never really able to describe them, particularly not at that age. I mean, we all have bad dreams, right? But it's usually pretty hard to recall them. That young boy did though, and so does Rosie. That incident is so real to her that she can't forget it and continues to dream about it night after night. That's what makes the reincarnation story believable to me. Carrie's consciousness is not letting Rosie forget what happened! It's almost as though, despite the fact that Carrie's screams were silenced, she is still able to make her voice heard through Rosie. It may give me the creeps but you know, I think I believe her." Juanita looked around at everyone, hoping to find others who agreed with her.

"I don't know," George said. "Remember the defense lawyer got that subject expert to admit that there have been fraudulent reincarnation claims. How do we know this isn't one of them?"

"Well," Susan said, "let's keep that question in mind as we discuss the evidence and see if we think fraud is a possibility."

For the next hour they discussed motive. All they could really come up with was that Mike MacShane appeared to be a real ladies man. Although he attracted women easily, he not only couldn't handle rejection, he refused to accept it. George kept sighing, as if to say "hey… are your really buying in to that as a reason for murder?" And every now and then he rose to prowl around the room and pick up more chips.

Their next step was to once more review all the facts they'd learned from Rosie. Most of them thought they were very believable.

"She didn't pick Mike out of the photo line-up though, and she couldn't really describe what he looked like," George pointed out, mid-prowl.

At that point, Susan pulled the photo of the six-man line up out of the exhibit pile. "Take a look at this photo. Each man has dark hair and is about the same build. I'm not all that surprised she didn't recognize him. They look pretty similar to me, and we've been staring at Mike for days." She passed it around and then noted, "She picked out Carrie's photo instantly," holding up that montage.

"You know, it's four o'clock now. "Why don't we all stretch our legs a little, get the blood flowing, use the restroom. Unfortunately you'll have to do all of that in here since we're not allowed out until we've reached a verdict."

==

Although the jurors at least had sandwiches for lunch, Samantha and David sat down the hall from the courtroom, with coffee and yogurt. There was no way they were going to go out for lunch and miss a possible quick return of the jury. They started down many roads of conversation, but always found themselves detoured by their own internal thoughts.

Finally David broke the ice. He put down his coffee cup and turned to face Samantha. "I think we should talk. Not about the trial, that's out of our hands now, but about us. Perhaps you can tell that I have feelings for you, or at least I hope you can. The closer we get to the end of the trial, the more I wonder about what will come next. In terms of us, I mean."

Samantha knew exactly what he meant and had given it quite a bit of thought. "There's no doubt that we've become close over the course of this trial. We've been together nearly ever day and have come to know each other really well. I think you're an amazing man; thoughtful, generous, smart, persistent, handsome… all of that. And I must admit that I'm very tempted…" She paused.

"I hear a 'but' coming."

"Yes. The fact is that I'm really committed to giving my marriage another try. Hank went through a lot of emotional upheaval which resulted in the dissolution of our marriage for four years. But, with medical help, he now understands the cause of all his upset and has worked very hard to move beyond it. All he wants now is to be the husband I married and a good father to Bonnie. I want that too, David. At least I want to see if it's possible. I hope you understand." She rested her hand softly on his arm.

Obviously disappointed, David nevertheless replied, "Of course I do. But if you find that it doesn't work, promise that you'll call me. You're a very special woman; a wonderful mother, beautiful inside and out, headstrong and determined. Without you, we wouldn't be here today. However this turns out, I owe you a debt of gratitude.

"And speaking of that, this is for Bonnie. I want you to give it to her when she graduates from high school." He reached into his jacket pocket and pulled out an envelope with Bonnie's name on it.

Surprised, Samantha opened it and pulled out a card with a unicorn on the front. Inside it said, "Dear Bonnie, Thank you for being one of a kind, and for bringing peace back into my life. Love, David." Also inside, was a check made out to Bonnie Mitchell for $100,000.

Samantha's hand went to her heart. "Oh, David! I can't take this!"

"You also can't refuse it since it's not for you! It's the reward money I offered to whoever could identify Carrie's murderer. Bonnie is that person, so this belongs to her. Think of it as her college education fund."

"I... I really don't know what to say." She sat silently for a moment. "Thank you. When Bonnie gets older I will tell her about the kind and generous man who met her when she was only three, but thought of her as a daughter." She had tears in her eyes and took his hand again. She held his gaze for a minute then gave him a long hug. Pulling away, she fished a tissue out of her bag.

Not quite knowing what to say next, Samantha diverted the conversation to the trial. "Oh dear, I'm getting nervous! I hope you've prepared yourself for the possibility of a not guilty verdict. After all, not only do they have to accept the evidence of a child, a child who is the reincarnation of the victim, but they also have to get inside Mike's head and decide whether the murder was premeditated or involuntary. How on earth do they decide that? I just hope we haven't come all this way for nothing."

==

After their stretch and a little chatting, Susan noticed that the jurors had become a more collegial group. Sort of like a family. One in which not everyone agrees... but still.

As she'd done after lunch, Susan again asked for a vote. "Okay, let's get down to business. We've covered a lot of ground so far. We voiced a number of concerns, and we reviewed all the facts we learned from the witnesses. This might be a good time to remind ourselves that the Judge told us our decision could only be based on the evidence presented in the trial. In other words, no hypotheticals. Do we believe what we heard? And is what we heard, enough to convict Mike? With that in mind, has anyone decided to change their vote?"

Juanita, Richie and Sandra raised their hands.

Juanita said "That review of the testimony really helped. As far as I'm concerned, there is just no way that he couldn't have done it. There is a string of facts that ends up pointing right at him."

"And," Sandra said, "as we talked over the evidence we heard, I kept seeing that little girl. She didn't seem to have a devious bone in her body. She answered all the questions as best she could. And she was honest when she couldn't remember Mike's description." Sandra directed some of her comments to George.

"The dad's testimony did it for me," Sanjay said. "A dad knows his own daughter. So if Kelly believes Carrie is speaking through Rosie, then I do too. Add me to the guilty column. I know I told you that I'm agnostic, but now I'm no longer sure about that."

"Thank you Sanjay. We now have eight guilty votes, two undecided and two not guilty." Susan erased the previous numbers and updated them. Maybe its time to hear from Mary Ann and Alice. Can you explain why you think Mr. MacShane is innocent?"

Mary Ann began. "Well, now I'm not as certain as I was before. But Mike just never looked guilty to me. He's been very laid back, stretching his legs out in front of him, smiling. Shouldn't he be nervous? I mean even when he showed us that tattoo he was smiling!"

"OJ smiled too when he tried on those bloody gloves. Did you think he was innocent?" asked Bill.

"No, I definitely thought he was guilty," Mary Ann said, "because they had so much forensic evidence; DNA, blood, all that stuff, which we don't. And although OJ was smiling when he tried on the gloves, he didn't look all that calm during the witness testimonies, the way Mike did."

"You know," said Richie, "I saw a TV movie recently about Ted Bundy, the serial killer. Boy did he look calm, cool and collected during his trial. I think we need to focus on the evidence, and not on Mike's demeanor."

"Speaking about the evidence," George interjected, "what about that snake? How do we really know whether it was put on five years ago or ten years ago? I wasn't too impressed with that tattoo expert. He looked kind of seedy to me."

Susan sighed. George's manner and tone were getting on her nerves. "I don't think we should go by looks. He was brought in as a subject expert, and after twenty years as a tattoo artist, I expect he is."

Bill weighed in. "To me, he seemed convinced that the snake tattoo was older than just five years. He definitely thought it was more like ten. Carrie died six years ago right? So, according to him, Mike got it about four years before Carrie's death, if the fading signs of age are now apparent. I think Mike came up with a clever explanation, never dreaming that the prosecution could get a professional tattoo artist into the courtroom so quickly."

Others nodded and then looked expectantly at Mary Ann. "Yeah, I guess you're right," she said reluctantly. "If I just think about the evidence, he does seem guilty. But I certainly don't think it was premeditated murder. Maybe he was just trying to lure her into making love again, but things went terribly wrong."

"So have you moved to the guilty column?" asked Susan, wasting no time in moving along.

"Yes. But manslaughter, not murder."

"Fine." She put another check on the white board in the guilty column. There were now nine guilty checks. "Alice?"

Alice looked uncomfortable being put on the spot. "I'm not sure I can put my finger on why I don't think he's guilty. He just doesn't seem like a murderer to me. He looks like a model, for goodness sake. He can get any woman he wants. Why would he need to kill someone just because she didn't want him?"

Susan decided to weigh in on this one. "Even though Mike testified, we really don't know what was going on in his head back then... if he did it. All we know about him is that he seems to like having sex with lots of women. His girlfriend commented on how pissed he was when she broke off their relationship. Danny told us that he crowed about his hookup with Carrie, and revealed that she wasn't the only woman in the building he'd had sex with. Even Mike told us that he'd felt annoyed when Carrie rebuffed him.

"So, we have a picture of someone who seems obsessed with sex, and who clearly thinks his self-image is directly related to his sexual conquests. Remember he didn't want to tell Danny that Carrie had rebuffed him after their one-night stand, because it would tarnish his image as a 'lady killer.' So he may have gotten more and more upset each time he saw her, when she ignored him. I don't know if we will ever really know why he did it. But we have to accept that the facts are not in his favor."

The remaining undecided jurors seemed to pause and think about her comments. Apparently Alice bought in to it, because she too moved over to the guilty column.

Susan knew what was bothering the last two hold-outs. Reincarnation!

"Daniel and George. You two are still undecided. What exactly is bothering you, and is there any more you need to know to help you make a decision?"

"I want some direct, irrefutable proof!" George said, slapping his hand on the table and making his Coke spill over the cup. He looked annoyed and wiped it up while saying "Just because Carrie was worried about Mike isn't enough for me."

"Actually," Bill said, referring to his notes, "I think she said 'terrified,' which was confirmed by Greta."

"Well, I could be terrified of someone, but if I got killed one night it wouldn't necessarily mean that that person had done it," George said.

"But would you find him guilty if there had been an eye witness?" Susan asked.

"Of course I would," George said.

"One who could even recall a snake tattoo on his arm?" she added.

"Oh God, the kid." George sighed, putting his head in his hands. "But don't I have to agree that reincarnation is real in order to believe her?"

"No. You just have to decide that somehow, in a way that we may not understand, she has identified Carrie's killer. If we buy into everything she revealed in David's apartment, then don't we need to believe her nightmare story too? Including her recollection of Mike's name and his snake tattoo?"

George was quiet. Susan suspected that he'd been sure there wasn't enough proof, but now, although he hated to admit it, things were adding up.

"Let me think about it for a while." George said. "Let's hear what Daniel has to say."

All eyes turned to Daniel. "As I mentioned earlier, I am an Episcopalian. I consider myself to be very religious. To even suggest that reincarnation is real feels like blasphemy to me. And if I rule out the reincarnation idea, there isn't sufficient evidence, as George said."

Sanjay spoke up. "Tell me Daniel, do you believe in miracles?"

"Yes, I do. Christ performed a number of them, such as the loaves and the fishes and raising Lazarus from the dead. Then there's the Virgin Birth, the Shroud of Turin, and lots more."

"Yes. Christians are raised to believe in those miracles, while non-Christians usually don't," said Sanjay.

"However," he continued, "reincarnation, another sort of miracle you could say, is believed in by billions of people from many different religions. According to Wikipedia, even 20 - 40 percent of Christians believe in it.

"The point is that just because you subscribe to one religion does not necessarily mean that you can't believe in something associated with another. Our inability to explain miracles or reincarnation should not prohibit us from being open to the fact that they might be real."

Bill had been searching around on his cell phone. "Listen to this folks, 'Though the major Christian denominations reject the concept of reincarnation, a large number of Christians profess the belief. In a survey by the Pew Forum in 2008, 24 percent of American Christians expressed a belief in reincarnation. In a 1981 Survey in Europe, 31 percent of regular churchgoing Catholics expressed belief in reincarnation.' Plus... give me a minute, okay here it is. 'An Episcopalian priest named Geddes MacGregor, who is Emeritus Distinguished Professor of Philosophy at the University of Southern California, has written a book called *Reincarnation in Christianity: A New Vision of the Role of Rebirth in Christian Thought.* He says that Christian doctrine and reincarnation are not mutually exclusive belief systems." He snapped his phone shut and looked at Daniel.

Daniel sat back and seemed to be absorbing these new facts.

"Does that move the needle for you at all, Daniel?" Susan asked in a quiet voice.

"Well, actually, it does. If there are well respected theologians who don't believe reincarnation is incompatible with Christianity, than who am I to say they're wrong? Okay, I'll vote guilty as well. Plus, if Rosie remembers that snake, I don't see any other way around it. It's just damming evidence, even if we don't think he had much of a motive. Don't you agree, George?"

George stared down at the table. Susan could tell that he didn't know how to disagree. He wasn't sure, but he wasn't not sure either.

"I guess I'm the last holdout and to tell the truth, I can't come up with an argument to persuade all of you to change your minds. So I guess I'll join you, however reluctantly."

Everyone applauded as Susan rose to tell the bailiff that they had reached a verdict. He departed and then returned with a document for them to sign, which also listed the charges that the Judge had read to them. They discussed each and unanimously agreed on which they thought Mike was guilty of, based on the evidence.

Chapter 36

Word went out at 7:00 p.m. that the jury had reached a verdict and were returning to the courtroom. People hanging out in the hall quickly made their way back, particularly the reporters.

Samantha and David looked at the jurors' faces, trying to guess what they had decided. They noticed that no one was looking at Mike, which they took as a good sign. Mike noticed that as well and for the very first time since the trial had begun, seemed nervous.

After all the jurors were seated, Judge Brown said, "Madame Forewoman, have you reached your verdict?"

Susan stood up and said, "Yes, Your Honor."

"Please read it aloud," the Judge requested.

Susan cleared her throat. "To the charge of murder in the 2nd degree, we find the defendant... not guilty. To the charge of manslaughter in the 1st degree, we find the defendant... not guilty. To the charge of forcible touching, we find the defendant... not guilty."

At this point you could hear a pin drop in the courtroom, and Samantha grabbed David's hand.

"To the charge of manslaughter in the 2nd degree we find the defendant... guilty."

The courtroom started to erupt with sounds of both approval and disapproval until Judge Brown interrupted. Looking at the jury, he said, "Do you all agree with this verdict?" Everyone nodded in agreement.

Apparently, Samantha thought, they were convinced he did it, but not convinced he meant to do it... ergo the lightest sentence.

"Very well," the Judge said. "My thanks to all the jurors. This was not a simple case, and I appreciate your efforts to come to agreement and render a verdict. We will have a sentencing hearing on November 18th. Bailiff, please return Mr. MacShane to his cell. I would like to thank the Defense Attorney, Ms. Washington, and the Prosecutor, Mr. Hubbard. We are adjourned." The gavel came down for the last time.

==

Jack Hubbard led Dr. Karadamand, Bob Williams, Martha Riddle and Greta Neilson into an adjoining chamber so that David and Samantha could thank them. They were all thrilled with the outcome, and everyone congratulated everyone else on their contribution.

When they were alone, David gave Samantha a hug and held her close. As they drew apart, he searched her eyes for any last minute change of heart before he gave her a soft kiss on the mouth. "Remember, call me if you change your mind."

Walking down the front steps, Samantha was separated from David when a reporter pushed through the crowd to ask him some questions. He answered only one.

"Are you happy with the verdict, Mr. Kelly?"

"After six long years, I can only say that I am very relieved that justice has been served."

Samantha melted into the crowd, satisfied that she had done her part to help David, Carrie and, most importantly, Bonnie, to receive that justice. She had gone through a lot of angst and fear, but in the end everything had worked out. She couldn't wait to get home and tell Bonnie that the "bad man" was going to jail, thanks to her.

It was after 10 p.m. when Samantha arrived home and bid Mercedes goodnight. After getting ready for bed, she tiptoed into Bonnie's room and gazed down at her sleeping daughter. She thought about all that had happened in the past seven months, leading to an outcome that none had thought possible. Sitting on the side of the bed, she gave Bonnie a soft kiss on the cheek.

Opening her eyes to half-mast, Bonnie murmured, "Did we win, Mama? Did you make Mike go away?"

Samantha slipped under the covers and put both arms around her. "Yes we did, sweetie. And thanks to you, Mike is gone. You don't have to worry about him anymore." She started to tell Bonnie all about the tattoo man, but when she glanced down, the child was fast asleep, with a little smile on her face.

Susan Burke

Epilogue

This case became one for the history books. The jury had believed that a little girl was an eyewitness to her own murder in a previous life. The next day it was all over the news, in print and on TV. Thereafter, it would be discussed in homes and schools all over the world, and spoken of from the pulpits of countless churches, synagogues and temples. The names of Samantha and Bonnie Mitchell were never mentioned.

Susan Burke

Postscript
May, 2021

"Daddy, Daddy! Come catch me!" Bonnie's joyful shrieks carried across the Great Lawn in Central Park while Hank chased after her, making monster noises.

As Samantha stretched out on their blanket and basked in the warm rays of the sun, she remembered another May day three years ago, when different shrieks had sent chills up her spine. What a difference between now and then. The nightmares had ended about a week after the trial, and shortly thereafter Bonnie had completely stopped asking for her other daddy. She also stopped talking about Carrie and never spoke of a man named Mike. Her pillow remained on her bed, she stopped begging to be photographed, and "Boofa" was long forgotten.

It was all worth it Samantha thought, as she touched her gold necklace. Hank had more than made up for the past. He was a doting father and loving husband. She stood up to adjust the bonnet of the carriage, and then leaned in to give their four-month-old baby a kiss. Lucas was a good sleeper, but even so, as his eyes gazed up at her, Samantha could not help but wonder whether someone else was peering up at her as well.

Susan Burke

"The soul comes from without into the human body, as into a temporary abode, and it goes out of it anew; it passes into other habitations for the soul is immortal. It is the secret of the world that all things subsist and do not die but only retire a little from sight and afterwards return again. Nothing is dead; men feign themselves dead, and endure mock funerals... and there they stand looking out of the window, sound and well, in some strange new disguise."

Ralph Waldo Emerson

Acknowledgements

The Witness is a fictional story but it was inspired by the ongoing work of The Division of Perceptual Studies, at the University of Virginia. All my descriptions of how possibly reincarnated children behave and are investigated, as well as the two case studies mentioned, are discussed in Jim Tucker's book, *Return to Life.* I also attended a lecture, in which Jim Tucker explained their work and spoke of the little boy who recalled being a World War II pilot. If you have any interest in reincarnation, I encourage you to read this book.

You may have wondered where the manicurist's understanding of reincarnation came from. I told it just as my manicurist, Christina, explained it to me.

For the past 3 years, I've taken classes at WriterHouse in Charlottesville. It was a privilege to learn from so many successful authors, and receive feedback from other "wanna-bes" like me. Their encouragement helped me to persist.

I am grateful to Billie Jo Powell, a former social worker with experience in child protective services, for guiding me through their investigatory process. And to Sally Jones, who graciously agreed to be my editor.

Lindsay Heider Diamond, an extremely talented artist, created the cover design, which I love. Cynthia Burke lent me her artistic eye and literary ear, and Christen Hubbard came to my rescue with technical support.

My family and friends, no doubt, became tired of me reading them excerpts, and then saying "what do you think?" I'm grateful that they always listened and were supportive of my effort.

About the Author

 Susan Burke, who lives in Charlottesville, Virginia, is now in her late 70's. *The Witness* is her first novel, proving the point that it's never too late to start something new.

Living in New York City for decades, Susan had a career in marketing and advertising, and worked for companies like MasterCard International and American Express.

Although at her desk during the day, Susan also performed leading roles in many Off-Off-Off Broadway plays at night. This passion continued when she moved to Charlottesville. But then… she discovered writing.

Susan Burke